# THE ADVENTURES OF MORRIGAN HOLMES

# NO CAGE for a CROW

## M.R. GRAHAM

NO CAGE FOR A CROW
Copyright @ 2016-2017 M.R. Graham
ISBN: 1-946233-10-2
ISBN-13: 978-1-946233-10-3

http://quiestinliteris.com
COVER ART BY
M.R. Graham

# More by M.R. Graham

## The Adventures of Morrigan Holmes
No Cage for a Crow
The Death of a Swan (Coming Soon)

## The Van Helsing Legacy
We Shall Not Sleep

## The Liminality Series
The Medium

The Mora

The Mage

The Martyr (Coming Soon)

In the Shadow of the
Mountains

The Wailing

## Poetry
Versos, or, The Things a Woman Learns on the Banks of the Great
River

Papalotes: Songs of Texas

## Also
The Siren

The Truth of the Matter

Proof: A Short Tale of the Undead

For you, Gran.

For your copy of the Adventures,
for the adventures we had in your living room,
thank you.

For you.

# TABLE OF CONTENTS

# Foreword

ACTUALLY telling this story presents some unusual difficulties, primarily because it is not mine. I want to make that clear: the most I've had to do with this work is a bit of editing, a bit of cleanup. Some of the words are mine, but most are not, and I have absolutely nothing to do with the ideas.

The bizarre truth is that the permission I have received to make this all public is conditional, and the condition is secrecy. I am not allowed to describe how this story came into my hands. I am not allowed to dig into its origins, and I have been assured that the real writer, whoever that may be, would find out very quickly if I ever began to make inquiries. I have no idea what would happen next, in that case. Maybe the story would disappear from wherever I've published it. Maybe I'd be sued within an inch of my life. Maybe someone would show up at my front door. I have to admit that I am curious, but not *that* curious.

I am significantly more interested in why I was chosen at all. Some of you may know that I am a voracious reader of mysteries, but not a writer of them. My usual work is comprised of tales of the supernatural and paranormal and is considerably more far-fetched than what will follow. At least, more far-fetched from some perspectives. I know some bona fide Holmesians who would be far more willing to believe in ghosts than in this. I am tempted to call it a gutsy piece of fiction, except that, regardless of whether the events recounted ever actually happened, I get the disconcerting impression that the author intended a *memoir* rather than a *novel*.

To be perfectly honest, it's possible that even this caveat may be Against the Rules, but leaving out any notice at all would have felt like plagiarism. Publishing this at all feels a bit like plagiarism, but at least any and all readers have now been duly informed.

We'll see what happens, shall we?

~M.R. Graham

# PART ONE:

# INTO

# THE

# STORM

# ONE

WITH THE benefit of hindsight, I am forced to admit that the howling heart of a January storm might not have been the most well-considered moment to run away from home. Of course, adolescents have never been renowned for their unerring wisdom, and I was no exception, although I had always considered myself reasonably clever until that night. All I knew then, the one thought running continuously through my mind as I belted on my dressing gown, stuffed my feet into layers upon layers of stockings and then into my brother's over-sized boots, and threw a heavy woollen coat over all of it, was that I had to get out. It was all my fault, I had ruined everything with a single, alarmingly stupid mistake, and the only thing left was to run.

And so I ran.

I had no plan—as I have said, this was not an intelligent decision. It was an impulse born of powerful emotion, fierce, chaotic, unpleasant, as thoroughly divorced from the guidance of intuition as it was from that of reason.

Divorced from self.

# GRAHAM

There was a bizarre sensation of separation. I felt I was barely in control of the hands that fumbled at the window latch and scrabbled at the sash. Rain roared against the glass, rushing in immediately to drench my legs as the window slid open. It seemed impossible that no one would come, that no one would hear. But the din of the storm drowned me out perfectly. My fingers, curled around the slick sill, became numb as I stood stone-still, perched on the balls of my feet until the faint sound of the hall clock reached me. The stroke of two broke me from my paralysis. They were not asleep. I could still hear their voices, even if they could not hear my movement. They were not asleep, but they were not coming, either.

I swung one leg outside and ducked through, arms splayed out to brace myself against the walls.

From the hall there came a voice, male, one of my brothers, though over the noise of the storm, I could not have said which.

'Morrigan!'

I did not reply, only leaned back inside to seize a book from the table and heaved it at the door with all my strength. It struck the wall with a thud and fell to the floor in a heap of soggy pages. An unforgiveable abuse of the written word, I realised with a pang. But the voice did not call again, and when I was sure that no siblings were about to intrude, I effected my escape.

At home, escape through a window should have been an easy matter. The ancient, ivied walls of Mycroft House afforded countless hand- and foot-holds, even in the cold and wet; I could have made my way from the first floor to the ground in under a minute, and the stables would have been shelter enough until the storm abated.

This place, though, had never been and never would be home. I had never hated it until that night, but I had always felt like a guest, there, even in the room that they called mine. This place was wet brick, without ivy, without anything to break the fall I recklessly chose to risk. It was only luck, or perhaps a miracle, that kept my neck and spine intact.

I leaned out the window as far as I could and stared down at the little court below, obscured by a haze of water and darkness.

A flicker of doubt made me pause, but then voices rose in anger from somewhere behind me, cementing my blind resolve. I turned myself around and slid out of the safety of my candlelit room, fingers gripping the sill, boots braced against the outside wall.

Leather skidded against brick, and I lost a couple of inches, body slamming against the wall. The breath whooshed out of me, and for a moment, I could only cling. It would not be a terribly long drop, if I were to let go. I had fallen as far before, at home, but at home, such a fall ended in the cuts and scratches offered by the evergreen shrubbery that encircled the house beneath the lowermost windows. The cobblestones here promised much worse.

I recovered, inch by inch, and lowered myself until my toes caught on the slight protrusion of the decorative line of white brick that divided the first storey from the ground. I lowered myself a little further still. There was no convenient ivy, but if I could get my boots to the top of the next window and my hands to the decorative white brick, then my boots to the window sill below and my hands to the top of the window frame, I could jump the rest of the way safely.

One toe found purchase, so I worked my numb fingers free of the window sill and dropped them down to seek the next handhold. One hand, one foot. Slow and steady.

'Morrigan!' Again, the voice from inside, barely heard over the thundering rain. I slid a little more and again was left clinging to the outer wall, my heart pounding in my ears. Again, I slowly recovered, inch by inch, regaining my hold and my safety. I felt like snapping at the owner of the voice, but what good would that have done? 'Don't distract me while I'm trying to run away'? He would not have heard me, anyway.

The other foot followed the first, and now I was stretched

awkwardly at my full height, pressed hard up to the masonry, spanning the space between my window and the next, one arm extended straight above my head, the other drawn in tight against my side and grasping at the decorative brickwork. Addled though I was by strong emotion, I saw at once the danger of this position. While the majority of my weight rested on my toes, only the hand grasping the windowsill above prevented my toes from becoming a pivot. For the moment, in this in-between stage, the other hand served no purpose at all. Four fingertips only prevented me from tipping backward and tumbling headfirst to the street.

'God,' I thought, for neither the first nor the last time that night. 'This is idiotic.'

I could hardly turn back, though. Going down was a challenge, but going up would have been impossible. Would have been unthinkable. The tone of the voices from within told me clearly that I was no longer wanted in that place, and even if they could eventually find it in themselves to forgive me, nothing would ever be the same. Perhaps they could forgive me, someday, but the thought that I might eventually forgive myself was laughable. The life I had known was over, no matter which way I decided to go; down, at least, gave me a chance at deciding for myself how things would be in the future.

One hand, one foot.

Lightning flashed just above me, followed less than a second later by a thunderclap that shook my bones.

I cried out in startlement.

And I fell.

I felt my fingers clench, and I lost whatever grip I had managed to secure. I began to slip. But I was not so numb in body or in mind that I could not anticipate the consequences of such a fall.

At first, I panicked and scrabbled uselessly at the bricks with both hands, clawing at the rough surface as though I could catch hold of the tiny irregularities and hold myself fast. That was no good, though, and I knew it. In a moment, I would overbalance, pushed further and further by my own efforts at holding on. It was much too cold, much too wet, and much too late for me to catch myself. My best, my only hope, was to make my inevitable fall a good one.

I arched my body forward, pushing away from the wall with both hands and feet so that I would fall straight, land on my back with room to roll, disperse the force of the impact so it would not shatter me.

As if time had slowed, the brick and mortar floated away from my fingertips, and though I thought I knew what I was doing, I was frozen by a moment of consuming panic. I had avoided the deadly somersault that would surely have killed me but the fall could still break me, all the same.

And what then? What if I were too badly hurt to cry for help? How long would it take before someone intruded upon my privacy and found me missing? How long before someone came to look?

A sharp, pale face appeared in the window above me, staring down with... Was it disgust? Doubt? The figure leaned out of the window into the rain, and a long, white hand reached for me, but I was already beyond its grasp.

The moment passed as quickly as it had come upon me. I tucked up my body and bent my knees and hips, spreading my arms for balance. I had fallen as far before, and I knew how to fall well.

The pavement greeted me without any regard for what I did or did not know.

Falling to the irregular cobbles was nothing at all like falling to the shrubbery beneath my window at home or like falling to soft grass beneath my favourite reading tree. No, London was out to kill me.

On any other surface, even overwrought and in the pouring rain, my landing would have been flawless. The cobbles thwarted me, and perhaps the startlement of the presence of that figure in the window. I landed squarely on my two feet, but my two feet did not land squarely on the ground, and the left flew out from under me, leaving the right to bear my full weight. My ankle rolled, despite the support of its boot, with a horrible sensation like a creaking hinge. I gasped and fell to one side, striking my hip and my elbow.

For a moment, I could only lie beneath the downpour.

All right, girl, analyse.

Finding myself not-dead was a relief, of course. I had not broken my neck or my back or my skull, which was honestly one of the best things that had happened to me all day. The ankle, however, was almost definitely sprained, and I did not look forward to finding out for certain when I tried to stand on it.

There were bruises, too, but bruises were nothing new to a girl who climbed trees.

No, the worst of it was the ankle, which, even as I lay, began to ache fiercely.

I rolled onto my back. The face in the window watched me, impassive as a sickle moon. Waiting. He did not disappear, racing down to the courtyard to see if I was all right. He did not begin shouting for our parents. Maybe he knew I had to go. Maybe he just didn't care.

I should have gone back, of course, and I knew it. I should have called out for help until someone came, or hobbled to the door and knocked. I should have mustered the courage to explain what peculiar circumstances had led me to the pavement beneath an open window amidst the blasted storm, wet and hurt and—now—sobbing, as well. I should have admitted that I was an idiot girl who did not have the good sense not to jump from great heights or to keep my mouth shut or to mind my own blasted business. An idiot unworthy of her own name.

I knew it. I considered it. I shied away from the eminent sensibility of it. What sixteen-year-old girl has ever had the grace to admit stupidity? If I was to be a fool, then by God, I would be a fool, and to the hilt!

And besides, I reasoned, I had not actually killed myself, and that had to count for something. Had to mean something. If I had been doomed to fail, then I ought to have failed immediately and completely, but I was still alive, and, deliberately forsaking reason, I chose to take that simple coincidence as a sign from above. Surely, I was fated to go.

Strengthened by that absurd conviction I pushed myself upright, shivering at the cold that crept up my legs and trickled down my back. The ankle screamed in protest, and I nearly screamed as well, but a quick rearrangement of my posture shifted my weight to my good leg, and I was able to take a few strange, hopping steps, turning my back on the face I knew was watching me still. I lifted a hand in what was meant to be a cocky wave, ruined by the quiver of my shoulders.

The drumming of the rain echoed strangely in the grey little courtyard of that house I had so come to despise. Before me, the gate yawned wide, resembling nothing so much as a huge, gaping mouth, with the dead branches of wisteria that stretched down from its arch becoming the fangs. I had the impression of waiting, of languishing in the rumbling belly of a beast that was finally about to spit me out.

Beyond the monster's teeth, the great, dismal city sprawled. If the house was a monster, then the city was its home, a jungle of brick and smoke and throbbing humanity.

I wiped the tears from my face, only to have them replaced at once with streaks of sooty rain.

Trembling now as much with terror as with cold, I stepped out into the wilderness.

# TWO

WITHIN the space of a few steps, the house behind me had vanished into the sheeting rain. A sly wind crept up behind me, only to reverse itself suddenly and come clawing at the hem of my overcoat. I was forced to raise my arm to shield my eyes from the stinging drops, or else be blinded.

The house stood at the end of what was, in ordinary weather, a pleasant boulevard, divided up by tidy privet hedges and iron fences, awash with hydrangea and climbing rose. The other houses were quite as nice as the one I had left, their inhabitants altogether much too respectable to let even a smudge of light reach the street at that hour. And not a smudge did. Not a flicker or a gleam or a glimmer. The rain fell thick and grey, faintly luminescent itself, and all the world turned blank and white with each flash of lightning.

Regrets surged in my throat—not that I was leaving, but that I had not thought to bring a hat, or to seek out more waterproof clothing. I should have waited. A day of preparation would not have gone amiss. I should have taken the time to pack adequately. I should have known where I was going before I set out.

Well, I reasoned, rather than dwell on my blunders, perhaps I should leap at the chance to test my resourcefulness. Anything, you see, rather than admit that my best course of action would have been hasty retreat. I had some vague idea that I could make my way to my aunt and uncle in Bordeaux, who, though by no means conventional themselves, had never gotten on especially well with my flagrantly unconventional parents. They might send me back, but they might not, which was more than could be said for any of my English relations. Reaching France would pose a problem for one attired as I was, but I did have five pounds in notes stuffed into my pockets, and another four in coin, the sum of which represented most of my life's savings. How much it would actually purchase, I had no idea, but it would carry me a lot further than would nothing. Some tidily mended cast-offs, perhaps, and as much street food as I could stuff into my pockets, transportation, and a cheap room to keep the rain off me until I could pull my situation together enough to travel.

There, so it was not as though I had no plan at all. I had, also, some foggy and half-formed idea, no doubt drawn from the works of Mr Dickens, that life on London's streets, for a capable young person of strong constitution, at least in the short term, would be more adventure than misery. In my agonising ignorance, I thought that sleeping in doorways could do me no harm, at least until I could find passage to France.

Already, the weather was doing its utmost to disabuse me of the childish fantasy. My shivers intensified into quakes as I trudged on down the street. And with every step forward, I repeated my ill-begotten plan to myself until I had nearly convinced myself of its wisdom. Each footfall fuelled the next, driving me further and further into the wilderness. My surroundings were invisible; all I could do was push a foot ahead, gingerly, lest I fall and utterly ruin my throbbing ankle, and then follow it with the other. Though I knew I would have to find shelter before I caught my death, I could not stop in any place where I might be found and recognised and dragged back.

Slowly, I lost all track of time or distance. Minutes blurred together in the absolute darkness, so that I could not be sure whether I had walked a quarter of an hour, or a half, or even if dawn might be breaking somewhere beyond the storm-clouds. I had no idea, either, whether I had walked far enough. Unable to see even to the kerbs, I could not know whether I had left my neighbourhood behind, yet.

And suddenly, a hideous doubt stabbed me with the certainty that I had not even left my own street. I tried counting my steps, but I had scarcely reached fifty when it occurred to me that my hobbling gait could hardly be compared to my usual stride. Ordinarily, I could measure out yards quite as well as any surveyor, but my blasted ankle and the blasted darkness conspired to limit me to mere inches.

Time and distance bled together into a shapeless dream. I pushed one foot ahead, and then the other, listening to the pounding of the rain meld with the chattering of my teeth. The most reliable measure I could think of was my own stamina. I would walk for as far as I was able, and that would have to be far enough. It either would be, or it would not, and if it was not, well, there was nothing more I could do.

I walked.

I had lost sensation in my fingers almost before I was out of the bedroom window, and now the numbness crept up my arms and my legs, followed by the dull ache and then the sharp sting of intense cold – one of the first tastes of my profound error. I had endured greater cold than this, but never with such grossly inadequate insulation. A seed of horror took root in the heart of the fantasy as some part of me began to understand how winter could kill.

My legs cramped, and my shoulders and back. My skull felt squeezed with the cold.

## GRAHAM

I counted my breaths instead of my steps and tried to follow the fatigue in my limbs.

After some time—who knows how long—my brain became numb, as well. The number of breaths melted into the number of raindrops biting into my skin and the number of lightning flashes stabbing my eyes and the unsteady tattoo of my chattering teeth.

At last, I misstepped. My brain continued to lag behind, and my first indication was the moment my knee struck the pavement.

The limits of my energy closed in around me suddenly, vise-like, and it was all I could do to pull myself upright and shuffle sideways until my outstretched fingertips brushed against rough brick. I followed it until it dropped away, and I slipped into the space I had found. It was not a recessed doorway, as I had thought at first, but a narrow alley about three feet wide, and the overhang of the roofs above left only a few inches between them. It was not a dry space, or a warm one, but the close walls blocked out the tearing wind and the stinging rain, and I collapsed to the alley's filthy floor in mute gratitude.

I was well-versed in the dangers of falling asleep in the cold, but to stay awake proved impossible. My numb limbs and numb brain refused to respond to my half-hearted protests, and I curled up on my side in the soot and the refuse, and I sank into oblivion.

I may never have woken at all, were it not for the foot against my shoulder, rolling me onto my back. I opened my eyes to a grey but daylit sky and the grinning faces of four dirty boys about my own age.

'I likes them boots,' said one, showing black teeth.

'Rather fancy the coat, meself,' said another.

A third, the one with his foot on my shoulder, tipped his head thoughtfully to the side. 'The bird's a tad skinny for my taste,' he said. 'Anybody else want a go afore I cuts 'er a smile?'

The other three chuckled, but not, I thought, because it was a joke.

My brain turned the problem over sluggishly even as the ringleader drew a long, slender filleting knife from his belt. The gleam of the blade and the immediate danger it represented spurred me into coherence.

'Don't hurt me,' I said quickly. 'I'll give you what you want. I won't fight.' My voice was hoarse and cracked.

The four exchanged a look of surprise.

'Awful dirty for a proper lady, ain't ye?' asked the leader, but the question was directed more toward his compatriots than toward me. They took a moment to understand his meaning, and I was able to watch comprehension dawn on the other three faces almost simultaneously.

The foot lifted from my shoulder, and rude, rough hands reached down and pulled me to my feet. I swayed where I stood, supported only by my captors.

'I don't suppose,' said the leader slowly, in a mocking imitation of my own speech, 'that there's anybody what would be *generously* pleased to 'ave ye back in one piece?'

Held for ransom was not an ideal solution, but it sounded far and away better than violated, naked, and dead. I nodded vigorously.

A dark smile oozed across the villain's face, and he nodded. 'That's a bloody good thing for ye,' he said.

I could not help but agree.

The others were not as sure.

''Ow do we do a ransom?' asked the one who wanted my coat. 'Ain't never done a ransom before.'

'An' what if she gets away an' squeals?' asked the one who wanted my boots.

'Aye,' agreed the last of them, who had not spoken before. 'Dead don't squeal.'

To my intense dismay, the leader seemed to be giving their words real consideration. I had to cut in.

# GRAHAM

'I write a letter,' I said hurriedly. 'You tell me what to put in it. How much you want and where to leave it and by what time. You post it. You make sure I never hear your names and never see where you stay, so I couldn't tell anybody where to look for you, even if I wanted to. My parents will leave the money. I know they will. And when you've got it, we go our separate ways.'

As hard as I tried to sound calm and sensible, my voice rose shrilly until the leader's hand tightened painfully on my arm, and he leaned in close to my ear to hiss. His foetid breath clogged my nose. 'Shut yer gob!'

I shut my gob. But I also realised that he was afraid of being overheard. The street beyond the mouth of the alley was quiet, but the hour must not have been so early that there was no chance of discovery.

He eyed me with suspicion. 'What's yer game, layin' out the whole plan for us?'

'I want you to keep me alive,' I told him candidly. That really was all there was to it. If my brain had been working better, I might have been clever and cooked up a plot that seemed solid on the surface but was secretly riddled with holes to trap my captors. This plan I expected to work much as I had laid it out, barring the obvious facts that the police would be summoned and that whichever of the ruffians went to collect their prize would be arrested instantly. At which point, those remaining would likely kill me. It was an issue I would have to address, once I was thinking more clearly.

'I want to live,' I repeated firmly. 'And I'm prepared to help with anything that will keep you from killing me.'

He stared me down silently until I was certain me meant just to 'cut me a smile' and save himself all the trouble, but he only shrugged his shoulders and began to move down the alley, dragging me with him.

But suddenly, one of the devils behind us gave a warning cry, and I and the tough restraining me turned as one in time to see one of the others drop to his knees. Something small and bright streaked through the air, striking my captor in the throat, and he uttered a hoarse exclamation and fell, also. I scrambled away from him, striking the wall hard, and tried to become one with the brickwork.

Three dark figures appeared silently in the mouth of the alley, and two more hemmed us in from the other side, emerging from the shadows like ghosts.

Friend or foe seemed to be the salient question. I squinted at the newcomers but could make out nothing much beyond the mufflers that covered their faces from collar to eyes, cloth caps drawn down low over their brows, and the shine of steel in their hands. Four of them carried a hodgepodge assortment of blades, and the fifth held a contraption of wood and leather. A sling, I suspected, remembering the projectile which had felled my captor—only by narrowly missing me.

'Hellhounds!' cried a voice, filled with mockery. It echoed strangely in the small space, so that I could not venture a guess as to which of them had spoken. 'I said we'd thrash you if we found you on our turf again. Well, whose turf do you call this?'

The two downed Hellhounds were rising unsteadily, rubbing at their individual injuries and glaring back and forth between the pair of human barricades blocking their way.

'Wrong Boys,' one of them growled.

And suddenly, four met five in a tempest of whoops and blades and fists and flying ball-bearings. The Hellhounds moved automatically into a tight square, back-to-back against the onslaught. Two Wrong Boys advanced on them from either end of the alley, while the fifth, the one with the sling, mounted a pile of rubbish and sent a barrage of little metal missiles into the midst of the Hellhounds' formation, raising bruises and curses and fouling their aim as they slashed wildly at the Wrong Boys.

The tips of the flashing knives passed alarmingly close to me, and I sank down against the wall with my arms curled instinctively around my head, unable to run in either direction for the blockade of Wrong Boys.

# GRAHAM

The muffler-wrapped figure closest to me staggered suddenly, propelled by a fist to where I supposed its jaw must be. It collided with me, and I shoved it back toward the fray, but not before an angry Hellhound scented his foe's momentary disadvantage and followed, swinging punches wildly.

I had no particular reason to be favourably disposed toward the Wrong Boys, not knowing whether they meant to rescue me or leave me be or pick up where the Hellhounds had left off, but I did have ample reason to despise their rivals.

As the boy surged toward me, I made sure my legs tangled with his. He stumbled into the side of me, kicking fiercely to free himself. My ankle exploded with pain. The Wrong Boy kicked the Hellhound's knees out from under him, and I shifted before the two could fall on me. The Hellhound grabbed at the Wrong Boy's coat, and the two hit the ground together in a flurry of churning limbs.

Then there was a quiet noise, something between a gasp and a cough, and everything stopped. The two brawling gangs froze and turned to stare. The Wrong Boy beside me regained his feet. The Hellhound did not. He lay on his side with his knees drawn up to his chest and his arms curled around his belly. The Wrong Boy's short, curved knife dripped red.

'Had enough?' asked one of the muffled figures.

None of the Hellhounds moved or uttered a sound, save the one who lay and groaned.

'Fine, then,' said the Wrong Boy. 'Get you all out of here. And you'll all have much worse, next time.'

Slowly, their eyes blazing with malice, the three standing Hellhounds dragged their comrade to his feet and carried him to the mouth of the alley and out into the street. The Wrong Boys stood aside to let them pass.

All was momentarily still as the Wrong Boys and I watched the retreat.

Then one of them turned toward me, eyes glittering between scarf and cap, knife gleaming in his hand. He watched me closely, and I watched him.

'Hold up!' one of them exclaimed. 'That ain't no Hellhound.'

'I should say not!' I agreed heartily.

The eyes above the masks widened.

'Coo!' exclaimed the smallest one. 'It's a wee toff!'

The one I thought must be their leader sheathed his knife and approached, offering me a huge, gloved hand. I pulled myself up, using the wall for support, and he hastily grabbed my arm when he saw I could hardly stand.

'Lost?' he asked with a sharp glance at the hem of my nightgown peeking from beneath my coat. I knew I must have looked a sight, by then, drenched and shivering, evenly coated with the alley's muck, every hair that had blown free of my plait now plastered to my face and neck. But for the quality of my clothes, I could not have looked very much different from any other girl huddled in a London alley.

'Anywhere we can take you, Miss?'

'No,' I said. 'Thank you. I'll be quite all right on my own.'

They exchanged a look, as though not sure whether I intended that as a joke. I stared them down.

'Haven't you a home to go to?'

An instant of clarity broke upon me as I realised how dearly any of these boys would have loved a room with a fire and enough to eat. They would have thought me an idiot if they knew what I had had and had left behind. But it was not really so clear as that, no. It had not really been a choice. I had destroyed what I had hours before I decided to climb out that window.

'I had,' I admitted. 'I haven't, any more.'

## GRAHAM

They all exchanged another look and seemed to come to some sudden, silent agreement. The chances were good that each of them had uttered something similar, once. Each of them must have had a first night on the street.

The one supporting me cleared his throat. 'You'll be all right on your own,' he allowed, with the obvious tenor of an obliging lie, 'but maybe a bit more all right if you're dry and can walk.'

'You make a fair point, sir.'

His eyes crinkled in a smile.

# THREE

I FOLLOWED the gaggle of boys down the alley. Or rather, pressed between two of them who helped me to hobble along, I was conveyed down the alley with increasing unease. There was one Wrong Boy to either side of me, one before, and two behind, and while their leader had suggested a chance to dry myself and recover, I was not entirely sure that I would be allowed to decline their hospitality, should I change my mind. They were a gang, living by their wits and by the points of their knives, and for all they were against the Hellhounds, I had no real reason to believe they might be on the side of the angels.

I stole a glance at the one on my right, the leader. When I was not hunched over with cold and fatigue, he might have been only about an inch taller than I. In that moment, though, I felt like he towered. He certainly thought me smaller than I actually was. Perhaps that could become an advantage, though I could scarcely see how. Weak and shivering and barely able to stand on my own, perhaps I could surprise him with my height.

The thought nearly made me laugh. Nearly.

## GRAHAM

I must have made some sort of noise, because the Wrong Boy turned his head and blinked at me. His eyes were china-blue, and the fringe of lashes around them was yellow, like lemon crème. Not blond or gold, but yellow.

'You say something?'

I shook my head. 'No, I... I was just wondering why, when they were so ready to kill me, you're... not.' I stopped, not wanting to present any novel ideas.

He shook his head at my stupidity and went back to looking straight ahead. 'Wouldn't put food in our bellies,' he said. ''Less you're thinking we might eat ye. Which, s'pose I might if you was already cooked up, but, honest, there ain't much meat on ye.'

Perhaps he was joking, and perhaps not. The uncertainty was not reassuring.

I did not ask why they did not strip the clothes from my back and run; on the chance that had not yet occurred to them, I did not want to bring it up.

Neither did I ask why they did not think to ransom me. Perhaps they were not as clever as the Hellhounds. Perhaps they were far cleverer, had already given thought to the entire scenario, identified the problems, and rejected the possibility. Or perhaps they had given it thought and rejected it on moral grounds, as unlikely as that seemed. There was no doubt in my mind that this raggedy lot had no choice but to steal if they wanted to eat, but perhaps they drew the line at stealing people. I might almost have been ashamed of my suspicions. Their circumstances made them my inferiors, as far as society was concerned, but circumstances were artifice, no more substantial than the drifting clouds. Circumstances could not be held up as a measure of human worth, a fact brought home to me by the sudden, dramatic change in my own. The poor were poor by circumstance, not by nature or design, and so I could not doubt their morals based on circumstance alone. And yet...

And yet, I could not say for certain what I would have done in their position, gnawed by hunger and presented with a short, if dubious, route to a full belly.

A problem.

My best guesses relied on my own understanding, what I myself would do in any given situation, and I could not understand these people. I was hungry, but they had grown up hungry, like as not. I was cold, but they were warm only when July sun warmed London's blackened stone. The life I had learned was different from theirs, and no amount of imagining could bridge that gap. I could not anticipate them.

The cobbles seemed to slide sideways beneath me, and I tumbled into the Wrong Boy on my left. He caught my arm and propped me upright, and as though over a great distance, I thought I heard someone say:

'Best make for the doctor, I reckon. Something's got in 'er.'

A doctor! Good Lord, a doctor was the last thing I needed. Doctors, by nature, tend to be moderately clever, and a moderately clever person could not fail to notice that I did not exactly match my motley companions. Beneath my filth, my coat was well-made, sturdy, and while the lining had been replaced more than once, even the replacement was of silk. The cotton of my night dress was soft and fine. My boots, though made for feet rather larger than mine, were nevertheless bespoke, of visible quality even after years of hard use. Even I, myself, stood out. Gawky, yes, and thin, but not for want of food, not for a lifetime of hard living. Even the Hellhounds, who might on a good day have matched wits with a Hyde Park pigeon, had known me for what I was the moment they heard me speak. A clever man would know I belonged elsewhere.

Worse yet, my understanding was that doctors tended to be responsible citizens. A responsible citizen who discerned a runaway would take her immediately to the police. Even if I had not yet been reported missing, I would be, soon. I would be back in that house by noon. And then?

I could not imagine what would happen then, and I did not want to try.

'No,' I tried to tell them, 'No, I'm fine, really not all that bad,' but only a vague mumble emerged from me. I tried to pull away, but all my strength seemed to have left me at once. Voices crashed in upon me, roaring and then receding like waves at the seashore, and I felt myself hurried along through the labyrinth that hid behind London.

It crossed my mind that this might be a kidnapping, after all. Might they be subtle enough to feign concern, to pretend to help me so that they might lead me wherever they pleased without risking screams? That would be quite the ironic turn, to be kidnapped in the middle of running away. Even worse to be fooled into thinking that one's kidnappers were actually one's rescuers!

It didn't matter, though. None of my thoughts mattered, because I was entirely incapable of acting on them. My ankle throbbed abominably, and the rest of me was so numb I could only be certain I was moving because the scenery was slightly different after each of my increasingly long blinks.

They could take me where they would, and, I realised, I didn't care in the least, so long as the end of the line was enclosed by four walls and a roof, out of the wind and the fine, piercing rain that had started again.

I may have made another try or two at breaking free. I do not know. I do not remember.

But when they did finally stop, and I with them, I relinquished any thought of getting away, because they stopped me in front of a *door*. A once-blue door, faded with age and darkened with soot and smuts and mildew and possibly things even nastier, but it was a door all the same, and a door promised the possibility of an *indoors*.

One of the boys rapped sharply at the mouldering door, using his bare knuckles rather than the tarnished brass knocker. After what seemed like no pause at all, the door creaked open, and I was hustled down a dim, damp hallway hung with artworks made grey and indecipherable with age, then shunted sideways through a second door and into a room.

A sudden blaze of light forced my eyes shut: paraffin lamps covering every surface, tallow candles clustered upon every wall sconce, a fire blazing furiously in the tiny fireplace, before which crowded a thicket of tattered, mismatched chairs awash in a drift of horsehair.

And it was *warm*. It could hardly be otherwise, so full of flames as to shame a volcano. I began to relax, but only for a moment before the feeling returning to my face became burning pins and needles. I winced.

The swarm of boys around me surged and then subsided as another, darker figure entered my field of vision. Quite suddenly, there seemed to be no boys around me at all. All that remained...

Good God, he may as well have been the spectre of Death! About my height, he appeared far taller, his arms and legs elongated by his incredible thinness. His huge, domed head hung forward on a spindly neck that looked as though it might snap under the weight of his cranium, and sharp, black eyes glittered at me from out deep, shadowed sockets. A quick, reptilian tongue darted out to wet the man's dry, grey lips. His attire was hidden beneath a long smock that hung nearly to the floor, its once-white folds brushing the cracked and scuffed toes of his shoes.

He looked over me with interest, rubbing his long, discoloured hands together before him like a child contemplating a present, as my insides knotted with unease.

Finally, just when I thought I might turn and run, regardless of my ankle and of who might be standing behind me, he stepped forward.

'You're tall,' he observed, 'aren't you? Been eating well? Taking a fair amount of exercise, though not for the past few months?'

## GRAHAM

He put his serpentine face inches from mine and squinted into my eyes, then abruptly seized my arm, pushed my sleeve up, and dug his sharp fingers into my wrist.

I jerked myself away from the bizarre person, and he grinned at me. He even had fangs, eyeteeth jutting out far beyond his long, overlapping incisors. His gums showed the stains of a long tobacco habit. In fact, a few glistening strands of the stuff remained behind.

'Come now,' the man chided. 'I am Doctor Peach, and I assure you, your friends would not have brought you to me unless they thought you needed my attention.'

I said nothing, for fear of my voice betraying me, though the thought going through my mind was that I could imagine no more incongruous name for such a colourless individual.

'You have a name?' he continued, then chuckled, as though fully aware that I would not answer. His tongue appeared again, passed over his lips, and vanished. 'You don't say much. Perhaps you would be so good as to step into my examination room, so I may form my own opinions?'

I did not want to be alone in a room with the man, doctor or no. But I was alone already, I discovered, looking around to find that the boys had silently disappeared.

He moved away and waited for me to follow.

Seconds passed, and then his sunken face twitched. 'Well,' he said, in a tone I might almost have called amused, 'come on.'

'I don't want to,' I replied, forgetting myself for an instant. The lifeless face moved again, scalp tightening, tongue making another darting appearance.

Then his eyes crinkled in unmistakeable humour. His voice, though, was filled with acid. 'Ah. New, are you? Well, little lady, you ought to know that no perceived impropriety can sully your reputation out here. Now, if you can stand on that foot you're favouring – balance on it for a full count of ten – you may go, and I'll say no more. If not, you will come in here and let me take a look.'

His glittering black eyes fixed on me almost in accusation.

There was no use in refusing to respond. My accents had betrayed me already, and I could do no worse by answering him again.

'Sir,' I said, thinking of the Hellhounds and their salacious, rotting grins, 'it is not the perceived impropriety that concerns me.'

A moment too late, I realised how a man might take offence at such a frank statement of mistrust, but instead, he froze as though absorbed in thought.

'Perhaps,' he said slowly, drawing out the second syllable into a shuddering hiss. His gaze fixed on the splinter-prickled floor a moment before darting back to me, stabbing into me like needles. It took in my boots, my coat, the soiled hem of my night-dress, the damp strands of hair clinging to my cheeks.

'Perhapsss... that is why you left?'

I did not answer, hoping he would take my silence at face value and not as an affirmation. The shrieking and chaos of home still rang in my ears. I did not want to think of them, even to count the sins of which they were not guilty.

The pause lingered uncomfortably, then abruptly shattered as he snapped his fingers. His smock rustled as he brushed past me and stuck his head out into the corridor.

'Sylvia!' he called, drawing the name out like a sibilant curse.

Almost at once, a woman materialised in the doorway. She was the wife to his Jack Sprat, as completely his opposite as a human being could possibly have been. Her nearly spherical girth filled the door, and her ruddy, pockmarked face was drawn into an expression that was somehow at once obsequious and demanding.

'Aye?'

# GRAHAM

'Ah, Sylvia. The boys are fed?'

'Aye.'

'Then, would you be so good as to supervise my treatment of this young lady?'

Sylvia looked at me as though I had just torn off all my clothes, perched a flowerpot on my head, and declared myself to be the queen.

'S'pose.'

Doctor Peach nodded his satisfaction, then crossed to the fireplace and picked up the shovel, which he handed her with a thin smirk. 'And if I cross any boundary whatsoever, you are to thrash me soundly with this.'

She coughed less than politely. 'O'course.'

'And one for you, little miss.'

The poker somehow made its way from the hearth to my fist, though I could not for the life of me have said exactly how.

'Good,' he declared. 'Well, then, shall we?'

On the one hand, I was not particularly reassured by the presence of Sylvia, whom I did not know, and who seemed just a touch too familiar with the idea of a hearth shovel as a blunt weapon.

On the other hand, it did seem to be an earnest attempt to put me at ease. And anyway, the way Sylvia was brandishing that shovel told me that crossing her was a bad idea. Whether or not the gesture actually was meant as reassurance, I suddenly realised that whatever chance I'd had of refusing had just been deftly removed.

I clutched my poker tightly and allowed myself to be examined.

There is no need to detail the process too closely. I was palpated within an inch of my life, stripped of my coat, boots, stockings—not without considerable protest, though the quilt that was provided in their stead was much warmer than my soggy things. He bound my ankle tightly, at which I uttered a number of words a person of my station and sex should not have known, and even a few I am certain I must have

26

invented specially for the occasion. I was prescribed hot broth, hot tea, and a crust of brown bread with jam, and Sylvia, who did not seem to be the maid but did not seem to be Mrs Peach, either, forcibly installed me in the crumbling chair nearest the fire while my clothes began to dry and my treatment was prepared.

Drenched in warmth, watching the shapes in the steam that had begun to rise from my coat, there was little chance of keeping my eyes open, not even for the promise of food. I found a spot to fit my back between the chair's lumps and settled in, not exactly secure, but knowing full well that there was little to nothing I could do about it if the situation did turn sour.

I allowed my eyes to close.

#  FOUR

AND A SOUND like the descending hordes of Genghis Khan snapped my eyes back open again. Five grubby figures stormed into the room, wiping grease from chins with even greasier sleeves. Flapping and guffawing, they arrayed themselves on the chairs around me, sending up clouds of horsehair and dust.

Startled, I sank down and simply watched them come.

The Wrong Boys had left their hats and mufflers somewhere, and the first thing I noticed was that not all of them were Wrong Boys at all. The smallest one, wielder of the formidable slingshot, had set free a pair of fluffy, ginger-coloured plaits that fell over her ears and to her shoulders. Her state of privation made it difficult to guess her age - no older than twelve, though not younger than eight. She gave me a gap-toothed grin.

An enormous heap of a boy with close-cropped black hair and wide-set eyes grabbed the poker from where it had fallen beside my chair and shoved the tip of it down into the fire. He sucked his thick, red lips with a pensive air.

# GRAHAM

One with freckles and a pointed chin scratched at a lump of scarring where his left ear had once been, watching me narrowly.

A fourth, delicate and pale, almost effeminate, seated himself primly on the edge of a cushion beside the girl. His long, elegant fingers plucked nervously at the spoiled, once-lovely cravat he wore about his throat. He did not look at me at all.

And I did not look at him for long, either, because the fifth had caught my eye and demanded all of my attention. He of the china-blue eyes and yellow lashes. I had never seen such a person, and if I'd had a little better sense at that age, I should not have stared as I did, shamelessly, gaping like a fish. And, God help me, I should not have said what I did.

'I'm sorry, I...' I stuttered, realising that I must look a complete ass. 'I'm sorry, I...' And then I sabotaged my own attempt with the stupidest, least necessary statement possible. 'I've never met a Negro before.'

He lifted his eyebrows and shook his head with a bemused smile, but with no surprise. 'Is this what you call black?' he intoned, as one who has recited the same words countless times before. 'Don't be daft. The word you want is "albino".'

Perhaps his grasp of the etymology was, indeed, better than my own. Beneath his London patina, he was whiter than I. I began to mumble some reply that doubtless would have placed even greater strain upon his charity, but he cut me off.

'I'm Magpie,' he said. 'On account of, I has something of a fondness for things what shine. Our big 'un's Billy. He don't talk much, and most like in French, when he do.' He pointed to the mountain before the fireplace, who nodded. 'An' this 'ere's Weasel,' he said, indicating the boy with the missing ear. 'An' Dart.' This was the slender boy in the cravat. 'An' our girl 'ere is Snail. What are we to call you?'

As he pointed out each of his compatriots in turn, I noticed that his hands, though by no means black, were much darker than his face, or than me. Not exactly albino, then, though I could not recall the name for the condition that resulted in patchwork skin. Black and white. Perhaps *Magpie*, then, did not refer only to his fondness for sparkle.

I opened my mouth to decline—I had not gotten a real name for any of them and saw no reason why I should give them mine, especially since it would doubtless be appearing soon in the papers—but the girl interrupted me.

'I think she looks like a crow,' she said with a grin and a giggle. 'She's got the beak for it.'

Well, it was objectively true, at least. Not even my own mother—I shied away from the thought of her—had ever suggested to me that I could be thought beautiful, but it was still something of a shock to hear the fact of my prodigious nose announced so bluntly. But perhaps it was well-deserved. The observation was just as true and probably just as unwelcome as my own comment to the boy called Magpie.

I ducked my head, on the chance my sudden flush of embarrassment was visible.

Magpie leaned forward with a twinkle in his eye. "Ow about it? You're sure smart like a crow. We 'eard you tryin' to talk down the Hellhounds. Smart is good. Bet you'd learn real quick, if you was to run with us... Well, soon as you can run again.'

It took a moment for his meaning to sink in, at least apart from the fact that I was apparently to be known as Crow. 'You would let me join you?'

He shrugged. 'You got anywhere else to go?'

I thought of Bordeaux, and the decreasing likelihood, given my adventure of that morning, that I would ever be able to get there on my own. Possible, still, but no longer probable. No longer easy.

I sighed. 'I really don't think so. Thank you.'

He shrugged again. 'You talk nice. Would make a goodish haul begging, maybe. But I doubt you have any practice breaking the law. Goin' to need to learn that if you're goin' to stay alive.'

I must have blanched.

The freckled boy, Weasel, snorted loudly.

'I'm not certain I can do that,' I told them. 'It's not that I'm not grateful, but I'm afraid I'd just be a liability. I'd be slow, or I'd trip up. And I don't think I can break the law.'

Sylvia reappeared with a chipped wooden tray bearing an equally chipped bowl and a mug, both steaming beautifully. I took it with more gratitude than I could express, and she seemed to sense my appreciation, for some of the sergeant-major melted from her features, and she nodded briskly.

Magpie waited until she had departed again before turning back to me. 'You can learn,' he said. 'We all learn. And,' he added, not unkindly, 'pilfering's easy when you're hungry enough. Even for you, I promise.'

He had a point. I looked down at the bowl in front of me. A soggy crust of bread swam bleakly in oily brown broth atop a mush of bloated barley and unidentifiable vegetables. It was one of the most appealing things I had ever seen in my life, and it had not yet been a day since the last time I had eaten. Another day or two, maybe, and I could almost see myself stealing for a chance at even that fare. Or going home... No. I would brave the workhouse before I went home.

I sucked in a breath and blew it out. 'I am smart,' I agreed, pushing aside thoughts of all the recent evidence to the contrary. 'Most of the time. I'll learn anything you need me to, anything you can teach me. Anyway, I'd have to be an idiot to refuse if someone offers to teach me to survive.'

I was an idiot, of course, but not a suicidal one.

A huge grin split the boy's face from ear to ear. 'Right!' he exclaimed. 'Eat up, then. Doc says we can all stay till your things are dry. 'Ope it takes a while. Don't know 'bout you, but I don't fancy goin' back out there till I 'ave to.'

The business concluded, the Wrong Boys broke once again into their chatter, centring mostly, it seemed, on who had done the most damage to the Hellhounds. They seemed to agree that the day's winner had been Billy, the mountain, and I thought it possible that he had been the one whose knife had found its mark. For a moment, I tried to hope that the injured Hellhound had found help and would be all right, but it was no use. I hoped he bled out and froze to death in a heap of dung, somewhere. It wasn't charitable or ladylike, and perhaps that attitude had contributed to the horrible chain of events leading up to my escape out the window, but I could not bring myself to be sorry for it.

I turned to my soup and the cup of weak, bitter tea as they recounted the adventures again and again, embellishing until even I was entertained.

But the stories died away as, encouraged by the heat of the fire, they dropped one by one to sleep, until I set the tray aside and began to nod, too. Only Magpie remained alert, like a sentry, leaned back in the chair he had claimed, but regarding me steadily through his yellow lashes. There was no trust, there, less even than I had for him. That would take time and effort from both of us.

'Sorry,' I told him quietly.

His eyebrows twitched, and he shrugged, raising one hand to tear at the nails with his teeth.

It was acknowledgement, but was I forgiven?

—

All of the boys were still asleep when I woke, and most of the lamps and candles had been put out, but I could see by the light of the fire that the girl called Snail was awake. A wooden crutch had appeared beside my chair, a little short for me, but still infinitely better than trying to hop around on that ankle. I spent a few moments staring at it, then looked up to see Snail's eyes on me.

I opened my mouth to address her, then glanced at the sleeping boys, then back again.

She chuckled. 'Couldn't wake 'em 'less you was actually tryin',' she told me, barely bothering to lower her voice. As predicted, none of the boys even stirred.

I smiled. 'All right. Can I ask why they call you Snail?'

She pointed to the floor beneath her dangling feet, where I could see a lump of something grey, with frayed edges. A scrap of tarpaulin, maybe.

'I 'ave belts,' she said. 'So I can carry it on me back. Better'n gettin' wet. Wet'll kill ye.' She squinted at me critically. 'You ain't lookin' so good, Crow. 'Ope we got ye dried out in time.'

'I feel fine,' I assured her, wondering how I could possibly look worse than her own poor, hungry little reflection. 'Much better than earlier, anyway, thanks to you and your friends.'

She beamed. 'Are you gonna be my friend, too?' she asked, and my estimation of her age dropped by several years.

'Well, of course. I have a lot to learn, though. Will you teach me to use a sling like yours?'

It was almost more than she could bear. She bounced in her seat, flushed with pride and pleasure, and nodded until I was sure her head had come loose.

'And you can teach me girl things!' she replied, freezing me where I sat. 'I don' know any other girls.'

The boys had woken. I could tell by the half-terrified titter of laughter from one of the other chairs, followed by choked silence.

'Yes,' I mumbled. 'I suppose that would be a good thing.'

They gradually came around more fully, garments were retrieved and shuffled from one body to another before being reclaimed by the

34

rightful owners, and Sylvia reappeared to begin the process of shepherding Wrong Boys toward the door. I pulled on my almost-dry socks over Doctor Peach's bindings, wincing as I did, and was helped with the boot by Snail. I probably shouldn't have attempted the boot, but if I had to carry it, I probably would have lost it, and I thought it might provide some extra support for the ankle. A tattered wool jersey appeared to go under my coat, and I was able to hobble out into the evening after the boys, leaning heavily on the crutch. Sylvia slammed the door behind us.

I tottered forward to catch up with Magpie as he was adjusting his muffler to hide his face.

'Who is this Doctor Peach, exactly?' I asked, glancing over my shoulder at the door we were leaving behind. The strange, cadaverous man had struck me wrong, very wrong, though I could not put my finger on exactly why, and it seemed bizarre that the boys should trust him as they seemed to. Still, it seemed rude to say as much. My leg was braced, if painful; and my stomach was full, if queasy; and my coat was dry. And, I realised suddenly, the money was still in the pocket. Whatever nefarious ends my unconscious mind suspected of Peach and company, neither he nor Sylvia was apparently the sort to go exploring other people's pockets.

Magpie shot a glance in my direction, and I saw his sharp eyes rove down and up again, assessing my ease of movement. 'Do-gooder, I guess,' he said. 'Don' know much about 'im, but 'e 'elps us out when we're 'urt, feeds us if we bring a new patient for 'im. Won't take pay. 'Elps out some of the ladies, too...' He trailed off with another calculating glance at me, and I nodded to let him know I understood.

A doctor who fed the poor and took no pay for his care sounded promising. But a doctor so inexplicably eager for new patients that he was willing to bribe urchins to bring them in... Well, it was all a matter of phrasing.

'How long have you known him?'

He shrugged. 'Five years, maybe? 'E stopped the bleeding when Weasel got his ear took off. Put my arm back when it got pulled out. Plugged up loads of 'oles for all of us.'

'And who is Sylvia?'

'Christ. 'Is sister, maybe? Who knows?'

I laughed at the tone of his voice, letting me know clearly that I wasn't the only one who had noticed the peculiarity of that relationship.

'I trust 'em,' he continued, and beneath the reassurance, his voice had an edge. My suspicions were obvious to him, and they were not allowed. I could see why he was the leader; there was no possibility of an argument.

'All right,' I allowed. 'And why are you the Wrong Boys?'

He relaxed a little and chuckled. 'Oh. That. Well, that's because if you think you're gonna pick a fight with us...'

'You picked the wrong boys!' the rest of them chorused.

We had passed from the dark, narrow alley into a proper street, and a respectably-dressed man jumped in startlement at the declaration and promptly crossed to the other side to avoid us. The Wrong Boys pointed and cackled and hooted, and he quickened his pace and disappeared around a corner.

'Having seen you in action,' I said when they had quieted down, 'I have to say your name is well-chosen. Thank you all, by the way. I think I might not be alive right now, if not for you.'

There was some mildly embarrassed muttering of acknowledgement, but in moments, they had resumed the circular retelling in which the fight gradually grew to legendary proportions.

The foot of my crutch slid on a damp cobble. Magpie caught me before I could land on my face.

'Sorry,' I muttered. 'I don't know how long it'll take before I can actually start learning to be useful.'

He set me upright and held on until I was steady again. 'Begging ain't hard on the legs. Set you up on a corner somewhere, and that'll be good enough for a while.'

The thought of putting myself somewhere highly visible made me nervous, but my pride did not object to begging quite as strenuously as my conscience objected to theft. 'That sounds like something I could do.'

He nodded matter-of-factly.

And a baritone cry rang out behind us.

Beside me, Magpie spun around, uttered a muffled roar, and sprang away from me. My ankle and the crutch prevented me from being quick. I wobbled around to see what was happening, being excessively careful not to fall. The crutch slid, anyway, and I lost another moment in keeping myself upright.

The scene had progressed without me. Without my noticing—I thought I could remember the grumble of its wheels approaching, but had not realised that it had failed to pass by—a canvas-sided delivery wagon had drawn up behind us and stopped, disgorging three masked men. Real masks of black felt with slits for eyes, not just mufflers, as the Wrong Boys wore. One had seized Billy, the mountain, by the arms, but had apparently underestimated the advantages granted by Billy's sheer size. The man's mask was slick with moisture. It dripped red onto his filthy shirt. I hoped the aggressor was the source of the cry.

Weasel and Dart had fallen upon the man and were trying to wrestle him away from Billy, but the other two masked men joined the fray. One seized Dart and threw him to the ground. Snail aimed a kick at the man's knee, and I heard a pop and then a howl.

I was useless. I was unsteady, and I was unarmed.

Well, no, that was not entirely correct.

On his knees, the man drew a long, wicked knife from his belt and lunged toward Snail. The rough, solid length of my crutch met his elbow, and this time, it was a crack rather than a pop. He gurgled and coughed, curled around his limp arm. The momentum of my strike had carried me forward, though, into the heart of the fracas. A gloved hand came out of nowhere and jerked the crutch out from under me. With no chance to steady myself, I expected to hit the pavement, but something caught me in the stomach, driving the air out of me, and I was roughly thrown over the brute's shoulder.

The moment lengthened.

My reason was not in top form at that moment, but I certainly knew that masked men didn't pick you up just to set you back down again. If he had picked me up, it was because I was going in the back of the wagon.

I was *not* going in the back of the wagon.

He had me by the legs, so I could not kick him. But he had me by the legs, and that made the shoulder under me a fulcrum. I straightened as much as I could and abandoned my ineffectual efforts to beat him down with my fists. Instead, I reached back and groped blindly at his head, hoping to pull the mask over his eyes. I could still hear the Wrong Boys around me. They had not abandoned me. If I could blind my attacker for a moment, they would have time to knock him down and get me free.

My fingers scraped across scratchy wool felt. Then across something wet and soft. Something that gave.

I thought I heard a police whistle, but it wasn't. It was the man's high, reedy scream. I struck the pavement and rolled away from him without looking back. I did not care to see what I had done.

The wagon creaked, and I vaguely sensed a fourth man descending.

'Scatter!' Magpie bellowed.

The boys scattered, pelting away into the darkness.

I regained my feet and ran, too. Never mind my ankle. Never mind that I had no idea how I would ever find the Wrong Boys again if I separated from them now.

'There!' cried one of the men. 'That one! There she goes!'

And heavy boots came pounding after *me*.

Two pairs, I counted. I ran harder. It should have hurt. I shouldn't have been able to run at all, but my body was all but numb, and I didn't have time to stop and think that perhaps there was something wrong about that. I was not going to find out what they had planned for me in the back of that wagon.

I left the sky's last feeble glow behind me as I plunged wildly into the warren of streets and alleys. If there were any lamps, here, they had not yet been lit, and the coming night grasped at me with needy fingers. A deeper patch of black opened up beside me, and I darted toward it, hoping to God it would not end at a brick wall.

The drumming of boots behind me began to recede. But only for a moment. It paused and then came thundering after me again.

I cut left. The boots followed. I cut right. The boots followed. I couldn't catch my breath. It had to be the cold of the air burning my throat, or the fatigue, or my over-excited nerves, because running had never had me gasping so desperately for breath. Or maybe Sylvia's broth. My stomach voiced its agreement with my lungs, and I had to stop, entirely against my will, as the need to vomit overcame me. My knees were shaking, I could tell, but at the same time, I could not feel my legs at all.

Big, thick fingers dug into my scalp at the base of my plait, yanking my head back so that I could feel the vertebrae grating against one another in my neck. I had to let myself be pulled over or risk a severed spine. I reached back and grabbed hold of a heavy, woolly wrist with both hands, but he had control of my head, and there was nothing more I could do.

'Got 'er!' a voice called out, with absolutely no regard for who might hear. He jerked me backward and put his muffled mouth by my ear. '*Bitch*,' hissed. 'I get the feelin' you're gonna be more trouble than use. But you gotta pay, now. May just kill you, 'stead of takin' you...'

He sucked in a breath with a strange, high little sound, and I was shaken like a doll as he spun around, holding me out in front of himself like a shield. From the corner of my eye, I caught the eerie, almost phosphorescent gleam of a blade. It wasn't coming toward me, though. It thrust out in front of him, beyond me, into the darkness. I twisted frantically in his grip, trying to see what else was out there, but he shoved my head into the alley wall, and that was the end of my struggle.

I heard a shrill yell, more furious than afraid, and more of the man's guttural profanity, and something pinged against the brick above me and bounced off my shoulder. I fought my way to my hands and knees, blinking away stars, and saw a tiny bit of shine beside my hand. It was cool and smooth beneath my fingertips, a little sphere of cold steel.

Steel shot, of the sort launched from a sling.

Snail.

The alley was dark as a tomb, but I could see blurred, inky shapes moving in the gloom. The man's monstrous hulk, gripping its wicked knife, and a small, agile form sliding eel-like through the night, much too quick to be caught. The little girl added her own stream of scatological taunts to the man's roaring oaths.

I staggered up, trembling, leaning heavily on the wall for support, and emptied my guts into the pile of refuse where I stood. I couldn't run anymore. The leg still didn't hurt—and it began to dawn on me now that that wasn't a good thing—but I was aware of a weird, tight feeling that extended to my hip and a similar sensation in my head.

Snail bounded and slithered through the darkness, and the man slashed fruitlessly at her, missing by a foot or more each time. Like a dance. A gorilla and a ballerina twirling around in a glorious farce. It was hilarious.

Good old Snail. Apparently, the benefits of being a Wrong Boy took effect immediately upon induction. It was a bit of a surprise that she had come after me, but it was hard to protest. My rescuer was small, but efficient.

I couldn't run, but I could creep, and I took advantage of the distraction she provided. That had to be what she was doing, hadn't it? She was fast enough to vanish into the night in an instant, but she had not disappeared, yet. She had to have been waiting for me to get away. All that darting back and forth had to be tiring; she wouldn't be able to keep it up long. I had to make my escape quickly, so she could make her escape, too.

I shuffled along the wall, through my puddle of sick, with one hand outstretched to guide me. They wouldn't be able to see in the dark any better than I could. If I was quiet and lost myself in the maze of streets and stayed very still in the shadows, they would never be able to find me.

# FIVE

MY HAND slid across the grimy surface, fingertips trailing over an inch of thick slime and soot. Beneath was either brick or stone, but there was no way I could have told which.

Behind me, I heard a girl's little grunt, and I turned in time to see Snail wriggle out of the man's grip and take off the way she had come, done with this game. I had moments to become invisible.

Luck seemed to be with me. My fingers slid out of the muck and into open air as the entrance to a side passage opened in the wall. Not a passage, exactly. The top of the wall had crumbled away, opening onto some adjacent space, the lip of the gap at about the height of my waist. As quietly as I could, with trembling arms, I heaved myself up to sit in the mouldering masonry and swung my legs over.

I had forgotten about the others.

A child's petrified scream froze my guts, the most awful thing I had ever heard. Then a crash, and a scuffle, and a meaty thud, and then only heavy boots, walking away.

I twisted to see a broken little body, still and lifeless on the alley's floor... I blinked, and it was gone. But there was a retreating back, and a limp form slung over the massive shoulder.

The sight slid away from me as I overbalanced, scrabbling uselessly at the slick rock, and tumbled sideways into the shadows beyond the alley.

It took longer to fall than it should have, the floor of the dark place being a good four feet lower than the floor of the alley, my brain having slowed to a crawl. The landing was soft, at least, something spongy and giving, filling my nose with the smell of good earth and crushed green things.

Without checking myself for damage, I scrambled up again and felt for the lip of the hole, but my hands found only brick. It was too high for me to reach.

Snail's name bubbled up in my throat, and I swallowed it before it could emerge. If I called out, they would have both of us, and then who would remain to say where we had gone?

The boots came back at a trot, and I crouched down low and held my breath. An amber beam of light, solid as an iron bar, blazed through the hole above me. I did not know why I had not thought they might have lanterns. It came closer, pouring down, and a head appeared beside it. I shrank away, but the light only deepened all the shadows around its revealing circle, and I faded into the dirt. The head turned this way and that and then withdrew, but not before the light had struck a flowerbed, and a worn path, and brick walls all around. I was in the garden of a home.

Then the light was gone, and I was left blind, blinking away the spots it had left in my vision. Safe for the moment. I sank down into the dirt, thinking as quickly as I could.

All right, girl. Analyse.

Snail was taken.

I was not taken.

But the men had come after me. Specifically me. *'That one! There she goes!'* After me, but they had taken her. What did Snail and I have in common apart from our sex? We were not of the same age or class or size. Surely, I had not been a Wrong Boy long enough for that to be a factor. Only our sex, then. They were after girls? I shuddered.

But why me first, and Snail only once I was out of their reach? If they just wanted a girl, they should not have singled me out. Or could they have taken her only because she was the one to come after me? Not girls, then, but me, and then whomever had interfered? Or had they taken her to get to me...

That house flashed into my memory, and the people inside it. Was there any possibility—any at all—that my *family* would send hired men to find and retrieve me?

Good Lord, no. We were not a normal family, but we weren't the sort to hunt one another.

But the men had come after *me*, and I still had no idea how badly they wanted me. They might be back in daylight, so I could not stay put. I couldn't get out the way I had come, though. There should be a gate, or at least a ladder, not that I thought I could use a ladder, in my state.

My eyes began to recover from the sudden glare of the lantern, and my surroundings gradually resolved from opaque blackness into faint shapes in the dark. There was something big and low and square, with a peaked roof, about five feet wide and four feet tall. I could not think what it could be, except a shed, and that was where a ladder would be found. It was worth a shot.

A few half-blind, tottering steps brought me within arm's reach of it. I felt out the rough edges of a weathered wooden door, then spread my hands and searched out a handle, cautious of splinters. There. But I could not depress the thumb latch. Flakes of rust crumbled onto my fingers and pattered softly to the ground. I pressed harder, but my grip was

**45**

alarmingly weak. My hands trembled. No luck.

Well, there had to be a gate. I made a slow, grasping circuit of the garden, clinging to the wall like a drunk. My ankle didn't hurt at all, but my bones felt hot, and my teeth, while the rest of me froze. There was no damn gate.

I realized with a terrible, sinking sensation that the only way out of the garden was through the house.

I had not been able to see much of the house. I had the impression of two storeys, or maybe three, but no amount of squinting could confirm it. It was hard to be sure, in the dark, but I thought perhaps my eyes were not focussing quite right.

It was completely dark, though. No light in any of the windows, if there even were windows. Was it late enough for everyone to be abed? Or was the house empty? Good God, what if there was no one to let me out of the garden? If I shouted, I could draw the men back. If I didn't, I could die, there.

Unacceptable. I had to get out and rescue Snail and get to Bordeaux. I didn't have time to die.

There was no gate, but I had found the rear door of the house as I made my circuit of the garden, and I assumed it must enter onto the kitchen. If there were a servant in the house, she would be quartered near the kitchen, and her room might not have windows to show me the light.

I made my way back and felt out the door handle, twisting it carefully. The door did not budge. Who locks a door that opens onto an inaccessible garden? I shrugged to myself in the dark, as though someone had spoken the question aloud. Anyway, even if it had been unlocked, sneaking into a house was a dangerous prospect. Sneaking into a private garden was little better, I mused, but at least I could say I had fallen, and it would not be a lie.

I raised a hand and brought it down forcefully to rouse the house.

My fist smashed through glass.

There was a little pain, then, cold and distant, and I waited to hear myself scream, but there was no sound other than the musical tinkle of shards cascading down my arm and a wet pit-pat of falling droplets. Now, that was curious. People who put bits of themselves through windows usually had something to say about it, didn't they? I waited a moment longer, in case the reaction were merely delayed. It was not.

No one came to investigate the noise. Empty house, or sound sleepers. After a few seconds' deliberation, I reached gingerly through the jagged hole in the glass and slid back the latch, then froze.

Silence reigned. Still, no one came.

The door shrieked on its hinges. Still, no one came.

And no one would. An inhabited house, even one inhabited by sleepers, could not have been so utterly still. I was alone, then, not in danger of being found and arrested for breaking and entering. I let out a breath and patted my way into the kitchen, closing the door behind me. Then, for good measure, I locked it.

I felt around until I found the range and the box of long kitchen matches I knew must be somewhere near it. The sudden spurt of light showed me a candle stub, and the candle stub showed me a basin and faucet. I washed the blood from my lacerated hand and found it not as serious as I had expected. It dripped sluggishly onto the cold floor. A cloth stopped the flow. There was an endless supply of pickled things in the pantry. I opened a jar of something I thought was apples and ate them all, then filled the jar with water and drank that.

I vomited the lot of it into a bucket and drank another jar of water. The candle was almost unbearably bright.

Trembling, I sought out coal and built up a fire in the range, huddling in front of it as it grew. The heat didn't seem to touch my skin, but my insides burned.

## GRAHAM

I did not feel safe, somehow, though I did not fear discovery. No one who meant to come back soon would have left a cold range. The homeowners had gone somewhere, maybe for the entire winter. I should go see if the furniture were covered. It didn't matter much to me, of course. There was no point in going back out, that night. I would never be able to find the Wrong Boys at night, or even find my way back to Doctor Peach. That could wait until morning. It would have to. One night was a necessity, but I could hardly plan to stay any longer than that, so it didn't matter whether my unwitting hosts returned in a week or a month. I would be gone by then, either way.

But I did not feel safe.

I inched closer to the fire, unable to stop my shaking. I should check the rest of the house, if only to see if I could find some blankets.

A sudden sting lanced through my eye, and I swiped at it in alarm. My fingers came away wet. I couldn't possibly be crying, could I? Now, of all times? I wasn't, though. The other eye stung, and I swiped at that one, too, realising that my brow was pouring sweat.

The water I had drunk gushed out of me and down the front of my coat, and it seemed to burn me. I struggled to peel the soiled layer away, but my fingers were impossibly clumsy, and I could barely focus my eyes well enough to see the buttons.

The house shifted suddenly, not with a creak but a deafening crack like a gunshot. I almost fancied I could feel the floor heave under me, pitching me, unresisting, onto my side.

*Crack! Crack! Crack!* Not the house. Terrible, monstrous footsteps, the footsteps of a colossus. Stertorous, watery breathing, and sharp, piteous gasps. The sounds Mother had made in the moments I first knew I could not stay. The sounds rang in my ears. The sounds of dying.

I knew it was her, but some part of me knew Mother was far away. Barring ghosts, that left only me. I hadn't managed to spit up all the water, and much of it had gone into my lungs. If only I could cough...

48

The attempt sent a spasm tearing through my insides, and I heaved again, curling into a tight, damp ball.

'Are you going to die, Morrigan?'

I started, but there was no one there. Certainly not my brother, who was far away, with Mother. It was his voice, though. The tone was biting, sardonic, but then, it always was. Sherlock showed his love in strange ways, and never in words.

'Not real,' I whispered to myself, exhausting all the breath I had been able to collect.

'I'd rethink that decision,' the phantom voice went on. 'It would be counterproductive.'

Not real, but I cursed him silently all the same. If I were going to die, I didn't think I really had much say in the matter. Few people did. Few... but some did make a choice.

'Exactly,' he said, responding to my thoughts. 'Dying now would be inconsiderate, too. Haven't you caused enough trouble already?'

I fought to catch my breath, fought against the cold leaching into me from the stone floor, to control the heaves wracking my body, but there are fights you cannot win alone.

'You might help,' I mouthed, forgetting for a moment that no one was there.

I retched again, and the glow of the fire seemed to wink out. Again, and the light died entirely.

Floating between pain and emptiness, I was sure I could see Sherlock's smugly knowing face.

'I suppose this wasn't how your brilliant plan was *supposed* to play out.'

'Shut up.'

'Don't die, Morrigan.'

## GRAHAM

'Leave me alone.'

'Don't die, sister.'

There was another sound, very far away, faint, so faint.

The pain faded, and the spasms faded, and my brother's face faded... I faded. But before I was quite gone, I imagined that other noise may have been a key turning in a lock.

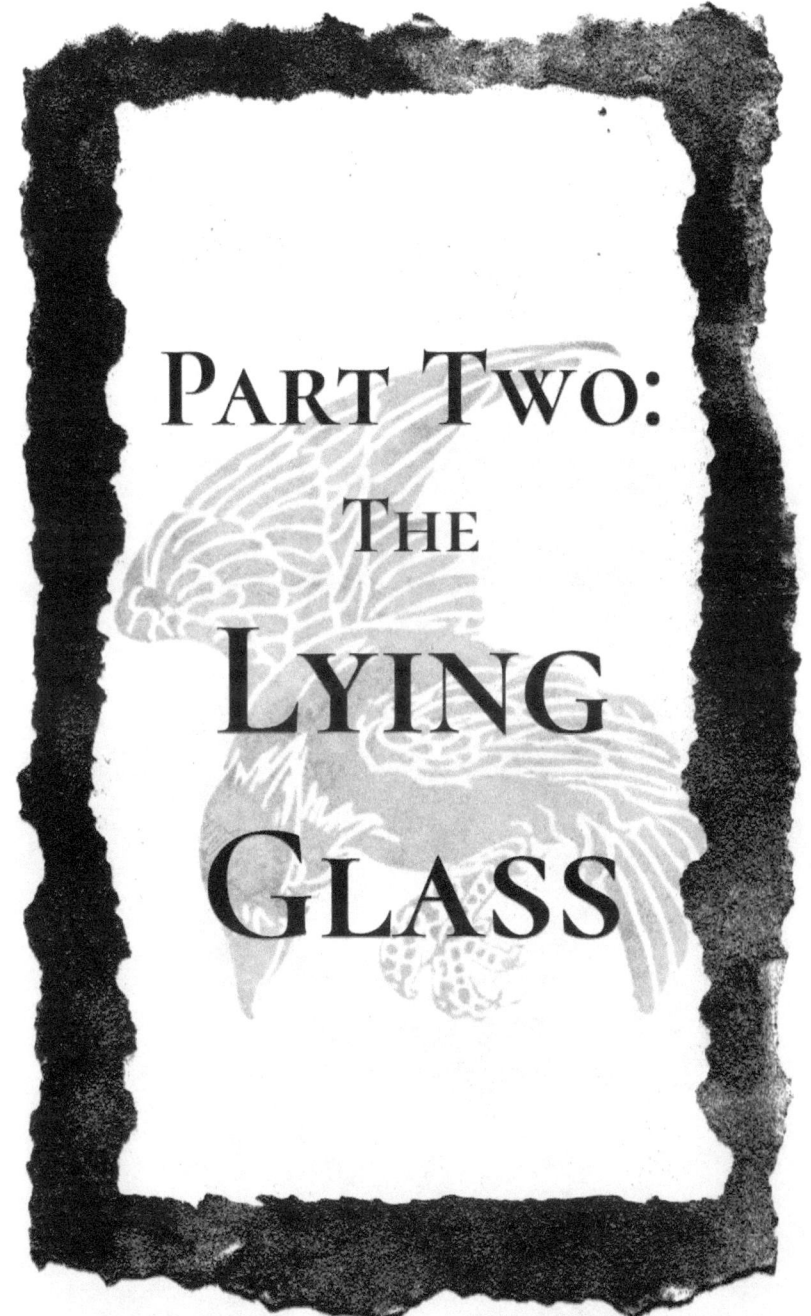

# PART TWO:
## THE
# LYING
# GLASS

# ONE

I WAS SURROUNDED by voices. They told me to hold on. They told me to give up. I had things to do, things I needed to fix. My life was worthless, a progression of failures culminating in this.

Live.

Die.

I dreamed. I sweated. I screamed in pain.

I focused on my brother's voice in the cacophony. Sherlock didn't accuse or encourage.

'It's a bad time,' he said. 'I can't tell you what to do, Morrigan. That's all your decision. But it would be a very bad time to die. Hurry up, though, one way or the other. Time's wasting.'

I tried to tell him again that dying people didn't have a whole lot of choice in the matter, but my mouth wouldn't work, and there was something impossibly heavy resting on my chest.

'There,' he said. 'Now you've done it. I can't see this improving, now.'

I slept again.

# GRAHAM

The fever broke with dawn. Grey-green light trickled between the curtains, slowly giving way to gold and rose. I watched it change and thought about going back to sleep. The ceiling was white. Just white, and I could see little else. It struck me that I wasn't actually dead. Death, as everyone was so fond of saying, was a better place, a surcease of pain. So I knew I wasn't dead, because my throat felt much like the barrel of a rifle must shortly after the bullet has passed through. My belly was not faring much better, nor were my joints. I would not have been surprised to learn I had been through a literal wringer and had all the strength squeezed out of me.

My mouth was terribly dry.

I did not recognize the room, but that hardly seemed important; I could not muster the strength to wonder where I was. All that mattered, the only important thing, was that I was desperately thirsty, and the glass on the table beside me was empty.

Sitting up was far too great an effort. It would have to be done in stages. I rolled onto my side first, then lay a while to rest. The next step was to gather my arms under myself and lever myself up, trembling, to brace myself against the headboard of the bed. After a while, I was able to push myself up higher with my elbows, enough that I could see the single paraffin lamp burning low on the trunk at the foot of the bed, a chest of drawers, a washstand.

It was a solidly practical middle-class room. A framed print of the Roman Coliseum hung above the chest of drawers. Beneath it stood a china shepherdess. Every flat surface was covered with crocheted lace. Not a speck of dust in sight. The mantel supported a clock and a candlestick and a little boy in blue lederhosen with a lamb across his shoulders, staring wistfully across the room at the shepherdess. There was no other decoration.

There. Part way, at least. I glanced down at the old, soft, woollen night-dress in which I had been clothed. I had been wearing a night-dress,

I thought. But this one was clean, and mine had not been. The sleeves ended inches above my wrists. I thought I'd had a jumper, too, and a coat and boots. The coat was mine, but the jumper had come from...

I squeezed my eyes shut and tried to concentrate. What *had* happened, exactly?

I was being chased...

No, that came last.

First, I ran away. Then, the Wrong Boys. Then Doctor Peach. The jumper had come from Sylvia, of course. The Boys found me, and Peach treated me, and Sylvia fed me. And then...

The dark, and the men in their cart, the men who wanted me. Wanted me, but took the little girl, Snail. And I ran, and I fell, and I broke into a house...

And then I was ill.

I looked around the room, but Sherlock was nowhere to be seen. Neither was Mother's pallid, vomit-soaked ghost, even though I knew— *knew*—they had both been there. I had seen them. I had heard them.

I had been very, very sick.

Something else seemed amiss, and, groggy as I was, it took me several minutes to place it.

There was no policeman watching me.

I could only be recovering in a bed, in a bedroom, in clean clothes, because someone had put me there, and only the owners of the house could have put me there. They had returned sooner than I had thought they would, and thank God for that. They had found me on the floor in their kitchen amid my own sick and the shards of their broken window, and they had not turned me over to the police.

They almost certainly would once they found me recovered, though.

I swung my legs over the edge of the bed and contemplated standing. Even the thought was exhausting. There was little chance I could sneak away before someone came to check on me. Maybe I could talk my way out of it. There was no need to lie. I had been chased, and the wall around their garden was crumbling, and I fell through and couldn't get back out. I only trespassed to keep from dying in the cold and the damp.

I sighed as I realised they would undoubtedly have found my money. I would have to surrender it to repair the damage to the window if I wanted to get out of this with my liberty. Without money, Bordeaux was very, very far away.

But...

I had been ragged and filthy, before. I had looked like an urchin. An urchin with a pocketful of notes and coins. Perhaps they would be understanding of my motives for breaking and entering, but I also looked like a thief. I couldn't explain without being sent home, but if I didn't explain, I'd be arrested. Maybe my educated accents could save me, where they had betrayed me before, but I could hardly rely on it.

There was really no choice, then. I had to make some effort to get away, before all control of the situation was taken from me.

I peeled myself out of the damp sheets and heaved myself upright, leaning heavily on the edge of the bed for support. My ankle throbbed, and I glanced down to see it freshly wrapped. A small, round carpet woven with roses protected my feet from the cold floor. My limbs trembled with the exertion, but I stayed standing.

The decanter to match the empty glass stood across the room on a small vanity. The cut glass and its desirable contents sparkled. The little chair was pulled away from the dressing-table, its needlepoint seat still depressed. Someone had been sitting there very recently.

They would undoubtedly be coming back.

I thought about reaching for the glass, but knew I did not have the strength of grip to carry it to the vanity without dropping it. In desperate moments, one may drink from a decanter.

Slowly, I let go of the bed and pushed one foot forward, off the little carpet and onto the cold wood. The house reminded me that it was winter outside, despite the sun trickling in through the window. I shook from cold and effort and growing fear. Someone would be coming. I had to be gone by then.

I achieved the vanity and gratefully moved my weight from my legs to the needlepoint chair, reaching for my object. My mouth felt coated with dust. I removed the circle of lace covering the decanter's mouth and gulped the contents. My stomach objected to the endeavour. I forced myself to slow and set the decanter down before I could be sick. A few measured breaths, and then I could continue. One. Two.

My eyes slid from the decanter to the mirror above, and the ghastly apparition staring back stole the breath I had gathered for a scream.

Have you ever failed to recognize your reflection?

The creature I beheld seemed every bit as startled by the revelation as I. Sharp grey eyes gleamed out from sunken sockets as deep and dark as caverns, riding atop cheekbones as sharp as knives. The gaunt face was sallow, the lips thin and cracked and pale. And the thick, black hair was cropped untidily only a couple of inches from the scalp.

My hair. The only part of me that had ever been called beautiful. Gone. I had not been raised to value beauty above all other womanly attributes, and so I was unprepared for the deep, biting pain that seared me as I realized the loss. My only loveliness.

I raised a hand and groped at the shorn fringe as though expecting to find it was only an illusion, but my fingers came up against the hedgehog tufts, and a low moan escaped me.

The face in the mirror wasn't *me*. I was thin, but it was *too* thin. I was pale, but it was *too* pale. I was plain, but... It wasn't me. It was someone else, a sickly, emaciated, terrified... *boy*.

But there was something else.

## GRAHAM

I had seen sickness, terrible sickness, as had everyone living in those times. Looking at the changes the illness had wrought in me, I knew I had not lain there a single night, nor two, nor five.

A whisper of movement in the corridor caught my attention an instant before the door clicked open. I turned, catching myself on the edge of the vanity as the motion threatened my balance.

A woman entered. She blinked at me in surprise, clucked her tongue, and strode across the room to seize me by the elbows. There were a few moments of incoherent protestation, but I was weaker than usual, and she was stronger than I had expected, and she succeeded in manhandling me back into the bed and rolling me tight into the blankets like an Egyptian mummy.

'*Call out* if you want something,' she chided. 'Don't just go staggering around in the cold with bare feet. There. That's better. Anyway, the water must be quite cold from sitting there all night. You'll have hot broth, if you can wait, and tea. Then you'll sleep.'

I didn't respond. She didn't seem to expect me to. She fluffed the pillows behind me rather more forcibly than was necessary, dropped a few more lumps of coal onto the fire, and stabbed the flames fiercely until they crackled and leapt.

I watched her. She was perhaps ten years older than I, in her mid or late twenties, and pretty. Her features were fine and even, skin smooth save for a single, tiny, indented scar beneath her right eye. Her hair was dark, tinted with red where the firelight struck it. A few prematurely silver strands glittered amidst the sable. She wore a loose, uncorseted gown in the style called 'artistic' dress, which told me either that she did not intend to go out soon, or this was a peculiarly Bohemian household. Her hands were long, but, strangely, the knuckles bulged. They were not red and coarse, as servants' hands often were. Well, she was no servant. But all the same, she had done work in the past that ladies' hands did not often see.

The room began to grow warmer.

She left and returned with the promised tea and broth, nothing at all like Sylvia's offerings. The tea was dark and fragrant. No grease floated atop the clear broth. She popped open the legs of the tray and set it across my lap. Good china. Nicer than the things around me, but old, chipped. Inherited from a wealthier family member, or purchased second-hand? No, mended once, twice, with great skill. There was some money, but she chose to spend it on mending rather than replacement. Sentimental. Inherited.

I shut my eyes.

'Would you like me to help you?' the woman asked.

'No, thank you,' I replied. She did not seem surprised by my voice. I must have talked during my illness. I must have raved. Fear gripped me that I had said something to identify myself, but my father was nowhere to be seen. What had I said, then? Could I ask without seeming suspicious?

I sipped the tea, my tongue curling at the sweetness. It was hot, though, and it would be rude to set it aside, even if it was sticky.

'My name is Theodora,' the woman said. 'You may call me Teddy, or Mrs Grey, if Christian names make you uncomfortable.'

She waited. I had not identified myself, then, not if she was waiting for an introduction.

'Crow,' I replied readily.

She tilted her head, her fine eyebrows arched, then sighed. 'You were very ill, Crow. We thought you would die. Or that your brain wouldn't be the same after such a high fever.'

I touched the prickling ends of my shorn hair. Long hair was too difficult to wash when it began to accumulate fever-sweat, and it held in a dangerous amount of heat. They might have saved my life by taking my beautiful hair away. I wanted it back.

## GRAHAM

'You've been here two weeks.'

I started. 'All of two weeks? Fourteen days?'

She nodded and pressed me back into the pillows with a firm hand. 'Twelve days. Don't upset yourself. You're not well, yet.'

I swatted her hand away. 'You don't understand. I was being chased. When I fell into your garden, there were men after me. I got away, but they took my friend.' I fell back again, exhausted. Oh, Snail. What could they have done to her in two weeks' time? Where could they have taken her? If she was even still alive, in two weeks, they could have left London. They could have left the country. If I had managed to find my way back to Doctor Peach the next day, he might have told me where to find the Wrong Boys, and I could have told them where to begin a search. Two weeks later, there would be no sign left to suggest our assailants' destination.

They had wanted me.

Theodora Grey's pretty face paled. 'I'll send for the police.'

The police would demand my name. They would send me home.

Theodora Grey stared deep into my eyes and understood. 'They hit you?' she asked. 'That ankle, and those bruises...'

I shook my head but made no reply. My family were not guilty of the sins Doctor Peach had suggested, and they had never hit me. My own sins had driven me out.

I did not think she believed me, even though she nodded. Her lips remained tight.

'It was very good of my husband's cousin to send you to stay,' she said emphatically. 'We always enjoy the company of family. But I suspect the police will want something more substantial than your charming sobriquet...?'

It was my turn to blink in surprise. She proposed to lie to the police. I had never had any particular dealings with them before, but I still had

**60**

the impression that wilful deception came with severe repercussions, should it be found out. But she did not mean to send me home.

I thought, weighing my adolescent powers as an actress against the fact that, if I had scarcely recognised myself, no one else could possibly recognise me, either.

'Morgan,' I decided. That would be easy. I would not arouse suspicion by failing to respond.

'Morgan Grey,' she agreed. 'Fondly known as Crow.' Her sharp gaze focused on me, gauging my resemblance to the bird, and she shook her head in disapproval, no doubt at the perceived unkindness. But Snail had given me that name, and the least I could do was keep it until she was found safe.

'I have to go, though,' I said. 'I have to find her other friends and let them know what happened to her. They'll be worried sick.' The hours I had known the Wrong Boys had shown me a strange little family, each dependent on the others, fiercely devoted. They fought for one another like wolves. I remembered Magpie, still and silent in the firelight of Doctor Peach's parlour, watching out for the others as they slept.

Those men had come after me. The Wrong Boys fought for me, and Snail came to rescue me, and she was taken. I broke my family, and then I broke theirs.

'Find her other friends?' Theodora Grey echoed. 'But surely...'

'I don't think she has any parents. Just her friends.'

'But where does she live?'

I shrugged. 'Nowhere, probably.'

I could almost see her train of thought change tracks to accommodate the new information. 'Ah. A gang.'

I nodded.

'Then you couldn't tell someone where to look for these friends. You just meant to wander around until you found them.'

## GRAHAM

Her use of the past tense suggested that she thought my plans had already changed.

'The outside is cold,' she continued, 'and the air is nothing but smuts at this time of year. You can barely stand, and you haven't enough flesh on you to stop you freezing. You're not leaving here for some time, I'm afraid.'

I would have loved to protest that she could not keep me against my will, except that she very obviously could. 'I have to find them,' I insisted. 'And her. She's only a child.'

A shadow of pain flickered across Theodora Grey's smooth face.

'Eight years old,' I pressed. 'If even that.'

'And if the cold is too much for your body, and you come ill again and die?' she snapped, revealing unexpected steel. 'Who will speak for the child, then? Who will remain to describe the men who took her, and who will remember where it happened, and what direction they took? You are not leaving here, for her good and your own. Tell the police.'

'I will. But—'

'But nothing.'

That ended the argument. I sipped my broth and waited for the moment I might escape. But the room was warm, and my body betrayed me. After a time, I slept again.

# TWO

THE POLICE DETECTIVE, Robbins, cared very little for Snail once he learned that she had no parents looking for her, but fortunately, he did not seem any more interested in me and my history. Theodora Grey had introduced me to him as Morgan Grey, her husband's cousin, and that seemed to be enough for him. He did not ask for my parents' names, or where I lived when I was not staying with Cousin Teddy and... I had never heard her husband's name, so I skirted around the necessity of discussing him.

I told Detective Robbins that I had been playing with the street children for want of anyone else near my own age. He did not question that a person sixteen years old might still be interested in play. I told him that we had gone rather far afield and were returning to the neighbourhood when the wagon appeared, and the masked men jumped out. He raised an eyebrow. I told him about the brief scuffle, about my companions scattering, the men pursuing me to the exclusion of the others, and Snail coming to my rescue as I raced through the alleys and mews on a weak ankle. I did not relate the fall through the hole in the garden wall, or the breaking-and-entering, as those were not things a cousin would have done. I said I realised I was home, just at the wrong end, and jumped down to the garden to hide until my cousins returned to let me in. Then I became ill.

'One of them has an eye out,' I added. 'He picked me up, and I struggled, and I put his eye out. By accident.'

Detective Robbins scratched at his monumental sideburns as he reviewed the notes he had taken. Then he scolded Mrs Grey for letting me associate with the street Arabs, who he said were likely the source of my disease. She bore the criticism serenely, but made no apologies. She had not changed out of her artistic dress, and her appearance and attitude made Robbins visibly uncomfortable, though she seemed entirely unaware of it. An uncorseted woman might be capable of anything, up to and including allowing family to interact with the lower forms of life.

The man stood at last, his shoulders moving irritably inside his greatcoat. 'If you had heard any of their names or seen their faces, I would be much more confident of a result,' he said. 'The eye is a useful piece of information, but I can hardly begin questioning every man with an eyepatch. Still, it is a starting place. We do have higher priorities, at the moment, but this will not go uninvestigated.'

By that time, my head was beginning to throb, and my chest ached. I knew very well that his priorities leaned toward money. The things that ended up in newspapers. Big things that earned promotions. Snail was a very little thing.

'Sir,' I said, 'they'd have known by looking that she was nobody. They know they can't ransom her. They took her for some purpose, maybe or maybe not the same purpose they had planned for me, but they've had plenty of time to enact it. I can't bear to think of even a moment being wasted.'

He sighed heavily, much more pathos in the gesture than I had expected. 'If I took the time to cry for every child who disappeared, I'd never get anything done. No time will be wasted, I promise you, but there are other people who need help, and I have to focus my attention where there is a higher probability of success. If you can remember anything more that might help identify these men or their destination, do not hesitate to send for me.'

I assured him I would continue trying to remember.

'Good afternoon, Master Morgan,' he intoned as he left the room. I blinked and felt again at the ends of my shorn hair, but did not correct him. There was no point. I knew very well I had not seen a face or heard a name, and so it was unlikely that I would see Detective Robbins again. And if he believed he had spent the last hour talking to a boy, he was unlikely to connect me to any reports he might receive of a runaway girl.

Still, it hurt. Somewhere, a dark, glossy braid as thick as my wrist lay like an amputated limb, a severed connection to the self I had been the night I crawled from my window.

Theodora Grey showed Robbins to the door. They did not seem to have servants. In a house of that respectable size, that seemed unlikely, but I had come to realise that I was among Bohemians, and so any strangeness could simply be called eccentricity. No servants, unrestrained women, taking in a runaway and lying to the police.

My captor appeared thoughtful when she returned.

'The rest of this gang aren't aware of the fate of their Snail,' she murmured.

She did not make it a question, so I did not respond.

'And you couldn't tell me where to look for them. But they ought to be told. Perhaps some other denizens of the streets might have heard of them and would know how to contact them. There are such children everywhere. Do you think one or more might consent to come back here with me and speak to you? Perhaps in exchange for a meal?'

## GRAHAM

I frowned at the mention of other denizens of the streets, thinking of the Hellhounds. There were horrible people in every walk of life, of course, but it seemed like a dangerous idea to invite strangers off the streets into a house, children or no.

'Doctor Peach,' I said.

Theodora Grey inclined her head and waited for me to continue.

'I don't know his Christian name,' I said. The thought of him made me uncomfortable. His peeling door, his deathly pallor, his inhuman movements, his sibilant speech. I did not trust him. But the Wrong Boys did. He seemed to have concerned himself with their welfare, and so Snail's fate was likewise his concern. And he may know where to find them.

'They took me to him. He bound my ankle. I think he knows them fairly well.'

She smiled, an unexpected tinge of triumph in the expression. Perhaps she thought she had broken through my reticence, and my own name would be coming next. 'There should be some way to locate a physician.'

I nodded. 'There was a woman with him named Sylvia.' I couldn't speak to the nature of their relationship, or to her surname, so I did not. 'I might be able to find them, from the alley behind your house.'

'Perhaps,' she allowed gently, 'if you could support your own weight.'

With that, she left me again, and I was forced to admit that she was absolutely right.

I did not escape that day, or the day after. Theodora Grey's logic was sound; I was not certain I could make it down the stairs, much less to Doctor Peach, wherever he was. I had run away very recently, and it seemed a bit excessive to run away again so soon, when I had Theodora's assurance that she was doing all she could to locate the Wrong Boys, and when my own power to do so was non-existent.

I did meet the husband, whose name turned out to be Edwin. He was older than his wife by perhaps twenty years, still very handsome, with dark hair and a neat moustache and the beginnings of a milky cataract in his right eye. He smiled constantly as if sharing a private joke with whomever happened to be in the room at the time. I intended to mistrust him, as I had resolved to mistrust everybody, but that smile made it impossible. He said that his Teddy had informed him of our recently-discovered kinship and that, after discussion, they had agreed that it ought to continue for as long as I needed. Theodora had, it seemed, shared her suspicions about the origin of my bruises.

I felt the need to set them aright, but neither had said anything aloud, and I did not want those words in the air. And their willingness to help removed the urgency of my flight to my family in Bordeaux, which allowed me to devote my attention to Snail's rescue without the distraction of my own difficulties. I could remain in London without wondering how I would live.

I did not ask them why. These people were eccentrics, and nothing they did required an explanation.

I thanked them both profusely, and Edwin Grey brought up books from their library for me to read while I convalesced. His interests were various. He brought me a history of Greek philosophy and a collection of folk tales and a romantic novel in three volumes. The lady of the house seemed to limit herself to botany. She brought me a volume on the poisonous plants of Provence and one on the families of flowering trees in the Indian subcontinent. I perused all their offerings in the hope of learning something more about the people who owned the books.

And in those first few days, I recovered enough that they were willing to help me downstairs to sit in their parlour in my borrowed night clothes. They did not seem concerned that unannounced callers would appear to take offence at my state of semi-undress. Edwin Grey, himself, barely seemed to notice that I was, by common standards, indecent.

## GRAHAM

Bohemians.

The eccentricity of that house was wildly different from the eccentricity to which I was accustomed at home. I had been raised in a set of rules and structures different from but equally as rigid as those subscribed by the masses. The Greys lived in an atmosphere of relaxation. They ate whenever they pleased and did not dress for dinner, as we were sometimes required to do at home. They talked about whatever appealed, and I listened. The government, Theodora's poisonous plants, literature, the weather and its extended effects on agriculture, crime in London and the countryside, and any number of other things one rarely heard discussed in mixed company, particularly when the mixture included an adolescent girl.

I slowly gathered that Edwin Grey had been a newspaper man, and both he and his wife studied each day's editions in depth to inform the evening's conversation. And Theodora, though she did not mention it, was herself an employed woman. I found a section of their shelves populated by the botanical treatises of T.D. Grey. She only smiled when I asked her about them.

And they did have servants. A house boy arrived each morning with a harried-looking cook who objected strenuously to the fact that both of the Greys occasionally invaded the kitchen to usurp her position. Their names were Dick and Rachel Dunn, and they took me in stride with the air of ones who had long since ceased to question anything that happened in their employers' home. They were grandmother and grandson, I thought. Dick Dunn was a couple of years older than I, but about the same height, and thin as a whip, with a peculiar sort of lanky grace that reminded me of the slow-moving storks in the pond at home. Slow-moving, that is, until a fish appeared. I was sure that, if he needed to, he could move like lightning. His grandmother was old, perhaps sixty, but untouched by senility, and a good three inches taller than Dick and I. She had a draught horse's muscular bulk and deliberation of movement, as though it took all of her concentration not to crush everything in her path. Mrs Dunn stuffed me with a soup made, it seemed, primarily from potatoes, onions, and fish heads, which she swore would cure anything. I don't know whether it accelerated my recovery, but it didn't do me any harm, either.

Within a week, I was able to make it upstairs and down on my own. Seventeen days since Snail was taken, and neither Doctor Peach nor the Wrong Boys appeared to hear my tale. The Greys assured me they were making their enquiries, but they did not have the resources of the police and were meeting with little success, trying to find four street children and a questionable physician in the whole of London.

I believed them. Doctor Peach I thought lived somewhere in their general vicinity, as I could not possibly have run very far before falling into their garden. But I was assuming that the space in which I had last seen him belonged to him, when it might have belonged to Sylvia. Perhaps he migrated, one place to another. And I was also assuming that, as a physician, he would want to be found. But Magpie had said that Doctor Peach helped out the ladies, and I had some vague sense that there was a particular type of help for which he could be arrested. Those who had accepted such help would be reluctant to admit they knew him.

The Wrong Boys had known where to find him, but that did not necessarily mean they stayed nearby. When they had found me in that alley, they had referred to the area as their turf, and it had been some distance from Doctor Peach's door.

I had asked Theodora Grey to search for invisible people.

Meanwhile, I sat in the warmth, adequately fed and as safe as a runaway could be. I told myself that it couldn't be helped as I sat quietly and listened to the Greys on the afternoon of the eighteenth day. They had tried for days to engage me in their conversation, but I resisted, and they stopped trying. Listening felt more productive than speaking, for the moment. If I spoke, I risked giving something away. If I listened, I might learn something of use.

'He admitted it?' Edwin was saying. 'Readily?'

'Proudly,' Theodora replied, her ankles crossed and her feet extended toward the fire. She had a glass of wine in one hand and one finger between the pages of a book in the other. 'And I wouldn't say "admitted" so much as "boasted". As though it's an inferior brand of research that requires one to leave the country. That nasty smirk when I told him I had brought back my samples from Australia, myself, rather than pay some brute to retrieve them for me! And of course, he studies people, not plants. He doesn't even get samples, just that brute's descriptions, as if some hired man with a gun would know what to look for...'

Edwin nodded sympathetically, drawing his thumbnail through his moustaches. 'I've never liked him. But it irritates me far more that people praise his armchair drivel.'

She sighed. 'I suppose it could be worse. He might be rehashing Pliny the Elder.'

Edwin laughed. 'Monopods!' he exclaimed.

'You laugh,' she retorted, 'but that is exactly what comes of relying on hearsay in anthropology. Monopods and worse, and nobody knows any better, because nobody has bothered to go and check. Have you any idea how many travellers have come home bearing reports of magical, panacea plants? One must wonder why we aren't all immortal, by now.'

Edwin leaned forward to reply, his hands spread wide and his teeth bared in that knowing smile.

Then there was a crash, and shards of glass rained into his hair as the bay window behind him shattered. Glittering fragments bounced across the carpet and skittered under my chair. So did something else, large and grey and solid, leaving a dark smudge in its wake. The curtains flapped in the rush of cold air, setting my teeth chattering as my heart accelerated.

Theodora leapt to her feet with a cry even as Edwin reflexively hunched down in his seat, his hands rising to protect his face. In the seconds following the event, all was unnaturally still, the silence deafening. Then I heard wheels in the street. I slid from my chair and would have raced to the gaping window, had I been able, but my body would not cooperate, and I realised a second later that, if one projectile could come through the window, so could another. I did not want to make myself a target. I only managed a couple of steps before stopping.

Edwin had put out an arm to keep me back, but as I stopped, he rose and completed the motion I had begun, approaching the window from an angle to stay clear of the path of anything else that might come through. His carpet slippers crunched on the shards.

'Gone,' he whispered, peering through the hole. 'The street's empty, now.'

He looked back at his wife, then at me, then drew the drapes in a feeble attempt to quell the rush of freezing air.

Mrs Dunn filled the doorway suddenly, her face flushed and eyes wide. 'What!' she cried. Dick's face appeared over her shoulder.

'Police,' Theodora said firmly.

Mrs Dunn nodded briskly, turned, and seized Dick by the shoulders, steering him away.

Theodora's sharp eyes turned on me. 'Your pursuers,' she said. 'They could *not* have seen where you went?'

I shook my head. 'They'd have caught me if they'd seen.'

She pursed her lips and surveyed the glittering floor. 'Or they did see and, like you, could not tell that we weren't at home and did not wish to risk waking the house. Or they took a guess and have been watching the house where they thought you ended up. You haven't been out, but you could be seen through the windows. It must be something. It would be far too great a coincidence for this to be unrelated to your presence here.'

'Teddy, dear,' Edwin said quietly, 'if they knew she was here, why would they not come in here and get her? What would frightening us accomplish? It may be no more than an ugly prank.'

Theodora's shoulders hunched, but she sat down slowly, her fingers twisting in her lap. In another woman, I might have thought that a sign of distress, but in her, it looked like deep contemplation.

'If they're angry that I put out that man's eye,' I said sourly, 'frightening us might suit them very well as a first step.'

I delved with a toe beneath the chair where I had been seated and nudged out a fragment of brick. It was black with spots of tar and speckled with salt, the two of which had resulted in the smudge on the carpet. There was something else on the flat side. I held it up.

'A message? Does this mean anything to you?'

The number '17' was painted in red on top of the tar. The paint was still tacky; smears of it stuck to my thumb. They may have made the mark *en route* to hurl it through the Greys' window.

'Seventeen,' Edwin said blankly. 'Seventeen what? Perhaps that was there already.'

'Still wet,' I said, handing it to him. 'They put it there to be seen.'

He turned it over in his hands, squinting almost angrily. 'Messages are usually more effective if the recipient understands them.'

'You have no idea?' I pressed.

'None. Do you?'

'No.'

We both looked at Theodora, who shrugged. 'Perhaps they mistook their target. They must have expected the number to communicate something, so perhaps it was intended for someone else.'

I couldn't imagine hurling anything through a window unless I was completely certain of the people on the other side of it. They had not mistaken their target.

'No,' I said. 'They had to know whose window it was. If we don't understand, I'm sure an explanation will be provided sooner or later.'

Theodora sighed. 'If the explanation isn't more detailed, we're going to run out of windows.'

# THREE

ROBBINS CAME back to hear the story. He talked to me and Theodora and Edwin together, asked a few questions of Mrs Dunn, and took the bit of brick. He cautioned us not to assume that this had anything to do with my near-abduction, but I did notice that he did not say that he thought the two events unrelated.

As he moved to leave, he turned to me once more, holding up the brick so that the scarlet numerals were visible.

'I don't suppose you are, by any chance, seventeen years of age, Master Morgan?'

I shook my head, not looking at the Greys. 'Not yet, sir.'

He sighed. 'It was worth a go,' he said with a shrug. 'I do hope your life continues uneventful for a while. Good afternoon, sirs, ma'am.'

Theodora waited tactfully until the police had gone to turn her smirk on me. 'Master Morgan,' she chuckled. 'I feel I must warn you that girls who pose as boys never have an easy time of it in the stories. They all wind up inconveniently in love with some unsuspecting chevalier.'

I glanced down at myself, wrapped in Edwin's dressing gown and a thick rug. It wasn't much of a disguise, but it worked well enough for a girl who had no curves to hide. The chevalier would not be impressed when I revealed myself.

'I have no intention of passing as a boy, but I don't want to go home, and nobody's looking for a boy.' I returned Theodora's smirk. 'And I saw no reason to embarrass the poor detective by correcting him.'

'Very considerate,' Edwin conceded, 'but there is a problem. You know you have to keep it up, now.'

That had not occurred to me. I frowned.

'Any news of your friend will come here, first, since the police have no other contact for the case, and you will have to be Master Morgan whenever they come back, at any time of day. If they even suspect that you have deceived them as to your sex—'

I began to protest, but he shook his head, moustaches twitching. 'Or that you have—*we* have—allowed them to deceive themselves. If they begin to suspect, your name will come into question, as well, and from there, your entire story. I'm not certain this makes anything easier for you.'

My back straightened, and my chin lifted. 'I do not expect or require ease. My freedom is less important than Snail's safety. I shall be Master Morgan as long as I am able, but if I must be found out in the process of saving her, then so be it.'

'You will be careful with your identity, though,' Theodora said drily, 'considering that we are also involved in the deception.' She sighed heavily and decanted another glass of wine for herself. It was her fourth since the intrusion of the brick into her parlour, but the spirit did not seem to have touched her. She sipped. 'We shall have to find you some trousers.'

The first pair of trousers that appeared to hand belonged to Dick, but it was Mrs Dunn whom the Greys paid for the use of them. I tried to pay them back from my own money, which I had found in the wardrobe in the room that had become mine, along with my boots and overcoat and the sorry remains of my night dress. They refused my coins.

Dick was visibly alarmed at the fate of his trousers, but knew better than to say so.

One of Edwin's old shirts joined the trousers, and obliging Mrs Dunn produced a waistcoat and jacket from the rag-and-bone. My boots were unsuitable, but would have to do until shoes were procured.

The ensemble was assembled by evening and laid out on my bed. I had planned to don it and wear it downstairs for critique. This was going to be different from the times I had worn trousers for their simple practicality in outdoor pursuits, like climbing and fishing. I had to make sure I could wear trousers like someone who had never worn skirts, and that might take some practice in private before the act's public debut.

But when I had folded the rug on the chair, I stopped and stood shivering in night dress and dressing gown, staring at the clothes lying there like a deflated person, like an empty skin I was about to pull on over my own. I had worn trousers before, but this was different. It was different, too, from sitting in a room with Detective Robbins and allowing him to think me male. That had been passive. This would be *taking steps*, an active deception. My fingertips explored my scalp, unaccustomed to the easy access. The prickly ends of my hair brushed my palm. If I put on those clothes and became Master Morgan, I would have to keep my hair short until I could move on and be myself again. I would have to become someone new, someone I did not know. The thought was ridiculous, but a nagging voice in the back of my head insisted that Morgan Grey was more than a disguise. He was a changeling, and if I brought him into that room by putting on those clothes, Morrigan Holmes would vanish.

I shook off the incoherent dread and threw off the dressing gown. Morgan Grey was a necessity. The police would find Snail if they were able, but they had other things to do, first, and she didn't have that time.

# GRAHAM

Morgan Grey would keep me from being dragged back home at least long enough that I could do something—anything—to help. He would last me until I found Snail and made it to Bordeaux.

I would never be that person again, anyway, the girl I had been the night of the storm, and I was not sure I wanted to be. She was dead. One of Edwin's books described rites of passage in faraway places, rituals of people whose names I could not pronounce. There were hundreds, spanning every continent but Antarctica, but the common thread linking them all was death. The child had to die before the adult could be born, like a caterpillar weaving its own coffin-like chrysalis, going still and cold before emerging with wings.

The muttering in the back of my head resolved itself into the pounding of rain and the rising, furious voices of my family. They haunted me.

Changeling, rite of passage, chrysalis. When I emerged from Morgan Grey, I would leave those voices behind and be *me*.

I shivered my way into the ill-fitting hotchpotch of clothing and hurried back downstairs without stopping to assess my reflection in the glass.

My appearance met with scepticism.

'It'll do,' Theodora allowed. 'For the moment. But you'll need something more suited to your station.' She blinked and checked herself. '*Our* station,' she corrected, but I was suppressing a smile at her unconscious inclusion of myself into her household. 'You'll attract attention if you look like you belong to a costermonger.'

Edwin Grey was not a costermonger. I eyed him as I slid into a seat at the table and helped myself to their vegetable stew and warm bread. 'What do you do, actually, now that you're not in newspapers?'

He laughed and flushed at the same time. 'Live idly on my father's money, I'm afraid. The journalism was my attempt at learning a trade, but it ended suddenly and sourly. I made a few other attempts, but Father decided I'd be less trouble if I stuck to managing his books.'

'Not too sourly,' Theodora objected with feigned affront. 'Edwin and I met through his work.'

He frowned. 'Something good came of the work itself, yes, but that doesn't make the ending of it any less unpleasant. Still, that was ten years ago. Plenty of time to forget the sour and concentrate on the sweet.'

The conversation turned to poetry, and thence to the tendency of every generation to lament the inferiority of its own art and literature when compared to the perceived glories of the past.

I rubbed my knees together beneath the table, not yet accustomed to the layers of fabric between them. Something more suitable to the Grey's station, I thought, would have to be made for me. They were not of the class that wore either castoffs or things made in the home. I did not think that either Theodora or Edwin had yet seen the difficulty with that plan: a tailor would have to touch me. Initial measurements would be taken, then there would be a fitting after. The process would take days, even if my suit were given priority. And new clothes were costly. I did not plan to remain with the Greys long enough to justify either the time or the expense. Better to obtain something nearly new and have it altered. That would sit better with my fictitious identity, anyway. No one would need all new clothes after an illness; even if one did take the common precaution of burning everything the invalid had touched, rarely would the invalid have touched every last article of clothing. But I might need old clothes altered to fit a ravaged body.

I touched my bony wrist and forced myself to scrape every morsel of stew from the bottom of my dish. I had piled on a second helping when the crash and tinkle of breaking glass once more rang through the house.

It was the study, this time, shards of glass covering the table beneath the window. A vase of dried lavender lay in pieces on the floor.

'Three,' Theodora said, picking up the missile that had done the damage and holding it for us to see. Robbins had taken the other bit of brick with him, but I suspected that if we put this one beside the other, we would discover two halves of the same whole.

'Seventeen,' Edwin mused. 'Three. Are we to take them separately, or together? Twenty?'

'Or one-hundred seventy-three?'

I stayed away from the window. 'Either way, it would seem not to have been a prank. Not now that there's been a second message.'

Cold air streamed into the room, stabbing at my bare hands and face. It was much too late to call back the man who had boarded over the smashed window in the parlour. Tonight, the heavy curtains would have to suffice to separate the indoors from the outdoors.

'I'm very worried that I've brought this down on you. The timing of it...'

Theodora slipped the tarry bit of brick into a pocket I had not known she had. Her lips thinned despite her attempts to smile. 'The timing would be extraordinary, if the two events are unrelated, no matter what the detective says. But even if it is your presence that's brought their attention here, please remember that you are not to blame for the actions of anyone but yourself. *They* are choosing to do this, whoever they are.'

Edwin nodded his agreement and motioned us from the study. 'I suggest we finish our supper and retire to an hotel for the night. The second message hardly explains the first, and I'm afraid there may be something larger on its way. I'd rather not be here if it arrives in the middle of the night.'

That thought made me shudder, as I wondered what sort of larger thing he thought might be on its way.

Theodora was wondering, too. She slid back past him into the study and shoved a bundle of papers into a leather case.

'If the next message happens to be on fire,' she explained, 'I should like to have my current manuscript safely with me.'

Edwin locked the study door behind her and pocketed the key, rubbing his hands together in the light and warmth of the hall.

The meal was concluded in silence, and when we were finished, Edwin and Theodora each packed a small bag. I caught sight of Theodora palming a tiny silver pistol, and a small, quiet part of me wondered what sort of people these actually were. They concealed a runaway and lied easily to the police, dealt calmly with an attack on their home and owned firearms. If they were criminals, I didn't much mind, for the moment, but I certainly would have liked to know for sure. 'Bohemians' was beginning to sound rather weak, in my head.

It was not yet so late as to make it difficult to find a cab or to arrange accommodations for a single night.

All three of us watched the street behind as we fled the darkened house. The steady golden light of the streetlamps revealed no shadowy figures watching our retreat, no carts waiting in the dim spaces between the circles of light to follow us away. Edwin found for us two adjoining rooms with a door between, and I left the door open through the night and watched the darkness shift around me. If I ever did fall asleep, it was only briefly, and I do not remember it.

We were not murdered in our rented beds, and no one came crashing through the window to take me, though with the blackness pressing hard on my eyeballs, I imagined all sorts of dangerous scenarios and tried my best to plan an effective response to each. With every creak of the floor, every voice without, every draught thumping against the window, my envy of Theodora's pistol increased. No matter what direction my life took, I wanted to learn to use one.

After a few hours, a light rain began, and I could no longer hear the Greys' breathing in the next room, so I do not know whether their sleep was as disturbed as mine, but I cannot think that they rested any easier than did I, waiting to find out whether their home would still be there in the morning.

At the very least, it had not burned down when we made our way back in the green dawn. The boards covering the broken parlour window were dark with damp, and from the other, the sodden curtains waved drearily.

Theodora pushed the curtains aside and peered through, careful of the glass remaining around the frame.

'The carpet,' she said with a sigh. 'But I think the books will be fine. Too far from the window to have gotten wet.'

'I'm sorry about your carpet,' I murmured.

She waved a dismissive hand, her brow beetled in displeasure.

Her anger was general, pointed elsewhere, because she did not know who was responsible. She was not angry at me. But I shut my mouth all the same and followed Edwin inside to view the extent of the damage.

The rain had only been light, with some breeze but no significant wind. A puddle spread beneath the table at the window, dispersing the dried lavender and some of the lighter fragments of the vase. The floorboards had begun to swell. When they dried, they would warp, and that whole section of the floor would have to be replaced. Two broken windows had been enough, but this...

A large Turkey wool rug had begun to absorb the edge of the puddle, and its fibres were dark. It would dry, in time, but some of the dye had run. That couldn't be repaired. It would have to be replaced, and such a rug would be an expense, and unwelcome one on top of two windows and a corner of floor.

Because of me, I couldn't help but think, no matter how many times I reminded myself of Robbins' caution against linking this with earlier events.

I shredded my family, shattered the Wrong Boys, and then quite literally broke the Greys' home. There was no such thing as a curse, or even really such a thing as bad luck, but I found myself scrounging for a rational explanation for the fact that I was very obviously cursed.

Edwin fetched rags with which to begin mopping up the mess. Theodora sent for a glazier and the police, who were getting very tired of hearing from us. Robbins confiscated the second bit of brick and interrogated us all concerning the significance of the number three.

'Rather a lot of effort for a prank,' he conceded, 'coming back again. You may be right that there's a third something coming, though I wouldn't count on it until something actually arrives.' He brushed his thick fingers thoughtfully through his facial hair. 'Mind, you may want to spend another night at your hotel.'

Theodora had taken it on herself to deal with the man, though I suspected he would have been more at ease talking with her husband. 'You think we may be in some danger, then?' she clarified, her eyes steely.

'I don't know,' he said candidly, making his best effort at conversing with a woman. He looked at the shattered parlour window and at the few spots of comfortingly conventional décor in the bohemian space. 'But I prefer not to take chances with people's lives. Better safe than sorry, I'm sure you agree.'

'I cannot be indefinitely banished from my house "just in case", Detective.'

'Sergeant,' he muttered.

She waved a hand. 'If you think our lives may be in danger, I assume some attempt will be made to apprehend the miscreant?'

He bristled. 'Of course. But you see, short of catching him in the act, there is little I can do. I shall leave a constable for that purpose, but if the brick-thrower chooses not to return...'

'That,' Theodora said crisply, 'would be ideal.'

That seemed to stump him. 'It would,' he admitted. His cheeks puffed, scarlet, and his shoulders writhed uncomfortably. 'But see here, I can't leave a policeman outside your door forever...'

'Best catch the responsible party, then.'

There was no way out for him. Whatever likelihood of success he estimated, there really was no way he could defer this particular problem. She had him on the hook.

Robbins turned to me in exasperation and eyed my peculiar attire. He seemed to decide that I was no stranger than the lady of the house, though, because his eyebrows returned to their usual position. 'Glad to see you up and about, Master Morgan. Did your cousin bully you into wellness?'

Theodora smirked like a cat in cream.

'That'd be one way of putting it, sir,' I replied, reflecting on the accuracy of the statement.

He grinned, the briefest flash of good humour before the business-like façade descended again.

'Two constables,' he allowed. 'I'd stay, myself, but that I have a number of other matters presently at hand. But I assure you, I will come at once if a third something makes an appearance.'

He fixed me with a piercing stare. 'Or if Miss Snail reappears. I have not forgotten.'

He replaced his hat on his head and skirted around the glazier's assistants with their paraphernalia. Theodora and I accompanied him to the door.

'Thank you,' I said as he descended the step. Perhaps there was more heart to him than I had thought.

He raised a finger to the brim of his hat and climbed into the waiting hansom.

As the cab drew away from the kerb, a child came into view across the street. He was not one of the Wrong Boys, but his bare, blue feet and hungry expression told me at once that he belonged to their class. He shifted, trying to balance a long wooden box while tugging at the tatters of cardigan draped across his shoulders.

He was watching the Greys' house with more than just the curiosity of the idle.

I prodded Theodora before she could turn to go inside, and the boy, seeing that he was noticed, scurried across the street to present her with his parcel.

'For you, mum,' he said, with a curious glance at me.

Theodora hesitated, looking long after Robbins' departing cab, then turned back to the child.

'From whom?' Her voice was tight, and sharper than the boy had expected.

It seemed to dawn on him that he had stumbled into a difficult situation. A flicker of worry crossed his face. 'Dunno, mum. A man. 'E give it to me to give you.' A pause. 'An' a shilling to do it.'

'What did he look like?'

The boy shifted from foot to foot, his jaw set, a frown spreading.

Theodora sighed. 'You shall have a sovereign. And a hot meal. What did he look like?'

The boy nodded, his eyes the size of saucers. "Is face was muffled. But 'e was big. 'Ad a patch over 'is eye.'

Theodora looked at me cautiously. I understood. It might be nothing but coincidence, but that would be a really extraordinary coincidence.

She let the boy and his box into the hall, where he and I watched each other in wary silence, he clutching his box, I wondering if I should snatch it from him and hurl it back into the street. When she returned to offer him a gold coin, he dropped his parcel. I heard wood crack and braced for an explosion, but none came. The boy cradled his prize in both palms like a bird's egg, his mouth a tiny O, and refused to put it in a pocket long enough to accept the offered meal. He took his bowl of soup there in the hall, his sovereign balanced on his knee, and watched curiously while Theodora prised the top from the box.

I hovered behind them, not quite close enough to see what was within when the lid came off and sensible, forceful Theodora let out a piercing scream.

I pulled her away and reached for the thing to throw it outside, but stopped. Inside was no ticking mass of a bomb, no deadly snake poised to strike.

In the box, half-buried in a bed of clotted, discoloured salt, lay the severed head of a bird, a grisly, eyeless thing as long as my forearm.

An albatross.

# FOUR

THE LOOK on Theodora's face told me that this was the explanation she had been waiting for. I could see no connection between seventeen, three, and a dead sea bird, but she clearly understood this message. She sat where I had pushed her, sprawled on the hall floor, supporting herself with arms thrown behind her, her skirts in disarray. Her eyes were wide, her face stark white, her mouth open as though she could not quite manage to catch her breath.

I struggled up and tried to help her to her feet, but she pulled her knees to her chest and buried her face in her hands, shaking her head.

'Ow, Gawd,' she moaned, her vowels suddenly descending to the vernacular of the Wrong Boys. 'Ow, Christ.'

I drew back in surprise at the change just as Edwin appeared and dashed to his wife.

'Is anyone hurt?' he demanded.

Theodora and I shook our heads.

## GRAHAM

'No,' I said. 'Your explanation arrived.' I nudged the box with my toe, but he did not look back until Theodora had raised her tear-streaked face to meet his gaze.

'They're back,' she said.

Edwin looked at her blankly, then at me, and finally into the box. He managed for a moment to remain expressionless, but I could tell by his sudden pallor that he understood the signal as well as his wife had. Then a shudder worked its way through him.

'Oh,' he said hollowly. 'So it's about the albatross.'

No. I heard a special significance attached to the word, one that warranted a capital letter. The Albatross.

'We should 'ave known,' Theodora whispered. ''Ow did we not put it together sooner? Masked men takin' gels off the streets... Oh, Edwin...'

My throat closed in alarm, and I rounded on her. 'What do you mean?'

'A ghost from our past,' Edwin murmured. He stopped and looked me over earnestly, his lips pursed, eternal smile gone. 'This message was meant for us, not for you. So maybe there is at least a small coincidence, here.'

He pulled his wife to her feet and led her down to the kitchen, leaving me to follow.

I paused and took a moment to close the front door. In the commotion, the boy had vanished, and I could not blame him. No one in that house would shoot the messenger, but he wasn't to know that. I suspect he wanted to disappear before the police made yet another inevitable appearance. I locked the door and kicked the box up against the hall tree before following the Greys.

The kitchen was warm, and Edwin was heating water for tea. I glanced at the back door and saw its glass repaired; that must have been done while I was confined to bed upstairs. The Greys must have been very popular with the area's glaziers, by that time.

Theodora sat at the heavy wooden table. Her tears had stopped, and her expression was distant.

I pulled out a chair and sat down beside her.

'Tell me,' I said.

She glanced at her husband's taut back and then looked at me. To my annoyance, she shook her head. 'Not now.' Her voice had resumed its original tenor, precise and genteel, the traces of the streets gone.

'You cannot leave me out of it,' I protested. 'Not if you think you know who took Snail.'

'I don't want to relive that part of my life. I don't want to touch on those memories unless I have no other choice. Not unless I'm certain.'

'You seemed fairly certain when you saw that head in the box! What is the Albatross?'

She bared her teeth in a terrible grimace and turned away from me.

Edwin looked at her with a frown. 'Are we not certain?' he asked gently. 'What other possibility is there?'

She shook her head. I could not see her face, but I thought from the angle of her shoulders and the tension in her neck that her tears must have started, again.

'You'll hear everything,' Edwin said to me as he laid a hand on his wife's back. 'But later. You will not be left out of it, I promise. But Teddy and I both need time to collect ourselves. Tomorrow, perhaps, in the morning. That policeman will want to hear the whole story, I'm sure, and I don't know that we'll be able to tell it all more than once.' He sighed. 'You can hear all about it when we tell him.'

That was not satisfactory, but I could tell it was the best I was going to get. For the moment, at least, I was wholly dependent on them—for my room and board, for protection, for whatever information they possessed. The least I could do in return was wait.

# GRAHAM

Wait on their story, that is.

I saw no reason to wait on anything else. With the amount of time I had lost already, I saw no reason to waste even a moment more.

Edwin took the kettle from the stove and prepared a pot and three cups, but I declined.

'Could you help Teddy upstairs, then?' he asked. 'I should probably go reassure the workmen that the world isn't ending. Heaven only knows what they think is happening in here.'

I said I would, and he bent to press his lips briefly into his wife's dark hair before retreating from the kitchen.

Theodora shook off my hand, so I put her tea on a tray and followed her up to the couple's room, where she dragged a chintz-covered chair away from the window before sinking into it. She pressed her fingertips into her forehead and sat silent.

I placed the tray on a table and watched her for a few moments, but she had turned to stone, pale and motionless.

'It's something really terrible, isn't it?' I asked.

She did not respond. For all I knew, she had not even heard. My heart rose into my throat.

'Do you suppose there's any chance we'll find Snail alive?'

'She's alive,' Theodora whispered.

I let myself breathe.

Then she continued. 'But as for finding her...'

The choking lump returned. I had no more time to waste. I tiptoed to the door, mind churning. Only one possibility presented itself. I did not like to jump to conclusions, but what other story could there be to tell? I turned back to her with my hand on the knob and voiced my suspicion, not truly expecting an answer.

'You know who took Snail because they took you, once. Is that right?'

90

She looked up, her eyes all whites.

'Do you know *where* she is?'

'No. I'm sorry. No.'

I nodded and withdrew, biting my tongue. My irritation would not calm her mind enough to let her tell me more. Time might do that. It might not. I thought she did understand the gravity of the situation. Better than I did, myself, if I was right. Surely, she wouldn't withhold any information that would be helpful in the here and now. I could wait for her story.

I shut the door quietly and passed briefly through my own room to retrieve my overcoat and Sylvia's jumper before padding back downstairs and to the kitchen.

Through the repaired panes of the door, I could see into the back garden and to the rear wall, to the patch of crumbled brick where my acquaintance with the Greys had begun.

I wondered whether I had left any skin behind when I went scraping across those rough edges to land in the earthen bed, below. Memory took me back. Darkness, my legs weak underneath me, the fury of the men behind me, cowering away from a searching beam of light. I wrapped myself in jumper and coat and pushed outside.

I had not seen the garden since that night, and daylight made it an entirely new place.

A few evergreen plants stood dark and glossy, but most of the beds were empty, the path a muddy morass from the night's rain. There was the shed that had failed to yield me a ladder. On closer inspection, I could see that it was not locked, merely rusty. My strength had not completely recovered, but when I depressed the thumb latch now, it gave.

And there was a ladder. I pulled it out and propped it against the side of the shed while I shut the door again. The handle had nearly disintegrated, a pile of rusty fragments growing at my feet. I took my prize to the hole in the rear wall and glanced guiltily over my shoulder as I contemplated an escape. That glance showed me, to my intense exasperation, that the garden did have a gate. It stood, prominently painted green, to the right of the kitchen window. There the whole time, and I had utterly failed to find it. Well, I had been very sick. And it was just as well; if I had found the gate and escaped through it, I might just have died in the cold. And I wouldn't stand poised to learn whatever it was the Greys knew.

Of course, I reminded myself irritably, if I had died of fever and exhaustion and exposure, I still would never have learned what the Greys knew. The one did sort of preclude the other. I stamped down a flash of irrational anger at the lapse. It was a little thing, a stupid thing, not worth the time I had given it. If I was to be angry about something, it should be that I had allowed Snail to be taken in the first place. A small illogic hardly mattered, in the long run. And yet, there I was, dwelling on it.

I shook myself and hauled myself through the hole in the wall and out into the alley.

It was dim, the high brick walls to either side blocking out the light that the open expanse of the garden had allowed.

I stood stock-still for a moment, half sure that someone would be watching me from the deeper shadows, and it took an effort of will to recall that it had been nearly a fortnight. No one could possibly have been waiting there for me for all that time.

A sound drew my eye, and I turned my head fractionally to see a scrawny cat dragging the bloodied carcass of a pigeon. It stopped and looked at me with what seemed more offence than fear, then turned around and dragged its prize back the way it had come, no more interested in me than I was in it.

I brushed myself off and stepped away from the wall. It was a close, claustrophobic space, with a stale smell that rose from the combination of black soot and grey-green mould caking the brick, from the stubs of decaying vegetable matter and the remains of birds, rodents, and other small things that had died in a place where few people ever bothered to go. The smell would become briefly worse when spring arrived and the bits of refuse began to thaw, but then more small vermin would arrive, drawn by the odour, and would pick the place clean. This was a decent part of London, though, like all decent parts, it abutted slums and hellish rookeries. What was distasteful here would be considered luxury only a half-mile away.

I toed my way through the frozen scum in the direction I thought I had come, that night, but every corner, every stretch of blank wall looked the same to someone who had only ever passed by them in pitch blackness, before. I was very much aware of how easily I could become lost, and it occurred to me now that I did not know the Greys' address to ask for if I could not find my way back to them.

Grimacing, I picked up the end of what I took to be a chicken bone and scored a deep mark in the sooty patina of the wall beside me. I did the same at the next turn I took, and the next, when a faint gleam caught my eye. I bent to pick up the object, a tiny, round bit of steel. One of Snail's slingshot missiles. Either she had launched it at one of the men while she was chasing them in pursuit of me, or she had dropped it as they were carrying her away. Not intentionally, I didn't think. At that last glance I had of her, she had seemed quite unconscious, so I did not think I could expect a trail of breadcrumbs to lead me to wherever she was, now. But a general direction was better than nothing. I pocketed the steel shot and crept along in search of the next. In a couple of places, there were two or three near each other, which confirmed to me that they were falling at random from her pouch, not dropped carefully, one by one, as a signal. By the time the trail had led me to a road, I had a pocket full of fifteen little steel balls.

But the trail vanished at the street. It had been nearly a fortnight, and any shiny little things would have been picked up or kicked away or driven deep into the gaps between the paving stones. The men would have hauled her out of the alleys back to their waiting wagon, and there was no way of knowing which way the wagon had gone.

No general direction, then.

I lingered for a few minutes in the mouth of the alley, getting a feel for the ebb and flow of the foot traffic and the carts and drays, carriages and cabs. I was not totally certain, but I thought this might be the point at which I had originally gone in. If it was, Doctor Peach's place—I found it difficult to think of those rooms as a medical practice—would be near. Hopefully, near enough that I could find it.

I did make a few wrong turnings, but after only fifteen or twenty minutes of wandering, I found the peeling blue door. It was shut, and there was no one around. I hesitated before knocking, considering the street I had left behind and the impunity with which I had moved through it. The invisibility. Even hatless, dressed in my bizarre mélange of mismatched apparel, no one had even seemed to see me. I was not a striking person. I had never drawn admiring gazes, like the daughters of some of my father's friends. But when I had gone out as myself, in the company of my family, passers-by made eye contact. If we were on foot, they and we performed that little dance of negotiation so that neither party would have to stop entirely as we passed one another on the pavement. Alone, as Morgan Grey, I hardly even existed. Pedestrians walked straight toward me, giving me no choice but to move out of the way, and no one looked me in the eye, their gazes sliding across me with the same unconcerned ease with which they slid over the names of familiar businesses. I had become a part of the scenery.

No one would recognise me as that runaway if no one even saw me.

I knocked.

And I waited.

For several long moments, there was no answer, and I was raising my fist to knock again, and harder, when the door opened a crack and

Sylvia's scarlet face appeared in the gap. She narrowed her eyes.

Trying to remember where she'd seen me before, I thought.

'Is Doctor Peach available?' I asked.

She looked at me again, harder, her broad mouth working in her concentration.

'Sorry,' I said. 'My hair was rather longer, the last time we met.'

Her eyebrows went down and then up in what I took for assent. 'Ah,' she said, and she opened the door wider to let me through.

'Doc!' she roared into the depths of the building as she led me down the grimy hall and to the room of chairs and lamps. The candles, lamps, and lanterns were all still there, but only about half as many of them were lit as had been last time. In the more moderate light, the place seemed closer, more inviting than it had when blazing like a furnace.

Sylvia gestured me toward one of the mouldering chairs and bustled out of the room, bellowing again for the Doc. I wondered whether she was capable of uttering more than a single syllable at a time. Not that it seemed to matter; she clearly got on very well with her minimalistic communication style. My ankle had begun to ache fiercely after so much walking, so despite my intention to remain standing, I took the chair. A puff of horsehair burst into the air as my rear made contact with the cushion, and I coughed furiously, but the relief of being off the ankle was sublime.

After a few moments, Doctor Peach loomed in the doorway like a creeping shade, a splash of darkness in the light of the lamps. He had discarded the long, stained smock in which I had last seen him and appeared now in a once-black frock coat, its shoulders and hems faded to the colour of rust. Some chemical had left blotches of greenish-white at the cuffs.

I could see that he recognised me without an instant of confusion.

'Oh,' he said. From someone else, that would have sounded like distaste, but from him, it was merely acknowledgement. I was there, and he had become aware of the fact.

'I need to speak with the Wrong Boys,' I said without preamble. 'Do you know where I can find them?'

He considered me silently for a moment before moving further into the room with his slow, deliberate gait, like a chilled lizard.

'I do not know where they are, at present,' he informed me. 'But Dart and Billy were here this morning, and one or another of them is sure to stop in tomorrow.'

He fell silent again, rubbing his skeletal hands together before him, drawing my attention to the flashing glimpses of his stained fingernails.

'You see,' he said in a lower voice, the second word a prolonged hiss, 'they have been visiting me religiously, in the hope you would find your way back here.'

I looked at him with surprise. 'Me?'

'You. Snail knows the secret location of their lair and would return there, if she were able. She has not. But you, if you had escaped, might reappear here. And you have.'

I mulled that over. The idea that they had been anxious for me was gratifying.

'Of course,' he continued, 'Weasel is of the opinion that you may have been accomplice in the whole ordeal and are welcome to rot in hell. After all, no one had ever tried to kidnap one of their number until you arrived.' He bared his tobacco-brown teeth in a wicked smile. 'I am sure whatever story you bring with you will be enough to allay his suspicions.'

I shuddered at the aggressive sibilance of his final word. 'What story I have, I've already told to the police. They...' I shook my head. 'They will do what they are able, but the detective I spoke to was not optimistic. We may have to turn vigilante.'

It was his turn to regard me with surprise. 'We? Well. What do you think you and four boys can do that the police cannot?'

I did not try to conceal my annoyance at his objection. 'For the moment, it is not a matter of what they can but of what they will. An active search is more than is being done right now, and I think the others will agree that something is better than nothing.'

He sighed. 'I cannot argue with that. But I cannot tell you where to find them, now. Come again tomorrow, earlier. They have no watches amongst them, so I do not expect precision, but they have been coming around ten o'clock every day.'

I assured him that I would come. Having found my way there once, I was certain I could find my way there again, though possibly not from the front end of the Greys' house.

I departed hastily, despite the pains shooting up my leg. I could find a reasonably quiet place to sit along the street, somewhere, and though it would be cold, I preferred it to staying there. My path wove through the gloom of the alleys and back ways, and I breathed a sigh of relief when I found the afternoon sun, again.

I had not been the accomplice, but that didn't mean that there wasn't one. In fact, the more I considered Doctor Peach's words, the likelier it seemed to me that an accomplice was necessary for the order of events as I had experienced them. After all, the men in the cart had come after me, specifically. In order to come after me, specifically, they must have known where I was, and the number of people who could have told them was small, indeed. I dismissed the idea that any of the Wrong Boys might have intentionally taken any action that would endanger Snail, though not that one of them might have been willing to sacrifice me but had not anticipated that one of their own would be harmed. That, I was willing to consider, though it did not seem likely, not with the way all of the boys had fought the abductors. It *might* have been any of them, but I did not think it was.

But it could have been Peach.

## GRAHAM

Magpie trusted the man, but I could not. He was like a serpent. And he paid street children in food to bring him new patients. It was an extraordinarily philanthropic gesture, if he did not have something to gain from it. It made me question his motivations as a doctor, and other signals made me question his motivations as a private person. A good citizen would have called the police for an obvious runaway; a crooked citizen might see an opportunity.

I had no choice but to come back tomorrow. I had to talk to the Wrong Boys and had no other way of contacting them.

But by God, I would not go alone.

# FIVE

THE WALK back was an agonizingly slow process. I should have known better. I should have secured a crutch, or brought my money with me in case I required a cab. I had enough, certainly, though I wasn't sure that a cab would stop for someone attired as I was.

My journey consisted of a few steps and a short rest, some carefully-selected oaths, a few more steps, and another rest. It wasn't long before I was limping badly, and I began to realise that my problems might extend beyond simple discomfort. I had thought that, because I could make it upstairs and down in the Greys' house, I was healed or close to it, but it was a simple fact that the Greys' staircase was a lot shorter than the trek I had chosen to undertake, and that there were chairs on both ends of it.

I couldn't stop for long in any place. I was invisible to passers-by for as long as I stayed moving, but every time I stopped, I caught strange looks from pedestrians and from a couple of police constables. A shabby boy in ill-assorted clothes was of no importance until he became a loiterer. Loitering was suspicious behaviour. I lounged for a minute or two at a corner, leaning my shoulder against the wall to take the weight off my leg, but I hurried along when a uniform began to move purposefully toward me, and had to stop again almost the very moment he was out of sight.

The afternoon was fading, and at that rate, it would be evening, or even night before I made it back to the Greys. I realised with a pang that they would be worried. They were good people, and I liked them. I knew they would understand. They had clearly stated their intention to keep me from going out until I was entirely recovered, and there wasn't time for that. They couldn't fault me for taking the afternoon into my own hands, or for not giving them a chance to prevent my going. They couldn't, but they would be hurt, all the same.

With that thought, I forced myself back onto both feet and tottered to the side of the street, watching for a wide enough gap in the traffic that I could make it through safely, even with my snail's pace.

One appeared, and I took it, stepping behind an omnibus and between two hansoms, then had to stop to let a brewer's dray pass. Looking for the next opening ahead of me, I neglected to pay attention to the rumbling wheels behind me, not until I sensed the flank of a horse passing much too close to my back for comfort. I glanced back and stepped forward at once, snapping an imprecation at the driver of the offending growler. No trace of his expression was betrayed between the brim of his hat and the thick, scarlet folds of his muffler, but his eyes fixed on me, and I saw the tension in his arms, traveling down the reins to slow his pair. Slower, slower, not quite to a stop.

There was a barouche blocking my way forward, away from the growler, and there was nowhere I could run as the door behind the driver swung open and scooped me in and slammed shut. A powerful arm settled me onto the rear-facing seat and withdrew.

The inside of the carriage was thick and dark after the light of a clear day. Blue and green streaks painted my vision, but through them, I could see a pair of glittering eyes like black beetles fixed on me through the gloom.

I shifted uneasily, aware that my every movement left a grimy smirch on the plush seat, aware that, though we had started picking up speed again, I might still throw myself out the door without hurting myself too badly, assuming that nothing was coming in the other direction. Aware, above all else, that a third gleam I could see in the dark was likely the metal knob of a cane, which would do a lot of damage if it came toward my skull with enough force.

A monstrous shape heaved in the shadows across from me like a dragon stirring in the depths of its cavern, and it leaned closer. I could smell pomade and cigar smoke. I blinked faster, willing my eyes to adjust, and the shape had almost resolved into the form of a gigantic man when a voice rumbled out of it like thunder. A voice I knew.

'Ah, Morrigan, I thought that might be you, but I couldn't be certain from a distance. I can't say I much like what you've done with your hair.'

My brother Mycroft loomed at me, expressionless. He held out his left hand, and a few more blinks showed me a crinkled paper envelope full of liquorice. I took a piece, not sure what shocked me more: that I was discovered, or that I was so changed that Mycroft, the cleverest of us all, had taken more than an instant to recognize me.

A smaller shape shifted in the shadows beside me, exiled from the fore-facing seat by our elder brother's incredible girth. Sherlock.

Mycroft sat back with a wheezing, growling noise, rearranging his bulk across the upholstery, and laced his fingers over the immaculate expanse of his waistcoat. 'This,' he said, exaggerated patience failing to conceal a dangerous edge, 'is the part where you explain yourself, my sister.'

# PART THREE:

# GHOSTS

## OF THE

# PAST

# ONE

THE RIDE was tense, with my brothers looming at me in the dim carriage, waiting for enlightenment. Perhaps I did owe them an explanation, but I was not inclined to provide one, and I couldn't find the words, and anyway, they should have been able to work it out. I wasn't sure exactly when Mycroft had arrived, that night, with Sherrinford in tow, but I knew he had been there long enough to hear Father's account of the day's events and to argue strenuously on the subject. I had heard some of it, when the rain had slowed enough to let me distinguish words amid the shouting. And Sherlock had been there. He had witnessed all of it. He had seen me leave and had made no attempt to stop me, which told me he understood or at least suspected my reasoning.

I left because I could not stay.

But I had never expected to have to justify that decision to anyone but myself. I realised suddenly that, with as much as I had feared being caught, I had never *expected* it. I had thought I'd made as close to a perfect getaway as possible. If I had left any tracks, the rain that night had washed them away. My movements since had been all but random, totally unpredictable, chosen for me by other people.

Surely, I could only have been found by unfortunate chance.

## GRAHAM

So I stayed silent, despite Mycroft's prompts, and waited to be taken home.

But I was surprised. The ride was short, and when we rolled to a stop, I recognised the front of the Greys' house. Any possibility that I was found by chance vanished. I stared at Mycroft, who stared back impassively.

'How did you...?'

He harrumphed and levered his bulk out of the seat and down to the pavement, setting the growler rocking furiously. I hesitated before sliding out behind him, but Sherlock caught my arm.

'A friend of his in the records office told him a man was looking for a London family including a Mycroft, a Sherlock, and a girl,' he whispered. 'He followed the name in the register to this address. He won't tell you that because he's angry with you, and he wants you to think he's done something more impressive than he really has.'

His lip curled.

'Oh,' was all I could say. I supposed that Sherlock's last statement didn't actually imply that Mycroft was the only one angry with me, but it sounded as though that's what he was getting at. But that couldn't be true. I had heard them.

'The Greys don't know who I am or why I ran away. I'd prefer they didn't find out.'

He looked at me curiously. 'It'd be hard for us to tell them about the latter, since we're not sure, either.'

I felt my eyebrows rise, and I began to reply, but Mycroft was pulling ferociously at the Greys' bell, simultaneously damaging the glossy paint of their front door with the head of his cane, and I pulled Sherlock out of the growler and hobbled up the step after our older brother.

A man on the corner began to stride toward us with an officious set to his shoulders. I assumed him to be a policeman in plain clothes, since

Robbins had led me to expect at least one to be lurking at all times.

"'Ere, now!' he objected.

'It's all right,' I told him. 'We haven't any bricks.'

He blinked at me uncertainly as Theodora Grey opened the door.

She was still pale, almost wilted, her dark eyes ringed with deep violet shadows. Her artistic dress did not so much flow around her as sag off of her, now, and I thought she must have slept in it since I had left. Her hair was untidy, as though she had taken it down and put it back up again with haste.

Mycroft, being half a head taller than either I or Sherlock and fully four times as big around, drew her attention first. She looked him up and down with minimal interest, then spotted me.

'Where did you go?' she asked, the mild words belying the relief in her face.

'I found Doctor Peach,' I replied, then gestured to my companions. 'These are my brothers, Mycroft and Sherlock. You were looking for them?'

She reacted to the names, her eyebrows rising, lips tightening. I must have called them out during my illness. There couldn't be so many Mycrofts or Sherlocks in London. Those two names would probably have been enough to identify me. I wondered how far she had gotten, whether she knew my name, too.

'A bit more information seemed to be in order,' she said, swelling to fill the door, blocking their entry. Her hand moved toward me of its own accord. She still suspected my family of abusing me.

'Well, they found you, instead. And I don't think they mean to leave, just yet.'

I hoped she understood. I would not necessarily have minded if she turned them away, but if she did, they might very well come back with police. Or with Father. That I had been brought back to the Greys' house meant that Mycroft wanted something more than to carry me home, which he could easily have done without the detour. He wanted to know what I had been up to for the last fortnight, and since circumstances had already dragged him out of his flat, he was satisfying his curiosity now rather than make the effort of leaving home a second time.

So if I wanted to preserve my liberty, I had to be very careful about what he learned.

Theodora frowned, but she stood aside, and I discovered her husband guarding her back with his hand in his jacket pocket. Of course, if she owned a gun, it seemed extremely likely that he would, as well.

Mycroft trundled past me, and I heard him snort as he perceived the concealed threat. I did not think he ought to have laughed. If Edwin did have a gun, it was because he had every intention of using it. I squeezed past my brother's bulk, made eye contact, and shook my head. Edwin relaxed, but not much.

'Mycroft Holmes,' my mountainous brother rumbled. He did not extend a hand, or remove his hat. 'But you already knew that, just as I already know that I am addressing Edwin Grey and Theodora Grey, formerly Poppy Cooper of the Old Nichol Street Rookery.'

Theodora's back stiffened and her chin shot up, but the last of the colour drained from her face.

'You should not have changed your name officially, if you wished to disappear,' Mycroft said with a shrug. 'There are no secrets where there is paper.'

'Mycroft is a clerk in the government,' I hurried to clarify, because Edwin's arm had tensed again, the hand in his pocket clenched tight. 'He has access to information that I'm sure is not public. And I doubt he has any intention of spreading it around.'

My brother shot me an irritable glance, but then nodded. 'I find that someone has been asking after me shortly after my sister vanishes. In your own words, Mrs Grey, a bit more information seemed to be in order.'

'We had probably better sit,' Theodora — *Poppy?* — said faintly. 'Won't you come through?'

She led the way to the parlour, and Mycroft and Sherlock followed. My younger brother seemed to have little to say, and I had to wonder why Mycroft had brought him. Perhaps Sherlock had insisted. He had seen me leave, though, and had made no attempt to stop me. I had assumed at the time that it was because he wanted me gone, but his presence now threw a kink into my understanding. Did he want me back? Did he want me punished? Edwin made up the rear of the procession, maintaining his threat.

The parlour was warmer than the hall, and I stripped off my coat and dropped it on the floor. Here and there, missed fragments of window glass still glittered in the light of the fire and the lamps. It would be some time before anyone could dare walk through there in bare feet.

Theodora settled herself into her usual chair and gestured for Mycroft to take the settee. It groaned beneath his weight as he removed his hat. I remained standing, as did Sherlock, as did Edwin.

My younger brother sidled closer to me. 'I am glad you're not dead,' he whispered in an impersonally bland tone, but the fact he bothered to say it at all warmed me from the inside out.

Theodora had arranged her dress and picked up a glass of wine that had been sitting on the table beside her. This must have been about where Mycroft's assault on the door had found her. She swirled the burgundy liquid, watching the light play in the crystal, but did not drink.

'There is a policeman outside,' she said, calm now. 'It may have occurred to you to call for him, but I do not advise it. We have been harbouring a runaway. That is indisputable. But when the case is tried, I think our defence will be solid. I have seen such bruises before, and I know what a hand's mark looks like, and for all she insists they were made after she ran away, I am also familiar with the victim's inexplicable need to defend the abuser. I've said similar words, myself, just as I've carried similar marks. You will not be removing my charge from this house unless you can satisfy me, and you should know that I am already significantly prejudiced against anyone from whom a young woman feels she must flee.'

Something of Mycroft's confidence evaporated. He did not show surprise—he never did—but Theodora had just demolished his expectations. He'd thought he had the unshakeable upper hand, that the most challenging part of the affair would be finding me, and, having done that, he would only have to claim me. He had not expected resistance, and he had certainly not expected to be dealt a reciprocal accusation.

I felt a little sorry for him.

'I've already told you,' I began, but she clicked her tongue and waved an imperious hand.

'I am aware,' she interrupted. 'And I do not doubt your honesty, but honesty has very little import in this sort of situation. I'm sorry, Morrigan.'

My mouth snapped shut. So they had known. Wherever they had gone looking for Mycrofts and Sherlocks, they had found at least one answer.

They were all looking at me, now, though. Theodora and Edwin were waiting for more argument, and Mycroft and Sherlock were waiting for explanation.

'Where did these bruises come from?' Mycroft asked.

I took Edwin's usual chair, stretching my bad leg out in front of me, and recounted in brief my misadventures since the night of the storm, carefully leaving out the things Edwin and Theodora – *Poppy* – knew. Their secrets were not mine to tell.

My brothers listened, Mycroft nodding and Sherlock staring into the fire.

'I don't intend to be dragged home easily,' I concluded, 'but I shall not be dragged home at all until Snail is safe and this thing, whatever it is, is uncovered and destroyed. Tomorrow, I will be returning to Doctor Peach to discuss the matter with the Wrong Boys. They won't have been idle all this time, and they're bound to have discovered *something*. But I would rather not go alone, please.'

I had meant the last comment for the Greys, should they succeed in keeping me out of my family's hands, but it was Mycroft who responded.

'Of course. You wouldn't be able to walk the distance again, I think. Or at least, you shouldn't. I doubt I would be of much use, but I am not your only brother.' Here, he looked pointedly at Sherlock, who stared back impassively.

I leaned forward. 'Why?'

He shrugged. 'Dragging was always a last resort, and you seem to be otherwise engaged, at the moment. There's nothing at home that requires your immediate attention. Father is intending to send you to school on the Continent as soon as you are located. His selection has an excellent reputation, which can only mean *you* would find it extremely objectionable. I will not allow you to continue endangering yourself, of course, but if you were to remain absent long enough for his temper to cool, well...'

I could sense Edwin's gaze on the back of my head and understood that fathers with tempers were well known for leaving bruises. I sighed.

'I've found you safe,' Mycroft continued, 'and in the hands of people who don't seem eager to give you up. There are some minor difficulties, of course, but this seems a stable place to leave the issue, for the time being.'

'Stable,' I echoed.

'And if it will persuade you to keep your nose out of trouble, I shall make enquiries regarding this investigation. Regardless of its priority—or lack thereof—there will be documentation. A pattern. I'll pass what I find to you. And to the police, of course.'

'But how could you possibly be on my side?'

That veiled expression returned and his eyes glittered coldly. 'Would you like to discuss our family matters here?'

I stopped talking and ignored the air of burning curiosity that had begun to radiate to either side of me.

Theodora's voice alerted me that, thankfully, a different subject had been chosen. 'You mean to help find Miss Snail and punish those who took her?'

'I do,' Mycroft confirmed.

Theodora twisted in her seat to send a pleading look in her husband's direction. Edwin frowned and came to perch on the arm of her chair, his free hand coming to rest on her shoulder. She finally took a sip of her wine and set down the glass.

'Then,' she said softly, 'there is much you have to know.'

And with a shuddering sigh, she began their story.

# TWO

*The Greys' Story*

POPPY COOPER was eighteen when she ran. It took her longer than perhaps it should have, but she was waiting for everyone else to be gone and safe, or at least gone. Mother was buried with the misshapen mass that had killed her, which she had lived long enough to name Christine, even though only God knew whether it was actually a girl under all that blue flesh. Davey was buried, too. Papa gave him to a chimney sweep, and he worked until he began to cough black dust, and he died. Peter was in the work house, where he was being taught to live by his hands. That would kill him, eventually, but it might wait until he was grown with a family, and that was all anyone could hope for. Poppy saved pennies, hiding them from Papa between her tattered stockings and the thin soles of her boots, refusing to limp even when the cold copper opened sores in her feet, until she had enough to buy Lisa a somewhat respectable frock. When the girl's hair was brushed and her face was washed, Poppy left her with Madam Pennacchi, who taught serious-minded girls to be housemaids and graciously let them pay for their lessons with their first three years' wages.

That left only her and Papa and the drink.

It wasn't really running away. At eighteen, she had not yet reached her majority, but she was as adult as it was possible to be. And if Papa insisted on his power over her, she had a dozen friends willing to swear before God that she was actually twenty-one. Somewhere, she knew, was a piece of paper declaring the date of her baptism, but as to the date of her birth, it would be Papa's word against the midwife's, and Widow James would be perfectly happy to misremember the year.

So Poppy felt safe, that morning, walking to Mrs Niall's laundry without any intention of walking home in the evening. She spent the day as always, carrying coal for the fires, hovering over vats of boiling water, thrusting her arms into the lye-laden clouds of steam to prod at other people's underthings with her wooden paddle. The work wasn't so bad in the winter, when the pounding heat was almost comfortable, but it was shattering in the summer. She had fainted, once, and woke red and swollen, feeling like her insides were trying to burst through her skin, but she had recovered, and of course it could have been worse. One of the other girls had fainted a few years back and fell forward into the vat she was working, boiled to death. The work was loud, and it was hard to see through the steam, and it had to have been several minutes before anyone knew what had happened. Nobody said much about it, after, and Poppy trained herself not to think of it, not to remember what a poached human looked like, and in a couple of months, she couldn't even remember the girl's name. They were all very careful, then. Mrs Niall even said that if anyone began to feel ill, she should go have a few minutes' sit-down and a cup of water. She said it was because heat sickness could make one vomit, and they couldn't afford the possibility that a whole batch of customers' clothing would be ruined, but everyone knew she actually cared for her girls. Mrs Niall was an uncommonly generous woman, even if she wouldn't admit it.

Poppy was having her few minutes' sit-down when she heard a noise from the other end of the yard, near the gate, and even before she was able to make out the voices, she knew it was Papa. The number of empty bottles beneath his bed had made her think she'd have most of the day before he found her things gone, but perhaps some of them had been there longer than she realised.

He was roaring her name and a bunch of words that would have made Madam Pennacchi go pale and fly into an Italian rage, the kind of words used by men who truly hated women, words that meant actions were soon to follow. There was never much conversation in the laundry, but the few murmurs left died quickly.

She heard Mrs Niall's voice join the row, Papa growing louder to drown her out, and she wiped her hands on her apron and went to see what could be done. The other women stood silently, their tasks abandoned, every head turned toward the gate and the invader.

Papa towered over Mrs Niall, swaying like a ship's mast on a stormy sea, his big, red and black fists waving in a threatening display. His eyes were glassy, and he had wet himself, fingers too clumsy with drink to unbutton his trousers. Poppy froze. The booze had made him too clumsy for fine work, but there was nothing fine about bashing heads into walls. He was conscious, and that made him dangerous.

Mrs Niall was telling him to go home. This yard was her place, she was a businesswoman, and he had no rights here. Poppy was an employee, she was saying, her pride ringing in that word, and he had no right to take a working woman away from her paid job, no right to come barging in there, making a scene, no right to hold up the entire operation of the place...

His fingers closed around Mrs Niall's throat, and Poppy found herself screaming, running, but before she could reach him, he dropped like a rock and Mrs Niall staggered away, clutching the reddening mark.

One of the other girls, Madge, stood over him with her steaming laundry paddle and hit him once more for good measure, wet wood on the bloated flesh of his face. Poppy thought she heard his nose break.

Madge and Mrs Niall met one another's eyes and nodded their mutual understanding.

It took four women to drag him out of the yard, and they simply left him there, secure in the knowledge that no one would really care what had happened to him, and that no one would believe a roaring drunk if he did try to tell anyone.

'No,' said Mrs Niall to nobody in particular. 'Absolutely no more o' that. 'E may try agin, but I think the Cotton boys'll be 'appy enough to discourage 'im.' She shoved a few stray strands of iron-grey hair beneath her cap and turned to Poppy. 'You got a place to go?'

'My Gran's,' Poppy replied. 'Mum's mum. I don't think 'e even knows where she lives.'

Mrs Niall sighed but said no more. Poppy understood. Concern was not the same thing as means. She wanted to know that Poppy would be safe, but had no way of helping, herself. It was going to be dangerous, a woman and her grandmother living alone, but still better than living with Papa and his bottles. They'd cope, somehow. And if they couldn't cope, well, there were advantages to owning nothing. It wasn't hard to vanish into the bowels of the rookery in the dead of night, emerge in another part of London. People did it all the time.

And they did cope. For weeks, they coped. Gran had gotten by on matchboxes for ages, clever fingers somehow getting the corners neat and square despite her failing eyesight, but with Poppy's income added, they could almost pretend to be comfortable. At least, there was food more often than there wasn't, and two bodies kept a bed warmer at night than one. Papa appeared at Mrs Niall's laundry twice more, but as promised, the Cotton boys chased him away. Ralph and Ed Cotton were big and mostly sober and almost always in a foul temper for want of work, and both were thrilled to receive a few pennies for nothing more strenuous than beating up on a boozy lout.

Everything was fine.

Until the evening Papa stood by Mrs Niall's gate and simply watched, rotted teeth bared in malice, simply watched as Poppy walked past him and hurried away. Just watched, dripping with grease and satisfaction, and while it made her cold and sick to her core, there was nothing she could do, nowhere else to run but back to Gran.

She knew she was being followed. The slum gave one an almost preternatural sixth sense for danger. Perhaps she heard a footstep in time with her own, or saw a shadow, the hint of a reflection in a sooty window. Perhaps she just knew, felt eyes on her back the way a rabbit feels a hawk. She pushed her exhaustion aside and walked faster, back to Gran.

Her building would be safe enough, she thought. The two of them lived in the third storey, packed like pigeons just beneath the roof. She had to go past the shop on the ground, then the four families in the first storey, six in the second, and if she did, so did whoever was following her. More than fifty people, in all. If she had to scream, someone would hear.

She clattered up the narrow stairs, ignoring the ache in her legs and shoulders and back, eager to be behind her own door. It didn't lock, of course, but it felt safer to be in than out.

Someone clattered up behind her, steps out of beat, now.

The building was quieter than it should have been. By chance or by design? No, it had to be by chance. Who could contrive to empty a building of fifty people just to make trouble for her?

She heard a muffled shout from far below, the rowdy sounds of laughter and cheers from the grim, muddy little yard outside the building. It sounded as though a fight had broken out. A fight broken out, and everybody gone to watch. An empty building. Not so much effort, after all.

The steps behind her gained, and she whirled suddenly to face her pursuer. A man, perfectly nondescript, much of his face concealed by a wiry black beard, the rest hidden by the gloom.

'C'mon,' he said, a smile in his voice. 'Your dad says you're to come wi' me.'

She had the higher ground, and she kicked him in the face. He reeled, hands closing around her ankle as he fought to steady himself, and as he began to fall, he jerked her feet out from under her. Her head hit the top step, and the darkness was suddenly absolute.

—

EDWIN GREY had really only set out to prove a point. He did plenty of things that were good for society at large, charitable work, land improvement. Study, of course; he had always believed that knowledge was power in a far more concrete way than most people who claimed the aphorism as a philosophy. But being good at things that produced an effect wasn't quite the same thing as being good at things that produced money, and Father thought that income built character more reliably than mere activity.

When pressed, Father said he wanted Edwin in a bank, or something, and Edwin took the 'or something' and ran. Something petty. Something disreputable. Something Father wouldn't want him doing for more than a couple of months, at most, so he could go back to the important things, the ones that cost money rather than bringing it in. Something that would highlight exactly how lucky Father was to have a son who had never lost a penny on wine, women, or wagers.

Journalism, obviously.

Edwin knew a man who knew a man who knew a man who owned a newspaper, a sensationalist rag called the *Albatross*. It wasn't even so much a newspaper as a weekly pamphlet, and, true to its name, it operated as a harbinger of doom, printing all the worst news for dreary people who enjoyed melancholy.

He signed on.

But because he really preferred to preserve at least a shred of public dignity, he wrote not as Edwin Grey, but as Peter Storm. The pseudonym entertained him enormously, but it lost some of its humour when he had to explain it to his friends. 'Peter Storm? Like a stormy petrel? You know, a sea bird? Like an albatross, but smaller?' By the time he had offered five or six such explanations, he had begun to regret the choice, but didn't want to expend the energy to come up with a new one.

'You'll have to find something really bleak to write about,' they told him over cards. He wasn't allowed to play, anymore, because he won annoyingly often, even though he never placed a bet.

'Poverty is bleak,' he told them, no longer joking, and they told him to go home because he was ruining everyone else's evening.

He did go home, and very early the next morning, he dressed himself very sensibly, picked up a small notebook and a pencil, and went to investigate poverty first-hand. May as well do some real good in his false profession.

By noon, he wasn't sure why he'd thought anybody at all would talk to him, because no-one did. His notebook was empty, his pencil unblunted, even though his shoes were caked with mud and offal and worse. He purchased a hand-pie from a stall and leaned against a wall to reconsider his strategy. Class was the issue, obviously. Money, it all came back to money. They could see it in his clothes, the way he carried himself. They could smell it on him, and it marked him as untrustworthy. He thought about acquiring something more worn, some old, discarded garments, but the idea of a costume seemed infinitely worse.

He was lost in thought when he became aware of a shadow approaching. He glanced up to find himself face-to-face with a man. A young man with a shaven head and a potato nose and cauliflower ears, no teeth to speak of. A brawler, a bruiser. He wondered whether he should have brought a stick, or even a pistol.

But the young man did not attack at once. 'I seen you aksin' questions,' he said.

'Yes,' Edwin agreed quickly, 'I have been, I'm afraid. I'm terribly sorry, should I not?'

The man squinted warily and folded his arms. 'You aksin' 'bout them girls gone missin'?'

'I am,' Edwin said, sensing that was the answer the man wanted to hear.

And that was how he met Ed Cotton, Jane Niall, and Madge Smith, and how he came to the bedside of Gertrude Bigg, who had a granddaughter named Poppy, and listened to her tell what she had heard through her paper-thin walls.

There was a fight in progress outside when Mrs Bigg heard someone coming up the stairs, her granddaughter's familiar tread. She usually came to the door to greet her, you see, but she had been sick abed for several days, and was too tired to get up. So she heard, but did not see. She heard a man's voice, the things he said carrying through the walls as clear as a bell, and a scuffle and a fall, a man's cursing, another voice. She didn't see Poppy, no, but she knew the sound of her boots. She was coming home... and then she didn't come home.

There were three others vanished, too. The police said they must have done a flit or run off with a boy, and sometimes that happened, but Poppy wouldn't. Poppy wouldn't, not with her dear gran sick abed.

Edwin returned home late with a pain in his heart and a fierce resolve.

He slept little, scribbling out his story for the *Albatross*. If he was able to *do* nothing else, at least he could spread the word. The people of the Old Nichol were used to bad things happening. It didn't fuss them, anymore. But this was strange, as well as bad, and the police had dismissed them, and they needed to know that someone was taking them

NO CAGE FOR A CROW

seriously. In the morning, he passed the inky wad of foolscap to Jones, his editor, who was sceptical about the truth of it but agreed it was a cracking good yarn, sure to sell, and sent him out to get more.

There was certainly more to be got. Other names in Church Street, in Jacob's Island, behind Petticoat Lane. Nine by noon, and then a whisper, a hint, a housemaid missing, as well. An upstanding girl who didn't go to the dirty places a woman might be seized. Happy in her position, and she left no note...

He stopped by his club for a cup of coffee, paranoid, horrified. London ate people. It swallowed them whole, left nothing behind. People were always disappearing, often by their own choice. It was ridiculous to think that every disappearance he'd heard of was related. They couldn't be. But he knew beyond doubt that some of them were. Many. There was a pattern, dots that, when connected, sketched out a shadowy beast prowling the city.

He added the housemaid's name to his article, copied the draft, and took it to the police. They hadn't listened to crazy, sick old women or frightened drunks, but they had to listen to him. Didn't they?

They did listen. He represented Money. They listened, took his list, thanked him for his information, and told him to stay out of it. Naturally.

Staying out of it, though, hadn't been a possibility for days.

He talked it over with his club friends, a few of whom were capable of being serious when they absolutely had to be.

'Only women,' he told them with a shudder. 'As far as I can tell.'

They exchanged pale-cheeked glances, desperately trying to think of more than one reason for kidnapping a couple dozen young women.

'I've got detailed descriptions of most of them,' he said. 'And we know where to begin looking.'

The glances became wide-eyed. 'You're joking,' one insisted.

'Do you have a better idea?' Edwin shot back. 'Are you a detective, now?'

'Do you have any idea how many women there are wandering the streets? It's needles in haystacks.'

He shook his head. 'They won't be on the streets. Outdoors, at night, there'd be chances to slip away. At least a few of them would have escaped. We're looking for an establishment.'

A collective shudder racked the group.

It took two weeks and a lot of money and considerable agony of conscience, asking after women with a certain interesting feature, and in the end, Edwin was not the one who found her. It was John Howard, an old school friend, who let it be known that he was looking specifically to be entertained by a girl with tattoos and was told in a whisper that no such product was currently available for let, but for an exorbitant sum, he could have one bespoke, all to himself, in perpetuity.

'Oh?' Howard asked, for all the world a revoltingly rich young man bored with conventional morality. 'How much do you call exorbitant?' Everyone had always said Howard should have been an actor, if only he could overcome his unhealthy preoccupation with politics.

The transaction was arranged out of a fashionable house in Chelsea, and a girl called Ellie was saved by the blue outline of a bird clumsily inked onto her left wrist. She did not object to being taken to the police station rather than being locked away again, and the story she told grew gradually louder and louder, peppered with language that reflected her fear and fury.

She had not been allowed to see where she was taken first, but she could guess. She knew her city, its smells, the voices of the street sellers hawking their wares, the timbre of each church's bells. She directed them.

In a great, many-armed raid, the house in Chelsea was stormed, and the brothel where Howard had learned of its existence, and a warehouse in Woolwich.

Edwin had done his part. He was not a fighter, and he was not police. They told him to stay home, and this time, he did, but the *Albatross* was the first to publish the details. Thirty women and girls rescued, between the ages of fourteen and thirty-eight. The police met with little resistance at the house and a perfunctory brawl at the brothel, but the warehouse became a battleground. Three of the villains shot to death, seventeen arrested, an unknown number escaped. The wooden building burned to the ground—no-one knew how the blaze had started, exactly—and took the little office with all its filing cabinets with it. Not a scrap of paper remained. None of those captured would confess to being the leader of the gang or to knowing who was.

But at least it was ended, Edwin thought, putting his pen down and folding the article into an envelope. Not happily, not really. There were still women missing, and those burned papers may have told where they had gone, who had bought them. But it was ended.

He delivered the article and his resignation and took a cab back to the Old Nichol to check in on Gertrude Bigg.

—

Gran's cough was worse since Poppy had seen her last, that morning that seemed a thousand years ago. Mrs Niall had been keeping her fed, sending one of the laundry girls each day with what food could be spared, taking the matchboxes Gran was able to paste together from bed and selling them for her. That was good and generous, but it wasn't going to be enough, and everyone knew it.

There was no time for Poppy to dwell on the things that had happened to her, no time to let the memories paralyse her, because they needed money, and they needed it now. Mrs Niall was a good woman, eminently sensible. She told Poppy there would always be a place for her at the laundry, but she added in a whisper that they would have to be discreet about it, that there was already self-righteous muttering about the diseases that might start spreading if blemished women were allowed to handle clothes, the moral stain that certainly would start spreading if she were allowed to work alongside other people's daughters. She'd be better off picking up and moving, coming down somewhere she could say her name was something else. Nobody mentioned that it wasn't her fault. They all knew it, and they also knew it didn't matter.

And they knew that picking up and moving would have to wait until Gran was dead. If she was going to get better on her own, she'd have done it already.

The knock on the door came as a surprise, but more surprising still was the fact that whoever was on the other side didn't just come on through. The visitor waited to be admitted.

Poppy sat frozen stiff, counting silently to herself, waiting for the next blow to fall, and still the visitor did not come through. There was another knock, a little softer, and Mrs Niall got up and opened the door by an inch, pressing her eye to the crack.

Then she opened it.

'Oh,' she said. 'Come in, then.'

The man standing in the doorway was a gentleman, dark-haired, warm-eyed, cradling his hat in the crook of one arm. Gentlemen didn't come to places like that, not for any reason. He wasn't there to collect the rent or to evict her, and Poppy felt her guts go cold.

'This is Mr Grey,' Mrs Niall said. ''E wrote the story what made the p'lice take notice.'

He smiled, not that superficial expression reserved for new acquaintances, but as though they were old friends. 'You must be Miss Cooper,' he said, meeting her eyes steadily and not looking at anything lower. 'I'm so glad to see you home and in one piece.'

He turned to the bed where Gran lay still, and his smile faltered. 'Mrs Bigg. I hope you're feeling better.'

Gran turned and coughed yellow fluid onto her pillow, and the gentleman turned ashen and ran, his shiny boots clattering on the rickety stairs. Poppy wasn't surprised, and she didn't have the energy to be disgusted. Men that clean and tidy didn't belong in places like that.

An hour and a half later, he returned with a doctor, and Gran lived eight more years.

# THREE

'THREE, seventeen,' Edwin repeated. 'Three dead, seventeen arrested. And the head of an albatross. I don't see how this could possibly be anything but more of the same. We never knew who was behind it all, whether he escaped. Clearly, he did.'

'Clearly,' Mycroft echoed. 'Unless someone else has taken over and is exacting revenge on behalf of a predecessor. And he seems to have been talking to some of your old friends, unless you were very public with your pen name.'

Edwin shrugged, pulling his thumbnail through his moustache. 'I wasn't very close about it. Not at first. Remember, I hoped to stir some things up, but I didn't think I'd end up writing about anything dangerous. But it's been ten years. I don't know whether they only just found out I was Peter Storm, or if they were sitting on the knowledge all this time.'

'It's a long time to wait,' I said.

Theodora shook her head. 'It isn't. People who make threats like this do so either because they have nothing to lose, or because they feel safe from repercussions. Ten years ago, there was nothing left to lose, the operation was destroyed, but nothing was done against us, so it seems likely that they didn't know who was responsible, who to blame. Now there is something to lose. The operation is running, again. But they've had a decade to grow it. It may be even larger than it was the first time. They want their revenge, and they don't expect us to have any way to defend ourselves.'

Mycroft made a dissatisfied noise, one that I recognised was in response to making assumptions, but he said nothing, and neither did I.

'We'll have to share all of this with the police,' she continued.

I agreed, hoping Inspector Robbins would not think to question the gang's interest in Morgan Grey after a history of pursuing only girls and women. I touched the fabric of my trousers and flexed my sore ankle, collecting my thoughts before I spoke.

'What we need, then, is to know who's responsible. Is it the same person, or is someone new in charge? How did they find you, and what's changed to make them target you now? We can only assume that, having made sure you knew who they were and what it was about, their next move will be violence against you, Mr Grey, and possibly Mrs Grey, too, if they're just petty and vengeful. We need to know whether they've organised themselves the same way, this time, with a central location where all their victims are taken initially, another where women are sold, and another where they're... rented.'

Theodora flinched, and I muttered an apology. She shook her head, though. 'You're not wrong. Obviously, last time, they weren't taken down as thoroughly as we thought. We have to do better, make sure this doesn't happen again another ten years from now.'

'We have to do better? So you don't intend to leave it to the police?'

She was silent, and I could see her weighing good citizenship against the depth of her personal injury.

'Of course,' Edwin answered for her, with an ambiguity I thought intentional. 'But for the moment, we have a plan. Your friends ought to know all we know. They'll be able to travel the city all but unseen, and perhaps discover more than we could. Tomorrow.'

—

Sherlock returned early the next morning. Mycroft, as I had anticipated, was not with him, and he seemed a lot more present, somehow, without our brother's massive figure and personality overshadowing him. He inhaled the breakfast the Greys offered him, saying little but watching everything, and when there were no more kippers left, he handed me the canvas bag he had brought.

Inside, I found a complete suit of his clothing, and a comb on top. It was uncommonly thoughtful, and I was about to say so when he explained.

'You'd look strange, walking with me dressed as you are now. You'd have to walk a bit behind to avoid attracting curiosity.' He frowned. 'And I don't think anyone should risk being alone.'

Impersonally sensible, as always. I thanked him, wishing we had a few moments to ourselves. Questions seared the inside of my mouth and clogged my throat, threatening to choke me if I continued to swallow them. Edwin and Theodora had trusted us with their story, but Mycroft had made clear that our family's story did not belong in that place.

And I did not want them to know what kind of creature they were harbouring under their roof.

The questions would have to wait, but they would not have to wait very long.

I excused myself and went upstairs to put on my brother's sober and tidy clothing. It didn't fit me, but it fit better than the hotchpotch I discarded in the bottom of the armoire. Anyway, the trousers were the right length, if the sleeves were a touch too long, and without holes or stains, I no longer looked like something fished out of a drain. I pulled on the old boots reluctantly, spoiling my momentary neatness, and failed an attempt to flatten my shorn hair.

# GRAHAM

Sherlock's sharp eyes lingered on the boots as I descended again, something like humour pulling at his thin lips.

'Well,' he said.

I ignored his mocking tone and straightened my lapels. 'Better, though not perfect. I appreciate the loan. It's a shame a pair of your shoes wouldn't have fit me.'

'They'd have fit you as well as those boots do. Didn't those used to belong to Sherrinford?'

'He was going to throw them out, and they were still perfectly serviceable,' I replied, checking the clock on the Greys' parlour mantel. 'We should go. Doctor Peach said to come around ten, though I suppose he'd ask the boys to wait rather than miss us.'

Edwin hovered nearby in the hall, pinching nervously at his moustache, his habitual smile uncertain. 'Are you sure you don't want me with you?' he asked as he helped me into one of his coats. It drooped off of my shoulders and felt like wearing a tent, but it was infinitely better than the soiled thing I had arrived in. 'Or Teddy? A larger group, safety in numbers...?'

I shook my head. We had discussed the matter at length the previous evening, and Theodora and I were in agreement. The delivery of the albatross head was meant for them, the timing of the vandalism so soon after my arrival almost certainly a mere coincidence. They were the intended victims, not me. The gang might still be seeking revenge for my putting out that man's eye, but they didn't know where I had gone and weren't likely to connect the girl I had been that night with the boy I had become. I did not think I was safe wandering the streets, not even in my brother's company, but I was definitely safer than Edwin or Theodora would have been. They had no intention of hiding in their house forever, but there was no reason for them to go traipsing around with targets painted on their backs.

There was also the fact that, in company, I could not put my questions to my brother.

'I appreciate it, really, but this'll be quicker and easier.' I thought of the interview to come and frowned. 'And with the two of you added, it'd become a crowd. The boys may not be willing to say much with you there.'

He nodded slowly, seeming unconvinced, as I glanced around him for Theodora, but she had gone, so Sherlock and I left.

Dick had fetched a cab for us, for which I was immensely grateful. The stabbing pains in my ankle had receded overnight, but they'd been replaced by a dull, persistent ache, and I knew I ought to stay off of it. Just to be safe, though, I pretended it didn't hurt much at all, so that no one would try to *make* me stay off of it.

We climbed into the hansom, Sherlock providing the driver with the address of the intersection where Mycroft had picked me up, and I at once lost the ability to ask my questions.

He stared straight ahead while I struggled, his expression closed. He had never shown any particular need to communicate with the people around him unless there was something specific to be said. I had rarely felt any such need, myself, but I suddenly understood the distress silence causes so many people. I could not speak, and he would not, and the void between us was almost physically painful.

But there was so little time. It wasn't a long way to Doctor Peach's establishment, and then there would be catching up to do, and then we would go back to the Greys, and then Sherlock would most likely leave. I couldn't let the silence go unchallenged.

'How can you bear to be near me?' I demanded. The moment the words were out of my mouth, they shocked and embarrassed me. After moment of thought, though, I realised that they were as much a request for information as emotional self-condemnation.

He gave me a sidelong glance and spoke quietly, the sounds of the street drowning his voice before it could reach the driver above us. 'What do you think happened, that night?'

'I'd rather you told me what actually did happen, since you obviously think my interpretation is wrong.'

His mouth compressed in dissatisfaction. 'You were there for the important parts. Nothing much happened after you had left. I think you must have overheard Father ranting about sending us both away, so you ran. I can understand that. It wouldn't matter much to me. He's sent me to stay with Mycroft for the moment, and I'll be going to school in the city later, but I've heard that girls' schools aren't very... informative. Running away seems extreme, though. You're more diplomatic than I am. You probably could have talked him around, given time. Not likely, now.' He grimaced, baring his teeth. 'It was very cruel of you to abandon us, right at that moment. I didn't expect that from you.'

'You must think me pretty shallow, then. The least I deserve is some time at an unpleasant school.'

'Deserve? Yes, you probably do. You've inconvenienced everybody.' He lowered his voice, forcing me to lean closer to hear him. 'Terrified everybody. Sherrinford's had another nervous attack. He might almost have coped with the facts of Mother's ordeal, but finding you missing on top of that prostrated him. It's not certain that he'll recover, this time.'

'Ordeal?' My heart seemed to stumble in my chest. He said ordeal, not death. 'She didn't...'

He swung his head around to face me, his eyes very, very wide. 'Oh. No.'

His hand found mine, and he squeezed tightly, equal parts comfort and caution. 'Don't cry quite so visibly,' he whispered. 'Boys don't, you may have noticed.'

I leaned back further beneath the hood of the cab and pressed my hand to my mouth, trying to lessen the burn of the freezing air in my throat.

'Morrigan...'

I shook my head.

'Nobody knew what she meant to do. Even Mycroft didn't see it coming. I didn't. If she'd asked me to go to the chemist instead of you, I'd have done it. You're not at fault for not seeing what nobody else saw, either.'

He stopped talking and turned away, his limited supply of comfort exhausted.

Neither of us spoke again as the cab rolled to a stop or as I led the way on foot the rest of the way back to Doctor Peach, and by the time we stood in front of the peeling door, my eyes were more red from cold than from tears.

Sylvia's reaction to the two of us was admirably subdued, despite the fact that, were I a little better groomed, Sherlock and I could almost have been twins. She let us in with no more than raised eyebrows and a wrinkled nose, eyeing his clothes on my body with veiled scepticism. I was a slightly different person each time she saw me: first a ragged girl, then a ragged boy, and finally a public school boy in ugly boots. I'd have to come up with something really interesting for the next time, if I wanted to keep it up. A girl again, hopefully. Morgan Grey was an uncomfortable skin to wear.

Magpie and Dart were waiting amidst the lamps.

Both leapt to their feet as Sylvia bustled us into the room, and I watched them freeze. Magpie stared between me and Sherlock, his expression closed and guarded, and a beat later, I saw recognition dawn. His full mouth pulled into a frown.

'That you, Crow? What've you done?'

'Got sick,' I told him. 'I thought as long as my hair was short, trousers'd make it easier to keep from getting sent back.'

# GRAHAM

His face registered scepticism, and he shook his head, glancing at Sherlock.

'My brother, Sherlock. He wants to help find Snail. And Magpie, there are other people who want to help, as well. They think they know what's happening.'

Once again, I related everything I knew, adding what I had learned from Theodora and Edwin, hurrying through it all before Peach could appear. If the man were involved, I didn't want him to know how much had already been found out, or that I was with the Greys. My description of them stiffened Dart's back, and I was glad I had decided to come without them. It took considerable explanation and reassurance to convince the Wrong Boys that the Greys were on the level.

A voice behind me made me jump, and I spun to find Peach himself listening in, blocking the door. He had come up in total silence. Sneaking.

'These crooks have had a decade to learn from their mistakes,' he hissed. 'If it is even the same lot. They're not likely to be caught a second time by a troop of carousing gentlemen.' His grey lips curled, the expression humourless.

I took a step back from him, glad I had not put myself at a disadvantage by taking a chair. Sherlock seemed to sense my dislike, and I felt him stiffen, his attention gathering on the reptilian doctor.

'Magpie said you sometimes help ladies,' I said sharply, remembering. 'If you heard anything...'

'Not such ladies as those,' he snapped. 'I know few who are especially fond of their managers, but none who are being held against their will. If the kidnappers care anything for the wellbeing of their victims, they'd have their own physician.' He bared yellow teeth. 'Do you suppose I might have heard something and kept it to myself?'

I didn't realise that he had felt my dislike, too, and I couldn't think of anything to say. That wasn't exactly what I had supposed, though. I had thought worse, that he might actually be the operation's own physician, if not the leader who escaped. I couldn't rid myself of the feeling that he was barely even human. Those dark, suspicious eyes bored into me.

Magpie stirred and appeared at my shoulder, and the brewing storm dissipated. He made no attempt to hide his irritation. 'No gentlemen carousing,' he interrupted. 'But we do got us, and your newspaper man found out what 'e did by askin' questions, first of all. If it is the same again, they'll be takin' more, and someone'll be sayin' somethin'.'

'That was chance,' I protested. 'He was *told* what questions he ought to be asking.'

Sherlock barked a laugh, shoving his hands into his pockets. 'We don't have to be told, *Crow*. We already know what questions to ask. And where to start, I should think. The slums?'

Magpie laughed right back at him. 'You'll look right pretty strollin' through the Ol' Nichol! A grown man I can see folk might think 'as a right to be askin' questions, but you two? That's a laff.'

'Find yourselves a grown man,' Peach drawled.

I looked at him in alarm. He couldn't mean himself. 'Don't you have to stay here, in case someone comes by in urgent need?'

It was bad enough that he knew what I knew and what the Greys knew; he couldn't be allowed along to keep an eye on our efforts, to take note of the names of the people we talked to. Or to sabotage us.

His curved shoulders rose in a shrug. 'If not I, then someone else.'

Somehow, the fact that he did not insist only heightened my discomfort. But Magpie was still between us, his presence reminding me that he trusted Peach and required that I do the same. Well, I was not obliged to obey. I swallowed my suspicions, but did not let go of them.

I withdrew a few steps, squeezing my eyes shut. 'But nobody ever saw,' I said, thinking aloud. 'No one could describe the kidnappers. And when we encountered them, they were masked. Asking questions will only tell us that someone else has gone missing, not who took them or where they were taken. What we actually need is to see it happen. To find the men with the wagon and follow it to wherever the victims are being kept.'

Dart piped up, his voice high and biting. "Ow do you mean to see it 'appen, then, if they always makes sure no one ever sees it 'appen?'

I looked at him, at his waifish figure, dirty face, and soiled cravat. 'We did see it happen, though. We just didn't manage to follow them. They didn't care, because you don't matter to them. Street children. Have you tried talking to the police? No? They knew you wouldn't. They know as well as you that the police wouldn't listen to you.'

Magpie's blue eyes opened very wide. "Ow many of us's seen somethin' an' didn' say? Cause nobody'd listen.'

'How many homeless children are there in London?'

I meant it as a rhetorical question, certain the number was enormous, but Sherlock had a ready answer. 'About thirty thousand.'

I didn't ask him where he had gotten the information. He wouldn't have said it if he wasn't reasonably sure. It chilled me.

'That's a considerable number of eyes,' I said, swallowing hard. 'More than enough to see something. More than enough to creep along after.'

Completely invisible. I recalled my own journey from the Greys' house to Doctor Peach's the previous day, how no one had even seemed to see me, much less looked at me. A raggedy child barely existed, as far as the city was concerned.

'There are other groups like yours?' I continued. 'Do you know any of them well enough to ask for help? One of their own was taken. That means everyone is in danger. Won't they be willing to help?'

Magpie nodded slowly. 'We can get a bit territorial, like, but that don't matter, now. We can find others, maybe even others what lost someone. Gimme a week,' he said, 'an' I'll 'ave you five 'undred eyes.'

# FOUR

THERE WAS no time to waste, and so we wasted none. Magpie sent Dart back to the Wrong Boys' hideout to relay the information and to send the other boys out on the same mission. With hundreds or thousands of children keeping their eyes peeled, there was almost no chance of the villains remaining undetected.

'You'll come wi' me, o' course,' Magpie said as he wound a muffler around his face and thrust his hands into a pair of tattered mittens. 'Since you 'eard the story first-'and and can tell it better.'

The thought of walking any distance made my ankle throb, but I swallowed my reluctance. Snail's life was more important. Peach watched me narrowly and wordlessly handed me a coarse stick. I didn't think it would make more than a small difference in my ability to cover ground, but at least it could be a weapon, in a pinch.

We left.

There was little to say. The boys to either side of me were pensive. Sherlock had his hands thrust deep into his pockets, and his expression was distant, though I did not know whether he was thinking so hard about our current situation or about the one back at home. Magpie wrapped his arms around himself, his head up and frosty eyes alert above the muffler. But his face moved as though, hidden behind the wool, he was talking to himself.

When I tried to think at all, too many thoughts crowded in at once and overwhelmed me.

Snail was gone, either to be prostituted or sold as chattel. Any number of other women and girls might be with her. If any of them were sold and taken elsewhere, they might never be found. Any good business had to keep detailed records, but the records kept by a monstrous criminal enterprise would either have to be well-hidden or unintelligible to anyone but the person who had written them, or both. Time was very short, and I had wasted a mountain of it just by getting sick.

Mother was alive. I couldn't imagine how that could possibly be, not after having seen her grey skin drenched in sweat and vomit, not after having seen the expression on the doctor's face. She asked for something for the pain in her broken hand, but there was nothing in the house, and the servants were busy preparing for Sherlock's birthday, so I went.

The note, penned sinister and almost illegible, said only *I'm sorry*, but Sherlock found her in her studio, stretched out in front of the painting she had been finishing when she fell in the street and a carriage wheel mangled her right hand. The painting would never be finished, nor would any other, and we should have seen it coming. I should have measured out the dose and taken the little brown bottle away with me. I should have handed it over to Hyde, who oversaw the medicine cabinet with as much diligence as the wine cellar. I should not have left the thing with her.

She might not be dead, but people weren't all right after things like that.

And now Sherrinford, too. Poor delicate, sensitive Sherrinford, Father's disappointing heir. He just wasn't built to cope with anything worse than bad weather. I hadn't considered the effect all of this would have on his nerves. He was bedridden for three months after his last attack, and Sherlock had said he might not recover at all, this time. My eldest brother possibly chair-bound for life, and that was my fault, too.

Too many thoughts. For the moment, I tried not to think at all.

The walk began to grow long, and my ankle ached.

'Who are we going to talk to, first?' I asked.

Magpie gave me a sideways glance, his eyes a little uncertain. 'Hellhounds,' he said.

Rotting teeth and long knives flashed through my memory. 'The ones who couldn't decide whether to rob and murder me or kidnap and ransom me? And then probably kill me anyway?'

He shrugged. 'Yeah.'

'I can't picture them caring what's happened to Snail.'

He shook his head and spread his hands. 'Doubt they do. But they'll know if there's a threat, they're in danger, too. May not want to 'elp us, but they'll watch out for theirselves an' won't mind if that 'appens to be 'elpful at the same time.'

'I don't recall seeing any girls among them.'

'Was thinking we'd leave that part out, actually.'

'You know how to find them?'

His eyes crinkled in a mixture of triumph and mischief. 'Yeah. Found 'em a while ago. I was just waitin' for a good time to let 'em know.'

'You're not afraid they'll run us off before we have a chance to explain?' And of course, I couldn't run. 'Or worse?'

'We'll knock, nice and polite.'

My back knotted with tension as the scenery became more and more familiar. I had forgotten that my first encounter with the Hellhounds had been close to home, that their turf bordered the Wrong Boys' domain, and both intersected alarmingly with my own former territory. I kept my head down, half-certain I would see Father walking past at any moment. Sherlock did not keep his head down, which made my effort useless.

I scarcely breathed as we walked past that arboured street. If I turned my head, I knew I would see the house, or at least a catch a glimpse of it, a brick corner, the slope of the roof, a single finial. Was Mother still there, or had she been taken somewhere else? A hospital? Back to Mycroft House to recover? I did not turn my head.

We walked on.

In a blink, we had crossed an invisible border between affluence and poverty, and the light and fragrant gardens vanished into grey brick, shabby but clean. In another instant, rags had sprouted from broken windows, and suddenly, the children wore a skin of dirt beneath their layers of threadbare wool. The buildings huddled closer together, hunched over as though trying to keep one another warm. I had never come this way before, and the close juxtaposition of wealth and need startled me.

Our little party attracted attention wherever it went. As we passed my street, the constable on the corner followed Magpie with a sharp eye, seemingly not reassured by my own presence or Sherlock's. Now, in the sooty shadows, Sherlock and I drew watchful stares, but Magpie stood a little straighter.

Suddenly, he ducked left, between two crates of cabbage. There one moment and gone the next, so fast and smooth that I doubt I would have noticed, had I not been following him. Sherlock and I scrambled after him into a narrow space between two buildings. It was not properly an alley, almost a tunnel, as it was clearly not intended to take any sort of traffic, not even on foot. My shoulders brushed each grimy wall, and the two boys had to turn slightly sideways to fit.

Twenty yards or so down, the crevice cut right, and we followed it until it came to a space about ten feet long and four feet wide. Nobody was meant to walk that way, but someone at some point had realised that foot traffic was at least possible and had erected a slatted fence, about fifteen feet high, to ensure wanderers could go no further. It was old, though, and at least one plank hung loose.

Magpie knocked.

'Oy,' he called through the fence, keeping his voice low. 'Pax, a'right? 'Ere to tell you summing important, like.'

No one appeared.

He knocked again, louder.

'Hellhounds!'

Sherlock pushed out a sharp breath through his nose, not quite a laugh. 'I suppose they can't be at home all the time. Shall we wait?'

'One-Arm Randy 'angs around near 'ere,' Magpie said musingly. 'Could talk to 'im and then come back later.'

'He sounds like a fellow with some stories to tell.'

Magpie snorted. 'You could say that. Just don't ask 'im unless you've got 'alf a day to listen.'

I hissed at them both for silence, and in the heartbeat that followed, I saw that Sherlock heard it, too. He met my eyes and nodded. From beyond the fence came a slow, regular thump, almost inaudible. It stopped for a few breaths and then resumed. Instinctively, I listened for a pattern, but the sound seemed random, certainly not Morse.

As one, Sherlock and I glanced up at the sliver of sky overhead. A thin splinter of wood hung loose from one of the crumbling rooves, clinging by only a few fibres. Not a breath of wind swayed it. It was not the weather making that noise.

Magpie followed our thinking half a second behind, and when I looked down again, he was staring balefully between the two of us.

'Wouldn't risk my neck for any of 'em,' he said simply.

'Neither would I,' I replied. 'But if one of them had seen something useful...'

He sighed and nodded, and suddenly, a gleam appeared at his right hand, a foot-long blade only as wide as my thumb, meant for fileting fish. He pushed one of the loose boards aside and slipped through.

I followed, struggling a little with my aching leg and the cane borrowed from Doctor Peach, and Sherlock came behind me, unfolding his little pocket knife, for all the good that would do.

Behind the fence was a small, grim yard, long abandoned. A refuse pile climbed the far wall, hard frozen at the moment, but still exuding a faint, rank air. There was a stack of wood fragments, bits of doors and sticks of furniture and corners of crates, some with nails protruding. In the middle of the yard was a pump with no handle. A green-and-black thread of algae connected the spout to the ground.

The building belonging to the yard was empty, with not a window left intact. I thought I saw movement in the darkness of the third storey and stiffened, but the momentary flash became a naked tail, vanishing inside, and I relaxed.

The thumping was clearer, now, more obviously purposeful. It came from inside.

We crept toward the boarded door, but the sound led us sideways along the wall, to a second door nearly concealed behind the stack of discarded wood. It slanted against the wall of the building, suggesting either a cellar or a shed. Jagged fragments of rust showed where a chain had once bound the handles together, but it had rotted away a long time ago, and nothing barred our entry, now.

Sherlock laid a hand on the frayed wood. His body was tight, and I could almost see his senses stretching out like quivering antennae, listening for footsteps or voices, anything other than the unsteady thumping. He pulled one side of the door open and we all flinched at the shriek of the hinges. For an instant, none of us moved, but nothing came charging out at us, no angry faces appeared in the staring windows above.

**144**

The thumping stopped, then began again with even greater vigour. A quiet sound joined it, like a muffled voice.

Questionable wooden steps descended into unrelieved blackness. Magpie frowned. 'Anybody got a light?'

Sherlock and I shook our heads, and I resolved never again to go out without a candle stub in my pocket.

He hummed disappointedly and shrugged. 'Carefully, then,' he conceded, and he crept down into the dark.

Sherlock followed.

I prised back the other side of the door to let in the greatest possible amount of light and made up the rear. The stairs were hell on my ankle, and I had to bite deep into my cheeks to keep from making a sound. Only the cane kept me from pitching forward and tumbling the rest of the way down.

The smell of dust and unwashed bodies pervaded the space, but fortunately, I did not smell anything I could guess was human rot. I had a vague understanding that there was nothing to compare to the smell of corpse, but I had happened upon a decaying horse, once, and that was bad enough. Whatever had happened, unless it were extremely recent, it did not seem to have ended in death.

The yard outside had not been extremely bright, and it did not take as long for my eyes to adjust as I had feared it would. The space came slowly into focus. Crumbling shelves lined the walls. Those that had not collapsed entirely were piled with odds and ends, shadowy mounds that I could not make out clearly. There was a dark splotch in the middle of the floor where rubbish may have been burned for warmth, but I imagined the smoke would be unbearable in a closed space. There were tangles of blankets, a three-legged stool, a few mostly-intact crates...

Magpie swore extravagantly, introducing me to a few turns of phrase I hadn't heard before.

## GRAHAM

I followed his gaze to the source of the thumping. The shadows were darker in that corner. And moving. Gradually, I was able to discern two separate shapes stretched out on the floor. What I had taken for blankets were two human beings, bound and gagged. One had worked its way up to one of the empty crates and was kicking the daylights out of it, boot leather on boards creating a hollow boom. Glistening eyes reflected the meagre light.

There was a flurry of motion as both Magpie and Sherlock sprang into action, knives working, and in a matter of moments, both the prisoners were free.

'You ain't Hellhounds,' Magpie commented blandly, and I could see what he meant. The figures stepping into the light were swathed in skirts and shawls.

The smaller girl spat and cursed. 'Thank God you ain't, either. They ain't gonna be gone long,' she concluded. 'Said they'd be comin' back with a cart. We all better get lost.'

The other shivered. Everything down there was colourless, but when I squinted, I could see that she wore a housemaid's black woollens. Her simple, sober cape was torn, and one eye was swollen shut.

Coming back with a cart.

That answered one question, at least. The men in the wagon had come after me because the Hellhounds had given them my description. They had made me their target, either because they blamed me for bringing the Wrong Boys down on them, or because they thought I would fetch a higher price than their usual class of victim, girls like these. They took Snail because I had disappeared into the Greys' garden, and they refused to leave empty-handed.

A crawling sensation rose in my throat, and I forced it down with difficulty before I could speak.

'We'd better go quickly. Back to the Greys' house.'

There was no argument. We climbed the stairs and ducked through the gap in the fence, alert for any sign of approaching Hellhounds. The dirty crevice between buildings was still and silent.

'Thanks, an' all,' the smaller girl said, 'but I don't feel like goin' off with you, either. Don't akshally know you're any safer'n' them, now do I?'

She sprinted away without waiting for a reply, small and thin enough to move quickly between the crushing walls. I drew in a breath to call after her, to tell her to wait, that we only wanted to help, but the thought of my voice echoing and of who might hear it silenced me.

The other looked as though she would have run, too, if she thought she could. She clutched her cape around herself and stared at the ground.

'You'll want to go home,' I said. 'But would you be willing to talk to the police, first?'

She pressed her lips together as though swallowing tears, but she nodded.

'We'll stay on busy streets where there are lots of people and nobody would dare hurt you. All right?'

She nodded again, her hands twisting furiously at the folds of the cape.

'And my friend and my brother both have knives, and I've got a heavy stick. Nobody will get near you, I promise.'

She glanced up at me, a flicker of a question in her one good eye, but then her shoulders lowered a fraction, and some of the dull fear left her face. She swallowed hard, exhaled loudly, and straightened up. 'All right.'

I tried a smile. 'All right.'

Together, we four sidled carefully through the cramped gap and back into the sunlight, Sherlock, Magpie and I making a close ring around our frightened companion.

Something loosened in my chest. I had done so much harm. Mother, Sherrinford... Mother was not dead. She could not possibly be well, and

## GRAHAM

I still felt the weight of that on my shoulders, but she was not dead. Sherrinford's nervous attack remained my fault. He had always been sensitive and sickly, and we all knew very well to mind that he never received a bad shock. I knew that very well. I couldn't escape that blame. Even Snail's kidnap had only occurred because I was nearby, and I was only nearby because of my own poor choices.

But the girl walking in front of me, with her tight, hunched back and furtive, fearful glances from side to side... I had done something to help her. I had done some good. She and the other, the one who ran, would have suffered Snail's fate if not for me and Magpie and Sherlock. I had done them some good. And if she knew something that would bring us closer to Snail, I might begin to undo one of my mistakes.

Only one. Mother and Sherrinford weighed heavily on me, still. But one was better than none. It was something.

So I gritted my teeth and hobbled along on my ankle, wearing my brother's clothes and layers of false names.

As we reached the end of the street and merged with the main road, I chanced to turn and saw a familiar dirty face, a grimacing mouthful of blackened teeth that had once threatened to cut me a smile. I saw dark, narrow eyes watching our backs, marking the escape of their prize and memorising the shapes of the three who took her away. Fists clenched, one rising to a knife at the belt.

It was as well he did not follow us, because I would not have been able to run.

But his eyes lit on Magpie, and his lips traced the words: '*Wrong Boys.*'

# PART FOUR:

## THE

# JAWS

## OF

# LONDON

# ONE

WE KEPT a brisk pace, each step sending a jolt up through my body. Somehow, nobody questioned our bizarre little parade. I with my limp, hatless, Sherlock stiff and alert, Magpie in his rags, all but masked, and the maid between us, her clothes torn, her face battered and bruised. People looked, but only briefly. Eyes took us in and then slid away, faces carefully blank or else twisting with the faintest hint of discomfort and disgust. Flashes of outrage as groups parted or crossed streets to avoid us. Where I saw pity, it was quickly suppressed, replaced by embarrassment. Those who did notice that something was wrong didn't know what to do about it. There was, as ever, the assumption that someone else would do something. Someone else would call for help. Someone else would ask what had happened and if anything could be done.

That curious tendency to defer allowed us to move unmolested through the city.

As the journey lengthened, my limp became more pronounced, and I began to fall behind. It was only a foot or so, at first, then five, then ten. I shuffled forward, lagged, shuffled forward, lagged. Sherlock glanced back with an eyebrow raised and gestured impatiently.

'Keep up, *Crow*,' he insisted, when he might just as easily have told the others to slow down.

I grumbled something unkind at him, but I hadn't really expected anything different. He could be infinitely patient when it suited him, but rarely when it suited anybody else.

So I tried to keep up.

Tried and failed. I knew that fear and emergency dulled pain, so perhaps if I'd had to run for my life, I'd have been able, but I was not able to walk at a reasonable pace through London. When next Sherlock looked back, feet had become yards. He only shrugged one thin shoulder and turned forward again, but thereafter he looked back every few steps. He wouldn't slow for me, but he wasn't about to let me be snatched, either.

And I was aware of that distinct possibility. From my position in the rear, separated from my little group, the crowds seemed thicker, and my senses quivered. Every passing face stood out to me, all the sounds and smells—hooves and smoke, voices and jellied eels, the rumble of wheels, peppermint water.

Alert and hyper-aware, it did not take me long to recognise one face, in particular. The first time it appeared, I suspected, and the second time, I knew. I had last seen it in the company of the boy with the rotted teeth, expressing an interest in taking the boots off my dead body.

We were being followed.

Two more familiar faces darted in and out of sight, never still even for a moment. Three of them, then. I recalled there being four, originally, but perhaps the one who was stabbed was still out of action. Or perhaps he had died of his wound. I tried for a moment not to hope for the latter, but then I remembered what they were doing, why they had two girls bound and gagged in a filthy cellar, and that they were most likely the reason masked men had taken Snail away. Death was too good. I hoped his wound had become infected and that he was still suffering it.

Then I wondered whether I had always had such a vicious streak, or if that was new.

The next time Sherlock glanced back, I gestured to him with a jerk of my head, and he shortened his stride to fall in step beside me. Magpie noticed and slowed as well, his hand on the girl's arm.

I described our pursuers briefly, being careful not to look round for them as I did, my voice low so as not to frighten the girl unnecessarily. As promised, we were keeping to busy streets, and I did not think the Hellhounds would risk an altercation in front of a few dozen witnesses. They had assaulted me in an alley before full daylight, and the masked men with their cart had come after dusk, and only when the street was empty but for a pack of boys who stole and begged to survive and so could never go to the police. Shopkeepers, costers, women visiting, men on business... There were too many eyes, here, and even those pretending not to see us would object to a row.

'We can't go back to the doctor,' Sherlock murmured, echoing my own thoughts. 'There are some lonely stretches between here and there. To the Grey house, then.'

Magpie tensed at the thought, but did not argue.

I looked at him, considering. He was not comfortable with the idea of sheltering among strangers. I didn't think any of the other Wrong Boys would be, either. Did the Hellhounds know that?

'Would they go to Doctor Peach anyway, if they lost us? Expecting us to go there? I know they recognised you, Magpie.'

Above his muffler, his eyes narrowed in anxiety, yellow brows lowering. 'Don' think they'd mess with the Doc, as 'e 'elps them, too, when they need. There's plenty what goes to 'im. They wouldn't...' He cut off, and I knew that he wasn't completely sure that they wouldn't. 'They wouldn't connec' us anything special with 'im.'

Peach treated the Hellhounds, too? I stared, startled by the unexpected link. It still didn't say for certain that Peach was involved. No, but it was suggestive.

'But they have followed you there very recently. They may not know how often you've been visiting him, but...' But if Peach were involved, they probably did know, and they probably knew at about what time the Wrong Boys could be found at the little medical practice, and they probably knew that it was only ever one or two of them at a time. And doctors possessed things like ether.

Magpie nodded. 'Somebody needs to warn 'im. I'll get you to your friends' 'ouse, an' then I'll go tell 'im. I can move faster on my own, prolly lose 'em.'

I pursed my lips, not sure if the misunderstanding was deliberate. 'Actually, I thought the other boys ought to be warned. About him.'

He was silent a long time, long enough to make it obvious that there had been no misunderstanding at all. 'Keep it up,' he said softly, 'an' I'll clock you, you know. You don' have any bleedin' idea what you're talkin' about.'

The possibility that he actually would clock me was not sufficient deterrent. 'I can't imagine anyone more perfectly positioned to be at the very centre of this. He seems to have a broad reach throughout exactly the class of people who are being taken. He's clever enough to manage it. He's connected to the Hellhounds, who we know have been seizing women for this... this thing. He's undoubtedly connected to any number of other people willing to sacrifice human lives for a fee. You said he helps the women, so that means he knows them, too. Which ones go walking where at night, which might disappear without anyone noticing...'

His shoulders hunched, and I heard his teeth creak, but his clenched fists stayed firmly at his sides. 'You're upsetting 'er,' he hissed, jerking his head toward the battered maid.

There were fresh tears on her bruised cheeks, and she was shaking with far more than just cold. I stopped talking.

No one said another word until we reached the Greys' house. I signalled the constable outside and bade him fetch Robbins, and as I spoke to him, a flicker of motion at the end of the street told me our pursuers had identified police and vanished. But they knew the address, now. That could not be helped. We could never have lost them, not with my handicap. Let them wonder what it meant that we had come back to Peter Storm, of the *Albatross*.

At least we hadn't put anyone into any new danger. The Greys were already under attack, and whoever was in charge knew where they lived. It could hardly get worse for them because we had led Hellhounds to their door.

Magpie slipped away as Sherlock and I hustled the maid up the step. I glanced back the way we had come to make sure no one was watching, anymore. They must have seen no reason to loiter once they knew where we had gone. I gritted my teeth and swallowed the words of caution I wanted to give. He was angry with me already, and returning to our difference of opinions would only make it worse. He was sliding out of sight when a horrible thought came to me: Magpie's loyalty to Peach seemed long-standing. He had known him for years, and certainly cared more for Peach than he did for me. What if he passed my suspicions on to the doctor? Peach had certainly guessed that I suspected him, but he had done nothing, because he had no way to know for sure. What would he do if he learned it straight from Magpie's lips?

I could not catch him up now, though. He had already disappeared.

Well, perhaps he would say nothing, to spare Peach's feelings. Assuming Peach had any human feeling other than cutting irony.

Theodora opened the door before I had a chance to knock, and her keen dark eyes took in the situation in a single glance. 'You were gone rather longer than I expected,' she said with some asperity, and stood aside to let us pass. A twinge of guilt stabbed me for continuing to worry her so.

We installed the maid near the fire in the little parlour, where she seemed extremely uncomfortable to receive tea and biscuits rather than being required to serve them, herself.

I collapsed into a chair nearby, the pain in my ankle bringing tears to my eyes that I could not quell.

Sherlock paced. There had never been much rivalry between the two of us—paternal attention was so scarce there was no point in competing for it, and Mother distributed her time and care according to a rigidly equitable timetable that would never favour any child over another—but I felt a pang of envy for his stamina. Even with both legs in peak condition, I could never have made myself pace after walking all day.

I drank some of the tea and tried to make myself relax.

'What's your name, then?' I asked the silent girl.

She looked at me without any particular trust, her expression shadowed. 'Ruth,' she whispered, so reluctantly that I knew she had thought about lying.

'This is Sherlock, and I'm... Morgan.' In a flash, I understood her mistrust. To her, I was male, as male as the Hellhounds, and they had stated their intentions very clearly when I encountered them. 'Ruth, did they only hit you, or did they hurt you in other ways?'

Her mouth tightened in dull comprehension and fear, but she shook her head. 'They said they would when they came back.'

Sherlock had stopped pacing and stood with his head bowed, his chin tucked tight to his chest. Listening to us, I thought, though his eyes were unfocused and he seemed miles away.

'When did they take you?' I asked.

She shuddered. 'This morning, early. I went out to post a letter, and there was no one else around, and suddenly...'

I wanted to tell her that I very much understood, about my own experience being taunted and nearly taken, but that would give me away, and Robbins would be coming soon. I had to be Morgan when he arrived, and I couldn't be sure Ruth wouldn't slip and call me 'she' in his presence. Even if I had time to make her understand my situation, my problems seemed stupid beside hers, almost a farce.

Sherlock looked at me sharply, at my hands plucking at the knees of my trousers, and read my mind. He crooked a finger at me, and I heaved myself painfully from my chair and followed him out of the parlour into the hall.

'What do you want me to say?' he asked in a low voice. 'If you call me your brother, I'll have to lie about my name, too. Or would you rather I left before the police arrive?'

'You can't,' I corrected. 'Ruth will say she was rescued by three boys, and I've already called you my brother in front of her. Magpie has no home, so no one will be surprised that he's disappeared. But if you vanish, as well, it'll begin to look even more suspicious than it already does.'

'Does that mean I'm Sherlock Grey for the time being?' he asked with a touch of humour. 'Isn't this charade getting rather involved?'

I tsked at him. 'I didn't exactly have time to plan any of it, and I couldn't have known I'd have to fit you into it, either. No, just be Sherlock, for the moment. Don't add any details. Now that the police are around so much, this is bound to fall to pieces sooner or later, and I'm going to be in trouble, when it does. There's no reason for you to get in trouble, too, and no reason to hasten the collapse. I can't be sent home until Snail is found, Sherlock. I can't.'

He studied me earnestly for a moment before nodding. 'There's already going to be at least a bit of trouble, for me. You've run away, and I know where you are and haven't turned you in. I can probably blame that on Mycroft, though. But Morrigan... Morgan. If it does look like you're going to be found out and sent home... will you come? Or will you try to run even further away?'

'Are you asking because you're hoping for one outcome or the other? Or are you just curious?'

He frowned and tsked back at me. 'I'm hoping for neither. The effect on me would be the same, either way. If you run further away, you'll be inaccessible, but if you come home, Father will send you to Europe, and you'll still be inaccessible. If it were up to me, you wouldn't go anywhere.'

A smile threatened to break, but I forced it down. 'Are you saying you'd miss me?'

Much as I had expected, gentle ribbing received little reaction.

'I would notice your absence,' he said in a clipped tone, 'and I would regret it.' Something else seemed about to rise to the surface, but he pursed his lips and held it back.

He so rarely expressed strong emotion, even when we were very small, that I knew it must have been something powerful. I caught him by the arm as he began to move back toward the parlour.

'Sherlock?'

'Morrigan.'

'Was there something else?'

He looked at me blandly, deliberated for a moment, and then shook his head. 'It wasn't important.'

'Not generally important, or not important to you?'

A dark tinge crept into his pale cheeks. Not embarrassment, I thought. Sherlock was never embarrassed. That meant it was anger.

'Not generally important,' he said evenly.

'Important to you, then. If something's wrong, I'd like to know, Sherlock. I can't do anything about it if I don't know.'

He glanced down at my hand still upon his arm, and then his eyes travelled up slowly to meet mine with icy intensity. 'You can't do anything about it, anyway, now. But the fact is, it was after midnight.'

I took my hand away quickly and rubbed it against my trouser leg, as if the cold of his stare had burned me. 'What was?'

'It was after midnight when you left home.'

I thought back. 'About two in the morning?' But the significance of the time escaped me. I squinted at him, desperate for a hint.

'A few minutes past. I remember the clock striking the hour.' He shrugged, the gesture tense. He was unhappy, angry with me, but I knew he would not have hesitated to tell me why if he thought the reason was a good one.

But trivia did not upset him. So it was something of questionably real importance, but still a large gaffe, something intensely personal.

'Sherlock?'

He thought another moment, then dismissed the conversation with a wave of a hand. 'It's nothing. Childish.' And he brushed past me into the parlour, his heels clacking smartly with his long stride.

Something childish? I was not certain I really considered myself adult, yet, but I knew I was no longer a child, and there were only ten months between us, so neither was he. With our upbringing, perhaps neither of us had ever really been children. For a few short weeks each year, we were the same age. I would turn seventeen, soon, the age at which girls were supposed to start looking for a match, even if there were several years yet before one could reasonably marry. Sherlock had turned sixteen on the sixth of the month...

My eyes shut, and I sagged against the wall.

Good Lord, no wonder he'd had so little to say to me.

I had gone to the chemist for Mother because the servants were busy preparing for Sherlock's birthday party. She drank what I had been sure was enough paregoric to kill her at about noon the day before. Sherlock found her quickly, and the doctor was sent for and arrived soon after that. Soon enough to save her life, I understood. And then the shouting. When I thought back, I couldn't remember exactly what I had actually heard, other than my name, over and over. It had been the tone of the voices that had driven me out the window, but I could not be sure that the tone I perceived was not influenced by the knowledge of what I had done.

And so, at two o'clock on the morning of my little brother's sixteenth birthday, hours after his mother's attempted suicide, he watched his sister throw herself from a first-storey window to a stone courtyard in the freezing rain, and when she did not die, she walked away with a jaunty wave.

# TWO

ROBBINS SPOKE with each of us in turn, preventing any attempt at editing our story during its telling. Not that I would have been tempted to edit very much — the Hellhounds needed to be found and prevented from doing any more harm, and any prevarication would only make that more difficult for the police. But such a thing would never have been permitted in Ruth's own home, where her master or mistress would certainly have been present for her questioning, to make sure she said nothing to incriminate the household, to shield her from undue aggression on the part of the police, and for the simple necessity of preventing a young woman from being alone in a room with a man. She said nothing in protest, though, and when she emerged from the parlour, where Robbins had planted himself, she appeared pale but composed.

I gave her a smile as I moved past her, next to be interviewed. Somehow, I had thought her very much older than myself, but some of her age seemed to have been fear. Now that she was calmer, she held herself straighter, her shoulders back beneath her torn cape, and her face beneath its bruises was smooth. I didn't think her any older than nineteen.

# GRAHAM

Theodora led her away toward the kitchen, no doubt to ply her with tea, and I entered the room to face Sergeant Robbins.

He met my gaze steadily as I sank into the chair opposite, my bad leg stretched in front of me. I expected him to begin grilling me at once, but he simply sat, a pad of paper on his knee, a stub of pencil in his hand, and watched me. The silence stretched, punctuated by the crackling of the fire.

'Didn't you want to ask me something?' I asked after a while.

'Is there something particular you'd like to tell me?' he replied.

The back of my neck prickled, but he only smiled. I could not tell if it was a knowing smile, or only a friendly one. I reminded myself that he probably thought he was being kind, allowing me to tell the events in my own way, rather than being interrogated like a criminal. But the way he said that made me feel as though he were trying to squeeze out something he thought I was hiding. Had he been asking the same questions the Greys had asked? Had my father circulated a photograph of me? I had hardly recognised myself in the mirror—Mycroft had hardly recognised me on the street—but my entire family had a distinctive look. It wasn't inconceivable that a clever man might connect the dots. My current situation attracted attention. My only real hope had been that those actively searching for me would be searching elsewhere. And Mycroft had certainly succeeded in finding me, even though it had nearly been a coincidence.

Mycroft. My muscles clenched, and one in my lower back began to twitch uncomfortably. He had said he would address the problem of Snail's disappearance. Perhaps he had already done so. If that were the case, it was possible that Robbins already knew exactly who I was and was only waiting for me to say it. But Mycroft, for all his intelligence, for all the strings he held in his massive hands, was only an uncommonly clever clerk. Could he possibly have said anything to Robbins that would inspire a police detective to let a runaway girl remain in the wild, disguised, however temporarily, as a boy?

'Something particular?' I repeated slowly, tilting my head. 'I assume you want to know how we found Ruth, and what we found around her. She'll already have told you some of it, but I don't know what, so I'm not sure what details you'd like me to fill in.'

He sat back, his mouth tightening in... what? Irritation? Disappointment? 'I'd like you to tell me all of it, in your own words. Even if I've already heard it, you may be able to add some trifling observation, something you saw that she did not, or even tell me exactly the same thing in different words, with slightly different shades of meaning.'

I let out a breath, no longer certain that he was trying to trap me, but still not entirely convinced of my safety. One way or another, though, I was less important than the issue at hand.

So I told him of seeking out the Wrong Boys, of telling Magpie and Dart what had become of their friend. I told him of our trek through London's streets in search of another group of homeless boys, our hope that they may have seen something of use, or at least that they could be made aware enough to protect themselves and any girls for whom they cared. Then the grim, filthy yard, the girls in the cellar, what the Hellhounds had meant to do with them, and the grimy, cruel faces that had followed us back to the Greys' home.

He listened earnestly, jotting occasional notes in his little book, particularly as to the exact location of the building where we had found Ruth and the other girl. I hesitated a moment as I came to the street where I had lived, tripping over its name, and his pencil paused for an instant in its path. He had noticed. But he did not look up until he had finished writing.

'You'll not try anything like that again,' he said quietly, so quietly I had to lean forward to be sure of his words, so quietly no one listening at the keyhole could have overheard. 'You'll not go out looking for trouble, do you understand? Not you, nor your brother, and you'll not encourage your homeless friends to go looking for trouble, either. That's three girls taken that you know of, by who-knows-how-many armed men. Don't you dare make me add a murder to my report. Am I clear?'

In that instant, I knew that he'd lost someone. His tight hands, fingers pushing the tip of his pencil so hard into the paper that the lead crumbled, told me it was someone close. A sibling, perhaps. Or a child. Perhaps that was what had inspired his police career. I was forced to admit that I had misjudged him badly. What I had taken for apathy was only practicality. It had never been that he did not care about Snail and the men who had taken her, only that he had known from the start that his hands were tied by lack of information.

Now I could identify by sight three different people involved in the crime, and if they could be identified, they could be caught, and if they could be caught, they could be questioned. I did not think for a moment that the Hellhounds might be kept silent by any sort of loyalty to the men who paid them to collect warm bodies.

I couldn't bring myself to promise. Perhaps Snail's kidnap was not really my fault—I had not known the danger—but it remained my responsibility. I pursed my lips.

'Very clear,' I said.

I thought he understood my meaning. The muscles in his jaw clenched briefly, but there was nothing much he could do. He could not arrest me on the chance I might involve myself further. Arrest was not a preventive measure. All he could do was express his objection and let me know what the consequences would be if I disobeyed. Well, what could he do to me? I had already sacrificed everything he might have taken away. All that remained was prison, and he'd have to be mad to bring an adolescent to trial for going outside when he had said not to.

I did not ask if I was forbidden from going outside at all, which was the only way he could keep me from interfering. Once I passed beyond the doors, I could reasonably claim that anything that happened was beyond my control. If the Hellhounds just happened to be wherever I was, or if I just happened to spot a cart and follow it... Well, there was little I could do about that.

He did not tell me not to go out.

I considered that a small victory, or at least a small grace, but the expression on his face soured my satisfaction.

He waved me out of the room and summoned Sherlock to hear his perspective. I smiled at my brother as he loped into the parlour, but he did not smile back. Already he wore that expression of boredom that, in him, always signifies intense concentration, and I hoped Robbins would not take offence.

I also hoped nothing unfortunate would come to light, but if this was the moment my charade fell apart, so be it.

I went down to the kitchen to partake of another cup of tea. Even hours after returning to the house, my feet and hands were cold.

Robbins spoke to Ruth once more, and then to Theodora and Edwin. They were with him a very long time, and I assumed they were repeating to him the story they had told me and Sherlock and Mycroft, connecting their past with the appalling present. Robbins would have something he could do, now, at least. He would have a place to start, perhaps access to a list of names of those arrested the first time around. The Greys had said that none of the men captured ten years ago had said or possibly even known from whom their orders originally came. They only followed the orders of one man up the chain, who followed the orders of one man up the chain. That seemed impossible, to me, but I did not suspect the Greys of hiding anything that could have helped. If no one knew who was at the top of the chain, that had to be deliberately built into the organisation's structure.

Robbins had information, now, a trail he could follow, and I believed that he would. In the beginning, I had involved myself because the police had higher priorities. I had thought Robbins didn't care for a parentless girl, no matter how violently she was taken, but I knew now that it had been more a matter of ability than will. But now that he had ability, I did not intend to step back. I had told Peach that somebody doing something was better than nobody doing anything, and the logical extension was that multiple somebodies doing somethings was better than just the one. With the Wrong Boys' knowledge of the streets and the invisibility provided by raggedy clothes, I could still go places the police would not be welcome and see and hear things that would be quickly hidden if Robbins bustled in with his official bearing.

When he left, he took Ruth with him. I felt bad for her. There would undoubtedly be more questions, more demands on her time and energy, simply because something awful had already happened to her. That was a bitter irony. And she would be taken home, at some point, and I knew very well that she might lose her position. Servants were expected to be of impeccable virtue, and society was certain that all manner of misfortunes reflected badly on one's own morals. Maybe her employers would believe that the Hellhounds had done no more than hit her. I could hope. I would bring it up to the Greys. They might not have room in their household for a maid, should Ruth be let go, but they moved in eccentric circles, and maybe one of their acquaintances would be able to find a place for a girl alone.

The door shut behind them with a snap. The light was failing, outside, and a light rain had begun to patter on the pavement, after the morning's fair skies. A carriage rolled slowly past, and I caught a glimpse of a pale face in its window before steps behind me made me turn.

'That's something,' Theodora commented. She turned to Sherlock. 'Will you be needing a room for the night? You're certainly welcome.'

He shook his head. 'Mycroft will be waiting for an update. May even have an update of his own to provide. I'll need to go.'

She nodded. 'Will you eat, first?'

He grinned.

The supper was laid in the kitchen, where the range kept it warmer than in their small dining room. We ate re-heated game pie and potatoes from incongruously fine china laid out on the scarred tabletop, and while we ate, Sherlock and I laid out all we had learned once more, this time including the obvious course of action.

'They're targeting the poor, first,' I said. 'Like the last time, it seems. They're beginning to reach higher, if they dared to take Ruth, and tried to take me, probably because of my voice. I imagine a small amount of education fetches a higher price, in that market.'

Sherlock made an uncomfortable noise, the edge of his knife screeching against the surface of his plate, and he covered by taking a long drink of water. The tendons in his neck stood taut. I could not tell whether it was the thought of that market, itself, or the idea of demand for education that provoked him. Or perhaps the reminder of my narrow escape, though I flattered myself.

'Will they have stopped targeting the poor, though?' I continued. 'Once they set their sights higher, socially? I don't think so. We'd have seen in the papers if there were a rash of disappearances. I mean, among people who are noticed if they disappear. They'll still be wanting a reliable flow of bodies from lower rungs. If we're to start asking questions, we should begin at the bottom. We tried with the street boys and found something unpleasant. Probably better not to risk continuing to ask around, there. We ought to leave that to the Wrong Boys, who know that set better. If anyone knows anything, or has seen anything, it's more likely to have been seen in the rookeries.'

Edwin glanced at Theodora, delving into his pie absently with the tines of his fork. He had not eaten anything, yet. 'Ask questions in the rookeries? That was where I began before, yes, but it was mostly chance that I discovered anything.'

'You weren't known,' Theodora said quietly. 'You were a stranger poking your nose where it wasn't wanted, and you wouldn't have found anything if they weren't desperate for someone to take notice of what was happening.'

'Precisely,' he said with a sharp nod. Then he frowned and rubbed at his milky eye. 'Teddy...'

'I'm known,' she continued. 'Probably not by very many, anymore, but I am known. Mrs Niall is still in business, and I believe Madam Pennacchi still moves in those parts. The Cottons are dead, I think. It's been a while since I saw them, at least. But there are those who still know me and will remember, will be willing to talk to me. In the morning, then?'

Edwin paled. 'Teddy, you don't have to, you know. Just because this ugly thing has reared its head, again...'

'Of course I do!' she snapped. 'Who more so than I? And if it's happening again, there will be those who remember the last time, and will be all the more distressed because they think they know what it is and can't be certain. I can't leave it to the police to speak to my old friends and acquaintances. They deserve to know it from me. And they are more likely to talk to me.'

She stabbed a small, red potato and shoved it whole into her mouth, quenching her ire in the act of chewing violently.

He sighed and slumped unhappily, nudging at his own food, and shook his head. 'It's not that I think you can't handle yourself, dear. But please consider what reliving all of that might do to you. You've never forgotten, and neither have I, but there's no reason to go plunging back in when the police can do the same job. More slowly, less effectively, perhaps, but the same.'

'Slowly is what we can't have,' she replied. 'They had me for a nearly a month, and I saw any number of women pass through and be sold on, to vanish forever. The ones the police were never able to trace. Prostitution is a terrible fate, but all the ones being held and used nearby can at least be found and freed. The ones who are sold away are... gone.

**168**

The longer it takes, the more are lost.'

She drank down an entire glass of wine in a single gulp. 'In the morning, then. Mrs Niall hears everything. She'll know if anyone's gone missing. Who, when, and where.'

'How,' Sherlock interjected.

All the rest of us looked at him.

'They went after Morrigan with a cart, and the Hellhounds were supposedly returning with a cart to transport those other girls. I suppose if we'd had the presence of mind, then, we might have followed it, but letting them loose seemed like a better idea, at the time. The most useful thing we can do, right now, is find one of those carts and see where it goes.'

'We can hardly hope to find another kidnapping in progress,' I objected. 'What are the chances of stumbling on one?' I paused, meeting his clear, grey eyes, as a thought began to take form. 'We'll have to engineer one, instead. At some point.'

'Find out where they're most active,' he agreed. 'Set a trap. Like hunting rabbits. Follow when the bait is taken.'

My game pie had suddenly ceased to appeal. I pushed my plate away. 'We'll definitely want police assistance for that part.'

# THREE

THEODORA APPEARED in the morning plainly dressed in grey wool, a worn tartan shawl over her shoulders. Still, her clothes were well-made, if drab. Where we were going, she would stand out.

I glanced down at my own clothes. I had left Sherlock's donated suit hanging in the wardrobe and resumed the collected bits and pieces I had first worn to go find Peach. I would stand out, too, but far less.

'Are you sure you want to go, yourself?' I asked.

She smiled with a touch of humour, despite the pallor of her cheeks. 'You think I ought to let you go by yourself? You and a few scrappy friends? On that leg?'

'No, but you might let Mr Grey go. It seems to be a dangerous time for women...'

She made a noise deep in her throat and tossed her head. 'It's always a dangerous time for women. This entire ordeal is nothing new, only better organised than usual. Or would you have all women stay inside at all times? Or only the respectable ones!'

She swallowed and picked at the hem of her shawl, shuddering. 'I'm sorry, that was unnecessarily harsh. I'm frightened and angry, and I can't stop thinking of poor Ruth. You know what's expected of respectable women. Follow the rules, and you'll stay safe. Break even one, and whatever happens to you, you've brought it on yourself. I grew up a short way beyond respectability, you recall. Quite a lot of people were very certain that I had somehow deserved all of my misfortunes. Even if they couldn't pinpoint exactly what I'd done wrong, they knew it must have been something, because good girls don't get hurt. It's almost inevitable that someone will think the same of her...'

She fell silent, watching me, but I had nothing to say. I was glad she had already thought of Ruth's precarious position.

'I don't mean to suggest that you're ignorant, of course,' she went on, as though desperate for any sound to fill the void. 'You don't seem to have had a very regular upbringing, but I'm sure you must know everything I've just said...' She trailed off.

I shifted my weight off my sore ankle. It was worse, this morning, after yesterday's walking. I would not be able to walk any great distance, again. 'Sorry,' I muttered. 'I think the usual response would be "I understand", but I'm afraid I don't. Knowing isn't quite the same as understanding, I don't think. I haven't had the most regular upbringing, but I certainly haven't been through what you have. I know about the rules, but my parents have their own set of rules, quite different. Honestly, I don't think they ever considered whether I or any of my brothers would ever be accepted in society.' I thought for a moment. 'Or whether I would ever be able to marry.' The idea had circled through my mind, before, but had never really struck me as it did in that moment. It occurred to me for the first time that I wanted to marry. I would be provided for, if I did not, or I would have been, had I not run away. There was more than enough money in the family. I might have lived forever at Mycroft House with Sherrinford, or been put up in a small place of my own in London. There was such a thing as a perennial spinster. But I didn't want to be one.

I shook off that train of thought and stared hard at Theodora. 'You've had some horrifying troubles, but you've become quite happy, haven't you? Without following the rules?' People like Poppy Cooper did not marry people like Edwin Grey. Like swanning about with no corset, or reading the newspapers, or authoring botanical treatises, it Simply Wasn't Done. And yet, she had.

She smiled, and this time, there was a flicker of conspiracy in the curve of her lips. 'Oh, incredibly. You know, Edwin and I discussed the possibility of my wearing trousers for today's excursion. You're very right that the danger to a person in skirts is likely greater now than usual, and I do own a suit of men's clothing.'

I felt my eyebrows rise, and her smile broadened into a grin.

'I use it at election times. So of course, neither Edwin nor I was totally shocked by your transformation. There are advantages to masculinity. But not for today. I am known in the Old Nichol as a woman, so I ought to go as a woman, if I am to speak with old friends.'

She paused, smoothing her dull skirts. 'Are you familiar with the writings of Miss Wollstonecraft? John Stuart Mill? Frances Cobbe? Harriet Martineau? I shall lend you some, when we're done with all of this.'

The most important point of that statement struck me as the fact that, after we were done with all of this, she expected that I would still be in a position to borrow her books. I smiled back.

Sherlock arrived shortly after we broke our fast. He was dressed in older clothes that I was surprised he had not thrown away, with his usually fastidious habits. Still, he was still nowhere near as shabby as I. The three of us squeezed uncomfortably into a cab, myself squashed between my brother and my hostess. The cab driver hesitated to take us on, but Theodora had money, and that was what mattered.

## GRAHAM

He took us only as far as Church Street, the outskirts of the slum, and would go no deeper, partly because he had no interest in going into a place like that, and partly because there were parts of it where a cab would not fit. We walked up Chance Street, from one world into another. I could smell lye, fish, and other things that would be much worse in warmer weather. My nose wrinkled, and I glanced at Sherlock. His senses were all much sharper than those of anyone else I knew, and his lips were pursed tightly as against the urge to retch.

Theodora – Poppy – did not seem to notice the smell. She strode confidently, trailing Sherlock and myself behind her like ducklings, down Old Nichol Street and turned on Nichols Row. Eyes followed her and then slid back to us, but she moved as though she belonged there, and no one seemed to spend too much energy questioning her presence. I needed to learn that trick.

She passed between two buildings and up to the rough wooden gate of a large yard. Rank steam billowed up from beyond the fence, and the sound of crackling fires, the rumble of boiling water, and a few voices, too low for the words to be made out. Theodora did not knock, but pushed the gate open and stuck her head in. She slipped partway through the opening, standing there in the small gap until a louder voice called out, and she moved further inside. Sherlock and I followed.

The stench was worse beyond the gate, so aggressively clean my lungs felt as scoured as the fabric women were pushing through vats of water with their long paddles. Sherlock pressed a handkerchief over his nose and mouth, his eyes watering. The handkerchief was snowy white and beautifully pressed, at odds with the rest of his costume. I would have to point that out to him, later. It would make me feel better about all the little slips I had made, trying to be a boy.

A heavily muscled woman was approaching us, wiping her hands on her apron. Her face was scarlet, as were her arms up to the elbows, and her iron-grey hair stuck to her face and neck. It was cold where we were standing, but she was covered in a mixture of perspiration and steam, and she looked as irritated as I would expect of one who had to step from immense heat into immense cold while damp.

'Do ye want summat?' she demanded, giving no deference whatsoever. When she had come within a few paces, though, she stopped and cocked her head to one side, studying Theodora.

'Poppy. Doin' well enough for yourself, I see. What're ye doin' back 'ere?' She seemed wary, and I thought I understood. She had known Poppy Cooper, but she did not know Theodora Grey. The woman before her had done some social climbing, more than was usual, and she was not sure how to react to her.

'Hello, Mrs Niall,' Theodora said seriously. She inclined her head in a gesture of respect, and I saw Mrs Niall's posture relax as the interaction became familiar. 'I... *We* need to speak with you. It's a matter of some urgency.'

Mrs Niall's sharp eyes travelled the length of Theodora's frame, then moved to myself and to Sherlock, taking in every inch of us with photographic retention. I understood why Theodora valued her information. She would remember every detail of each of us until the day she died.

'What's urgent, then?' Mrs Niall asked cautiously. The wariness was back, perhaps because of Theodora's meticulously educated speech, perhaps because of the peculiarities I knew she must have seen in the three of us. We were dressed for the occasion, to blend in, but not well enough to fool her completely, just enough that she was aware of the effort.

'It's to do with ten years ago,' Theodora replied, leaning forward, her voice a mere whisper.

Mrs Niall stiffened and stared, her scarlet face rigid, then nodded and gestured for us to follow.

## GRAHAM

We passed through the yard, between a dozen vats filled with foaming mounds of cotton and linen, surrounded by ruddy, sweating young women with their hair secured beneath grimy kerchiefs, and entered the building to which the fence was attached. A flight of dark, narrow stairs led us up to the next storey, where Mrs Niall seemed to live. She pushed through an unlocked door and bade Theodora sit in one of the bare wooden chairs beside the single table. She sat in the other and waved Sherlock and myself to the edge of the bed. We sat as well, the bed creaking ominously beneath us, and I glanced around as Mrs Niall reached for an oily clay pipe, tamped tobacco into the bowl, and lit it with a small flint and steel. No matches to be had.

The plaster walls were cracked. They had been papered with newsprint, adhered with who-knows-what, and the thin sheets were peeling off. There was a window for light, but a pane was broken, and the slivers of glass were held together with white paste and wads of rags. There was a small fireplace, and the coals inside were still warm, but it had been allowed to go out, and the scuttle beside held no coal or wood. On the mantel were a pitcher, a stub of grey wax with no visible wick, a chipped vase holding a bundle of dried flowers, and a large ball of string. A box sat in one corner, and a pair of shoes sat beside it.

There was nothing else in the room.

'What's this, then, Poppy?' Mrs Niall asked calmly when her pipe had begun to smoke adequately.

Theodora's hands clenched in her lap. 'I was hoping you could tell me. My fear is that it's exactly the same as last time.'

'Why?' The word cut through the freezing air like a knife, nearly making me jump.

'For the same reasons as before. Women have gone missing. This young lady here.' She indicated me with a sharp gesture. Mrs Niall did not even blink at the revelation, nor did she look to see which boy Theodora was calling a girl. 'She was set upon in the street by masked men who took her friend, instead. Edwin and I have had two bricks through our windows. And then a gift.' Her mouth twisted in distaste. 'An albatross head delivered to our door. And on further investigation, we have discovered at least two more girls taken, though they were found and released before they could be sold. I am certain it is the same as before, or at least some of the same people are involved. They must be, to have thought to frighten me and Edwin. Revenge, most likely. If it is the same, there will be many more missing. You know everything in the Old Nichol, and quite a lot elsewhere. If anyone else has vanished, I must know who, where, when they disappeared. Clearly, the gang was not destroyed last time. We knew that many of the villains escaped, and probably the man in charge, though we can't be sure. This time, it must be crushed utterly.'

She took a long, shaking breath, her shoulders tight, and stared at Mrs Niall with fierce intensity. 'Am I right?'

The older woman dragged deeply at her pipe and expelled a cloud of blue smoke. She scowled. 'Seems likely. There's others. Three 'ere. Two what I know of in Limehouse. Two from St Giles. A few's gone looking for a rozzer what'll listen, but no luck, this time. Should'a come lookin' for you an' yer man, I s'pose.'

'Yes,' Theodora agreed. 'You should have. You know you always can.'

'I know that.' Mrs Niall shrugged, throwing a shadow of doubt on her words.

Theodora's shoulders sagged, just by a fraction, and I could sense the gulf between the two women. They had worked side-by-side, once. I thought Theodora must have come to visit at least sometimes, over the last ten years, or else she could not have been as welcome as she seemed to be, but she had moved beyond Mrs Niall's circles, into a separate world. Their friendship had become stale, and it was only the present danger that threw them together again. The fact pained both of them.

'Tell me,' Theodora said softly, drawing paper and a tiny pencil from her skirt pocket. 'Who are they, and when did they disappear, and is there anyone I could speak to who might know more, or have seen something?'

Mrs Niall listed the names. A few had exact dates to go with them, but some had no one to notice when they didn't come home, and she could only give a rough guess, a span of several days. Some had exact locations, those who had been on their way from point A to point B and must have disappeared somewhere between the two. Some had gone out, no one knew where, and simply never came back. Theodora jotted each down neatly and then sat watching Mrs Niall, her expression clouded. To judge by her reactions, a few of the names had been familiar to her.

'May I take you for a cup of tea?' she asked after a pause. 'Or something stronger?'

The other woman's back straightened, her thin eyebrows pulling together. 'You feel like you have to buy information off me, do you?'

'You know that wasn't what I meant.'

'Maybe. But you oughter know that's 'ow it sounds.'

'I'm sorry.'

'Yeah.' For the first time since they had sat down, Mrs Niall's gaze swept around to me and Sherlock. A veiled intelligence burned in her eyes. 'Which of you was it?'

I raised a hand, not sure whether to be satisfied with the quality of my disguise or offended at the implied insult.

She nodded. 'An' the other one?'

'My brother, ma'am,' I replied.

She smirked at the honorific. 'Ye're plannin' on doin' summat about this?'

'They came after me and took a child, instead. They may have more children, and they certainly have other women, to be used and owned like objects. I'll do whatever it takes.'

'Well, that's summat.'

'And the police do know,' I continued, 'and they are doing something. I don't know how successful they'll be, but they're not ignoring it. Would you speak to them as well, if we told them where to find you?'

Her eyebrows twitched in something between amusement and affront. 'Runnin' a laundry's perfectly legal, you know. Why wouldn't I talk to 'em?'

I took her meaning.

'Yeah, you send 'em. I'll talk. 'Spect a few more will, as well. Don't much like rozzers pokin' around, but it's for our own.'

She leaned her chair back on two legs, making the wood creak dangerously, and sucked on her pipe. Her attention returned to Theodora. 'Talk to Madge, too. You remember Madge. Seen 'er at all? She's married. Four little 'uns. She was the first one what noticed Liza Jakes gone, since she lived in the next room. May'a seen summat, 'eard summat. Maybe not.'

Theodora thanked Mrs Niall and obtained directions to Madge's room and a warning that the occupant and her children were more likely to be out hawking hot eels than at home. If Madge were not home, there was another woman, Bess, who made her meagre living from the floor of the room she shared with three other women, assembling matchboxes. She might know something, or at the very least, she may have learned something in conversation with Madge.

'An' you watch yerself,' Mrs Niall muttered to our backs as we re-entered the yard and the chaos of the laundry. 'Yer ol' man's not got any sweeter since you left!'

She saw us through the yard and shut the gate behind us, leaving Sherlock frowning and Theodora silent and troubled.

# FOUR

MRS NIALL's building had been run-down, sunlight leaking in through the walls themselves, small animals boldly peering out from beneath the floorboards. Madge's building was a heap, to put it mildly. There were holes in the floors through which an unwary child might fall, and the place was thick with the stench of the midden. Scraps of rags served as doors where hinges had rusted through. Theodora's face was stiff and blank, but not the least bit surprised. I wondered whether she had lived in a place much like this one.

We climbed the stairs, pressed against the wall, where we were less likely to fall through to our deaths.

'They pay to live here,' Theodora whispered. 'Most of them more than they can afford. They go without food, sometimes, for the privilege of living in a hell like this. And there are worse places, if you can believe that. But any roof at all is better than nothing. On the street, you simply freeze in the night.'

I glanced back at Sherlock, knowing he would have heard, as well. His eyes were round as saucers, his mouth hanging open. It was easy to forget, sometimes, growing up so close together, that he was younger. Girls were sheltered, but somehow, those extra ten months of life had prepared me better to understand what we were seeing. I caught his hand and squeezed.

Madge and her children were not at home, so we continued up one more flight to visit Bess and the other matchbox women. They were at home, squatting on the floor as Mrs Niall had predicted, pasting for all they were worth. The boxes would be sold back to the manufacturer once they were assembled to be filled with matches and then sold to people who could afford them. These women could not. They could not even afford a fire. They crouched on thin, straw-filled pallets, huddled beneath layers of blankets and shawls, their fingers sticking out blue and white from their gloves.

They glanced up at us as we entered without knocking, fingers still moving at their task. Somehow, they got the edges straight, even without looking. None of the four seemed to recognise Theodora.

'Eh?' said one.

'Which of you is Bess?' Theodora asked.

They exchanged looks, and one lifted her chin in acknowledgement. She was square, though very thin, her nose red and crusty. 'An' you?'

Theodora hesitated before answering, barely a fraction of a second, but enough to raise the women's suspicions. 'My name is Poppy Cooper,' she said. 'Or it was, and that's how Madge will know me. I hear she's married. What's her husband's name?'

But that moment's hesitation had raised a wall between them and us, stiffened their backs and closed their lips. 'Why'd you wanna know?'

'I used to know her. We worked at Mrs Niall's laundry. I wanted to talk to her.'

One of the other women, one with extremely fair hair and yellowish skin, dug her thumbnail between her teeth and curled her lip. ''Bout what?'

'A woman went missing from here. Liza Jakes? There have been others as well, I'm afraid. I have to find out where they've been taken. And where they've been taken from. There may be more victims, unless we can stop the men doing it as quickly as possible.'

All four shifted in discomfort, and then in fear as they realised what she meant.

'Went missin', yeah,' Bess said, 'but nobody thought she were taken by anybody. More like jus' went out an' found trouble.'

'Liza worked at night,' the fair one added.

'Worked? Do you think she's dead?'

They exchanged another glance. 'Maybe. Maybe not. Just, I know she did work at night, and I don' know if she does anymore.'

'She's a prostitute?'

A jaw jutted defiantly. '*I* didn' say so.'

Theodora did not react to the woman's challenging tone. 'No, but it does make a difference as to what times she would be out and where she would go and who may have seen her. Was she?'

But she had failed to convince them. 'Didn' say so. Just, she worked at night when she lived 'ere.'

Theodora sighed. 'Do you know what time Madge usually comes home?'

'You gonna pester 'er, too?'

'I don't mean to pester anybody. But whoever is kidnapping women—and I believe you know exactly why somebody would—they'll continue doing it. How often do *you* go outside? How often might you go somewhere, however briefly, where there's nobody to see if something happened to you?'

Bess wiped at her nose with the back of her coarse glove. 'Don' doubt you. Just don' think there's anything you can do 'bout it. You better leave.'

'What time does Madge usually come home?'

## GRAHAM

'You better leave before I start shoutin'. Buildin' manager's awful big.'

Theodora's chin went up, but I caught hold of her sleeve and gave it a tug before she could get us into trouble. She wasn't one of them, anymore, and I thought she had forgotten that, for a moment. They really would start shouting, bring a large man to throw us out, because we were interlopers, strangers who did not understand them or their world. Even Theodora had been out of it long enough that she may have forgotten. She was not one of them, anymore.

She exhaled hard as she looked at me and then nodded, relaxing.

'Of course. Thank you for your time. I'll try for Madge later, but if I miss her, please tell her that I came by. Mrs Niall will know how she can contact me.'

Four heads shook slowly in exasperation and disbelief and bent back to their matchboxes. We retreated through the curtained doorway and onto the dim stairs.

'If Madge is hawking,' Theodora said thoughtfully, 'she's not likely to return until after dark. We can find more people to ask questions of before returning here later. We may need to take an omnibus.' She glanced at me. 'I think we'd have to walk some ways from here before a cab would be willing to pick us up, and you probably shouldn't.' Her forehead creased. 'How are you managing the stairs?'

The stairs were difficult, more so because the rotting wood required extreme caution.

'I'm fine,' I said.

She very plainly did not believe me, but she nodded, and we started down again, passing Madge's empty room. I wondered for a moment about the safety of leaving one's possessions in a room with no door, but then I thought perhaps she did not own anything worth stealing. On the other hand, virtually anything could be useful to someone who had

184

nothing. Any spare clothes, any piece of furniture, or anything that could be burned might be tempting to someone who lived like the women upstairs, or like Mrs Niall. But one could not protect one's possessions when every member of the family was required to bring income.

Theodora preceded Sherlock and myself down the stairs, pausing every now and then to test a particularly questionable board before placing her entire weight on it. The stairs switched back and forth, toward the front and then toward the back of the building, with a small landing between each flight.

We had descended two storeys when she stopped abruptly, staring at something around the corner, beneath the landing, tensed, and turned.

'Back up,' she instructed. 'Now, quickly.'

She spread her arms as if to shepherd us back the way we had come, blocking any chance we had of seeing what she had seen.

My first thought was that it had to do with the kidnappers, that there must be a masked man down there. But it was broad daylight, and there were three of us in an enclosed space, not like before, when cover of darkness and an empty street had given them the ability to appear, seize, and disappear again. There were people in this building and out on the street who would see or hear a struggle.

Something else, then. I turned, trusting that she knew what she was about, when I heard a thud and the breath whooshed out of her.

'My girl,' a voice growled. 'You popped out some right ugly spawn, didn't ye?'

In the next instant, she was gone, dragged through the nearest curtained door into the empty room beyond by a massive, blurred shape. A few vicious words trailed after them, both voices contributing.

Sherlock appeared beside me, his open pocket knife in his hand, his face taut and alert. He hesitated a moment, waiting for his brain to supply a course of action. We both decided in unison that, whatever had happened, it needed witnesses. He had his knife, and I had my heavy stick, and there was only one attacker we could discern. Three of us, two armed, against one.

As one, we burst through the curtain, the flimsy cloth tearing away from the tacks that secured it to the wall above. It fell and draped over my shoulder.

The man was large, and appeared older than I think he really was. His hair was receding from a pockmarked forehead, and it may at one time have been brown, but it had gone to an unhealthy, yellowish grey. His skin was bad, nose and cheeks marked with burst capillaries, his eyes red and watery, but incredibly sharp, in spite of the fact that he was obviously extremely drunk. His hands were enormous, and one gripped a large, sturdy knife with a blade that was half-serrated, half smooth, something that looked as though it could hew through wood.

His other hand was tangled in Theodora's hair. She gripped his wrist tightly, unable to lash out as long as he kept her off balance.

'Meet my father,' she said sourly.

He grinned, showing broken, blackened teeth. 'Yeah, meet yer granddad.'

There was no point in correcting him. But at that precise moment, there was also no point in charging him. His knife was close enough to Theodora's throat that any sudden move, any surprise, might kill her. He was drunk, but still savvy enough to have made sure of that.

'Shame they won't take yer, too,' he slurred. 'It's ladies only. If I'd known ye was comin', I coulda found somethin' for ye, but all I got's the river.'

His watery eyes focussed on our faces, searching for a reaction. He was drunk and angry, and he wanted us to be afraid of him.

That meant this was not a professional effort. 'They' could only be the kidnappers. He had to be involved, somehow, but not on the same level as the masked men in the cart. Well, that made sense. A drunk was unreliable. He would make irrational decisions, like attacking a woman in broad daylight. His emotions had gotten the better of him, and he had made a mistake. But he also knew something about them. If he intended to give Theodora over to them, he must have had a contact, one of them he knew by sight.

'Saw yer in the street,' he was saying, dragging Theodora's hair toward his mouth, his face turned down so she received the full impact of his breath. 'Couldn' believe me eyes, at first. Thought, that can't be me own Poppy, that fly bitch wi' such powerful ugly pups. Heard talk ye got married after ye run off. Musta got on with it quick, didn' ye?'

Sherlock bared his teeth in an expression of absolute contempt. 'So quick as to be retroactive, in fact,' he cut in. 'Since I was five when she got married.'

Cooper did not know what 'retroactive' meant, and he was too drunk to spot sarcasm. He reached the wrong conclusion. His arms tightened, muscles and veins bulging in his enormous fists.

'Slut,' he hissed into Theodora's face. 'Knew the cathouse was the right place for ye. Well, ye got out, then, but ye'll learn yer place, this time.'

'You are stupid, aren't you?' Sherlock shot back. 'We're not her children. Are you so blind you didn't notice? Or can you not tell when a woman is with child?'

He was trying to make Cooper angry, angrier than he already was. That did not seem like the right course of action, to me. Yes, an angry man might lose focus and make a mistake, but Cooper was already homicidal, and as long as he had that knife poised to end Theodora's life, we did not want him to make any mistakes.

But then I saw the man's eyes narrow, and the knife moved... down. Of course. He was already as angry at Theodora as he was going to get. He wanted to hurt her. He wanted a prolonged torture for her, a lifetime

**187**

of use and abuse. He had plans for her. But he had already decided to kill me and Sherlock. We were not part of his plan. If he lashed out, he would lash out at us, and the distance he had to cross to reach us would give us a moment to strike back.

The goal was to get him to cross that distance.

Making him angry was not the fastest way to do that.

'Don't let him out the door,' I said under my breath, but still quite loudly enough for Cooper to hear. 'I'm going to fetch the police.'

His entire body stiffened, and he shoved Theodora away, behind him. She hit the wall, but clearly not as hard as he had intended her to. She was rising again, even as he lunged toward us.

'Call 'em, then!' he roared, his huge hands shooting toward my throat. 'Fields an' me escaped last time, an' we would again! But ye won't, I promise ye.'

I stumbled away and escaped his grasp only by falling sideways. Sherlock stabbed a foot into the man's path, tangled with his legs, and the three of us went down in a pile. I reached for Cooper's knife, but only succeeded in knocking it across the floor, out of anybody's reach, which was good enough.

Then Cooper was moving again, his mountainous bulk heaving.

There was a quiet click, and he stopped. I scrambled out from under him, rescuing my stick, and saw Theodora with her revolver pushed deep into the lumpy flesh of his back, just behind his heart.

'That'll be quite enough,' she gasped. Her face was flushed, eyes wide and very bright. 'Do bring the police, one of you. I think they'll be interested in what he has to say!'

Sherlock and I exchanged a look and silently decided that he would be quicker than I. He regained his feet and dashed down the stairs.

'Don't try to get up,' she said. The round maw of her pistol dug deeper into his back, and I flinched, but her finger lay alongside the trigger, not poised to shoot. 'I'm not the girl you used to push around, *Dad*. This Poppy'll kill you.'

I could see the side of his face, his cheek pressed into the floor, and it seemed to be screwed up in contemplation. He was trying to decide whether she'd actually do it, and I was sure my expression mirrored his. Would she? She owned a gun, but I was sure that most people who owned guns had never actually killed someone before and probably couldn't if it came down to it. And he was her father. She had told us very little about him when she told her story, only giving a general sense of drunkenness and abuse. What he had done to her then and meant to do to her again was unforgiveable. He deserved to die for it, in my opinion. But to wish death on someone was not the same as being the one to inflict it.

I looked up into her face and saw the same confusion. She didn't know whether she'd do it, either.

'Don't kill him,' I whispered.

Her gaze slid toward me.

'Shoot him where it'll hurt, if you have to, but don't kill him. Snail needs what he knows.' He'd die in prison, anyway. Or be hanged. Someone like that must have committed murder at some point.

She nodded.

Perhaps he'd had the same thought. Perhaps he decided he would rather be shot in the back by his own daughter than die of prison fever or at the hands of criminals who had more honour than he did. Perhaps he didn't believe she had the courage to shoot at all and thought he could get away free.

His arm swung back, partially dislodging Theodora as he lurched to his knees and then to his feet. She wavered for a moment, balance precarious, but her aim stayed true.

She could have shot him. She did not.

He staggered and twisted to look back at her, uncertainty and then triumph painting his features. He smirked. 'Ye gonna do it or not?'

Her finger slipped beneath the semicircular guard, resting on the trigger, but did not tighten.

'Yeah,' he said. 'Course not. Can't tell the p'lice ye shot me in the back. Not self-defence that way, is it?' He moved toward the door.

'Stop,' she said.

He did not.

She shot him in the arm, close to his left elbow. He jumped, howling, and grabbed at his wound. Blood gushed between his thick fingers and pattered on the bare floorboards. His eyes rolled toward her wildly and saw something there that convinced him she would shoot again. But that did not inspire him to sit still. He staggered back through the door, one bloody hand in front of him as though to ward off a bullet, and disappeared onto the landing. His heavy footsteps started down the stairs, uneven with alcohol.

Then there was a hoarse shout and a crash that seemed to go on forever. Then silence.

# FIVE

IT MAY NOT have been fair, but Theodora's obviously educated manner and the address she gave saved us from the suspicions of the officer Sherlock brought. She said that she had been visiting a friend fallen on the hardest of times when she was attacked, failing to mention her relationship to the attacker. She said that the gun was his, and that it had discharged accidentally when she fought it away from him. Because it had killed a man, she was required to surrender it. She related the threat he had made and mentioned that Detective Sergeant Robbins should be informed.

By the time we had been taken to the closest station and given tea, questioned once more, and transported back to the Greys' house, it was too late to hope that we might return and learn anything from Madge.

Edwin burst from the doorway as we alighted, his face grey with worry, and scooped Theodora into his arms without the slightest regard for the police driver clearing his throat uncomfortably behind her. Sherlock watched blankly, as though bewildered by the display.

I touched his arm and gestured toward the open door. 'Come on.'

## GRAHAM

He complied, as meekly as I'd ever seen him do anything. Concern rose up instantly, and I moved him to the parlour, where the fire was warm enough to stop my shaking. He dropped into a chair and spread himself out, long limbs sprawling, head sunk on his chest. I dragged the other chair near and sat beside him.

'You'll stay tonight, won't you?' I asked. 'Mycroft won't be worried. You know he doesn't worry.'

The hand dangling over the arm of his chair twitched. 'I suppose,' he muttered.

'You should,' I pressed. 'I'd like you to. Please.' If he went back to Mycroft, he would be all but alone. Our elder brother slept little and worked late into the night and became testy if interrupted. I did not think Sherlock ought to be alone.

'All right,' he conceded. Then, after a very long time: 'I don't ever want to see a dead body again. The way his back was all...'

'I know. I don't, either.'

'The bastard deserved no better.'

'No. He didn't.'

'He deserved a lot worse.'

'Yes.'

'But it ought to have been done right. A trial.' He shoved his hair out of his face, exposing a sharp, grey eye. 'He said he escaped last time with someone called Fields. We have to find out who Fields is.'

I sat up straight and stared at him. 'Sherlock, I'm very glad you're here, but you don't have to keep doing this. This is my problem. And Cooper died accidentally, but last time there was an actual fight, a shootout, and lots of people died. It's completely possible this will get worse before it gets better.'

The front door clicked closed, and I heard the Greys' footsteps in the hall, but Sherlock's reply drew my attention back to him.

'Of course it's my problem, too. It's everyone's. And if it must get worse before it gets better, all the more reason to stop it as quickly and efficiently as possible. And anyway, you know I can't leave a thing unfinished.'

It was true. He had gone for four days without sleep once, determined to solve a particular mathematical problem as he taught himself calculus.

'Thank you.'

He shrugged. I still was not forgiven, then.

Theodora trudged into the room and sank onto the settee, her shoulders hunched. Edwin followed and sat beside her.

'Are you all right?' I asked for the hundredth time since that morning. Once again, she only smiled wanly and nodded.

I didn't think I saw any sadness in her. Her father had betrayed her, and there had never been any particular tenderness between them, as far as I could tell. There shouldn't have been guilt. She'd had the opportunity to kill him, but she hadn't done it. Perhaps it was just the strain.

Or perhaps... perhaps I would feel the same. I did not deceive myself that I knew anything about what must be going through her mind. That man, Cooper, was no real father. He had broken any bond that blood had forged between them by his cruelty. But he had been the closest Poppy had to one, and she had seen him dead. No, I had no way of knowing what she felt. No one did.

'Fields,' Sherlock said again. 'We'll have to find him. If he was involved last time, he may well be involved again. Cooper knew something, but the police can hardly question him, now.' The words were callous, but he hesitated, and I saw a shiver pass just beneath his skin. Seeing that man dead had done something to him. 'We only know the one other name.'

Theodora tensed, her head swinging back and forth, not quite in denial. 'You don't know what life is like in that place. This Fields may have been involved ten years ago, but the chances he's still alive at all are very slim.'

'No,' I cut in. 'He said that he and Fields escaped before, and they would again. *They would again.* I think Fields is still very much alive, and he is certainly involved now, too.'

She was silent for a moment, then nodded. Her torso jerked back, as though she were physically pulling herself away from an abyss. Withdrawing from her bereavement to focus on a problem she could actually solve.

'Yes. Of course. Father makes... *made* himself known in the Nichol. He likes to make a scene. People remember him.' Her mouth twisted, not really a smile. 'Never fondly, but people certainly do remember him. They'll likely remember anyone they saw him with, as well. We can ask.'

'We'll have to,' I agreed. 'But we'll have to be careful. We've no way of knowing whether this Fields knows about us. I doubt he'll have any idea that we're looking for him, but he may have been in the street today. He may know whom Cooper was following when he died. And he may not realise that the death was an accident.'

'I'm not sure that matters,' Sherlock said with a shrug of one thin shoulder. 'He's bound to be extremely dangerous even when he's not especially angry.'

'Well, yes, that's true. But he's also able to report to whomever is in charge. Whomever sent that albatross head. Someone who is already especially angry with you.' This last, I directed with a nod to the Greys.

Edwin grimaced. 'Speaking of. You've been hunting about on the streets so much, I'm afraid we've neglected that issue. I went out while you were gone, today.'

Theodora twisted to look at him, alarmed. 'Edwin!'

He smiled. 'I was very careful. I only went to see Jones. Editor of the

*Albatross*, you remember.' The smile died on his lips. 'He's dead. His wife said he was pulled out of the Thames about two weeks ago, terribly bloodied up. He never used a pen name, so he'd have been easy to find, and I'm afraid he's probably how they found me. I'm sorry, Teddy.'

'They killed him!'

'That's certainly how it appears. Poor man. I hadn't spoken to him in years. I wish I had.'

Sherlock stirred, his eyebrows drawn into a hard line. 'But then why the games, with you? You wrote it, but he printed it, so why is he dead, but you've only got two rocks and an albatross head?'

Edwin's face froze, and I sensed that he had hoped that question would go unasked. 'Oh. Well... I wouldn't say *only*. They got the rocks and the bird bits, as well. Thought it was a prank. An ugly one, but harmless. Mrs Jones didn't make any connection between that and her husband's death until I mentioned receiving the same deliveries.'

Sherlock's eyes widened incredulously. 'Didn't make any connection? How!'

Edwin shrugged. 'The *Albatross* printed a lot of things that upset a lot of people. I'm sure he must have seen the connection to the paper, just not to the kidnappings. I understood at the time that he'd been receiving angry letters for years. Mice in the morning post, dogs' droppings on the doorstep... I don't blame him for thinking nothing of it. Teddy and I only ever had the one experience with the *Albatross*, or we might not have been so quick to understand it, either.'

'Then they're going to make an attempt on our lives, as well.' Theodora frowned. 'They'll have a harder time of it, here, with a policeman out front, but I doubt that'll stop them. The next time we go out...'

Indignation straightened my spine. 'We have to, though. We have to find Fields! We have to find out where these women are being kept!'

## GRAHAM

'Detective Sergeant Robbins can find Fields,' she said reluctantly. 'We know more now than we did, and we shall tell him. This is larger now than it was before. When he first came, it was only a single child taken and next to no chance of finding her. Then vandalism. This is much more, now. Enough, perhaps, that it'll get a proper Inspector. It'll receive the attention it deserves.'

The gentle crackle of the fire filled the sudden silence, each little pop like a gunshot.

'Nothing's actually changed, though,' Sherlock said slowly. 'It isn't as though you didn't *know* they'd kill us if they caught us. Why is it any different now that we know they mean to kill you one way or another?'

Theodora and Edwin exchanged a look, but neither seemed to have an answer. Edwin slumped in his seat and rubbed at his eye.

'It doesn't make sense,' Sherlock pressed. 'There's no reason to be more afraid now than before. If anything, knowing for certain that they intend deadly revenge should only make it all the more necessary stop them as quickly as possible. To use every resource available. All of us.'

He was stretching logic to make his point. He was right: nothing had actually changed. Someone meant to kill Edwin and Theodora Grey one way or another. The only difference was that they were sure of it, now. But really, that meant that it was no more necessary to stop them now than it had been before. Still necessary. Vital, at this point. But not more than before.

Just a small misrepresentation, an emotional argument to get him what he wanted.

No, I realised. To get me what he thought I wanted.

I swallowed a smile. I didn't think I was forgiven, not yet, but I believed I would be.

Something occurred to me, and I turned to Edwin, feeling a small frown tugging at my mouth. 'How long after the albatross head was Mr

Jones killed?'

He took my point and frowned, as well. 'Mrs Jones said it was a few days later that he didn't come home. Three or four, but she couldn't remember exactly when the head was delivered. It was a few days yet after that he was found dead.'

'Then they probably meant to try something on you already, or very soon. Thank God for the police constable.'

The windows were still boarded—the glazier would be back in a few days' time with cut panes that would fit perfectly into the gaps the chunks of brick had left—but I had seen the man in his plain clothes lingering in front of the house. His shadow sometimes passed before the glass of the front door. He was not conspicuous, but he was noticeable. Anyone seeking to make mischief would know this house was protected.

Something stabbed at my memory, a problem with that feeling of safety, a warning that it was an illusion.

I didn't think the criminals would attack the policeman. Not if they were clever, not if they were cautious. They clearly wanted their revenge, but every action they took brightened the darkness in which they had to work. They had to know that Edwin and Theodora would understand the messages they had sent. They had to know the house was protected by the police, and by logical extension, they had to know that the Greys had told the police about the events of a decade earlier. If they were *really* clever, they'd take their revenge and then vanish for a while, stay silent long enough to force the police to abandon the search. But they were also arrogant, daring to take people who would be missed as well as the invisible women of the streets, daring to send a calling card to their victims' doors. Still, that was a calculated arrogance, taking risks they obviously thought they could handle. To attack the policeman would be a declaration of war against law enforcement, and their organisation had not survived the last war.

That wasn't the problem.

## GRAHAM

Sherlock leaned toward me, his eyes narrowed. 'What is it?'

'There's a policeman out front.'

'Clearly.'

I tsked at his tone. 'I'm *trying* to...'

It came to me, then.

There was a policeman out front because when Robbins had assigned him to watch the house, his object had been to prevent further vandalism, anything else thrown through the windows. He had not been posted to prevent attempted homicide, and there was more than one way into the house. If one really wanted to kill somebody, one probably didn't march in through the front door.

There was a hole in the wall around the back garden.

'The back. There's nobody watching the back.'

Three or four days after the delivery, Jones didn't come home. We needed another policeman. No, if *we* were really clever, we needed somewhere else to stay.

I hauled myself up as Sherlock leapt to his feet, nearly knocking me back over as he strode to the door and wrenched it open. He stopped, and a moment later, I was struck by the stinging reek of smoke.

# SIX

'YOU COULDN'T have realised this sooner!' he shot over his shoulder.

'*You* didn't notice it, either!' I fired back.

He hesitated, as much acknowledgement as I was going to get, then leaned into the hallway. 'I'm going to go see how bad it is. You should probably get out the front and have someone go for the fire brigade.'

'Going to go see!'

'Well,' he said reasonably. 'If it isn't too big, yet, we might be able to put it out, ourselves. I'll let you know...'

A thump interrupted him, at once sharp and round, as of a giant hand striking a leather chair, and in its wake, a growl and a crackle, louder than the fire in the grate. A finger of scarlet light brushed Sherlock's cheek.

'I would say it's already too big.' My throat and eyes began to burn. I stood, picking up my stick, and began to make my way toward him.

Theodora surged to her feet, past me and out into the hall, knocking Sherlock aside. He caught himself against the doorframe and stared after her in amazement as she raced, not out the front door, but toward the study. She stooped immediately inside and straightened with the leather case she had salvaged when leaving, before. Her manuscript.

'Everything else can be replaced,' she said firmly as Edwin appeared at her side. He was pale, but he nodded in agreement, glancing backward at the burgeoning glow with a wince for everything her statement encompassed.

I thought with a pang of the patched china, the money spent on repairing something that could as easily have been discarded. Everything else could be replaced, but the loss would hurt, all the same.

There was another thump. It was an aggressive sound, a hungry sound, eager, brutal. I thought it was the sound of the flames eating through doors, gushing into new rooms through the first small holes that gaped in the wood. Somewhere in the house would be a store of paraffin for the lamps. There would be rags, thin cloth, possibly impregnated with beeswax for the furniture. The curtains. The coke for the kitchen range.

My eyes flicked to the light fixtures. The very walls were full of gas.

Life is so very flammable.

The growl became a rumble, a landslide sound. There was another thump. A crash. The constable's voice rose outside, high and harsh with alarm. There was no way to make out his words, but the message was clear.

Theodora settled her parcel over her shoulder and seized my arm, dragging me up the hall and out the front door. The freezing air slapped the breath out of me. Sherlock followed, shepherded out by Edwin.

From the middle of the street, I turned and looked back. The front of the house still looked as it should, for the moment. Even in the dark, the brick was light and warm. White trim glowed around the windows and door. But smoke was already beginning to rise in a billowy plume from the back, reflecting orange and crimson from below.

The cold dug into me, all the more intense for the knowledge that soon, there would be heat. I shivered.

Edwin had already thought of the cold, and his arms were full of coats snatched from the hall tree as he passed. He draped one over his wife's shoulders and distributed the rest. The wool did little to quell the cold.

The constable was talking, demanding to know if we were all right and what we had seen, but no one had the energy to answer.

'No, there's no one else inside,' Theodora murmured.

The Dunns had gone home. Thank God.

A crack split the night, and sparks fountained into the air.

Neighbours had begun to trickle out into the night, their pale faces shining above woollen wrappers and layers of blankets. The light of the fire was growing bright enough that I could see their expressions. Dazed horror, puffy-eyed alarm. But some turned with vindication on their faces and strode back inside. Those Bohemians had finally gotten what was coming to them. You reap as you sow. Follow the rules, or you'll find trouble.

'My fault, my fault...' The constable's hat had disappeared, and he gripped handfuls of his hair in two gloved fists. It was a different man than I had seen before. He was very young.

'We can stay with Mycroft tonight,' Sherlock said quietly. The fire roared, and I barely heard him.

But no one moved.

We stood and watched the fire engine arrive, but they were not there to save the Greys' house. They laboured through the night to keep the fire from spreading down the street while a couple's life crumbled to embers.

# PART FIVE:
## IN
# FULLEST
# MEASURE

# ONE

MYCROFT was not surprised to see us in the first seconds after we arrived. Then he smelled the smoke in our hair and took in the flecks of ash we brushed from our shoulders. He checked his pocket watch and realised the time. One of his monumental eyebrows twitched, and he stepped aside to allow us entry.

Given his own way, I had no doubt Mycroft would have lived in a single room, probably one without a bed. It would have held a desk, a cabinet for his papers, endless shelves for his books, and a table on which he could take his meals, the one indulgence he allowed himself.

But it wasn't his flat, really. He had the use of it from Father, and nothing Father owned was less than respectable. In this case, respectability included spare rooms.

My brother called for hot baths to be drawn, for beds to be hurriedly made, and suitable clothing to be found. We soaked, we ate something reheated none of us was able to taste, and we fell into the beds prepared as dawn bloomed over London.

The beds were large and soft and warm. Mycroft scoffed at any luxury but the culinary, but I appreciated the comfort, after such a day. I felt cold through, and scorched at the same time. I pulled the coverlet up over my shoulders and neck, where gooseflesh erupted in the absence of my stolen hair.

The bed quaked, though, rocked by Sherlock's endless turning. He rolled onto his side. Rolled onto his back. Threw one long leg over the edge of the bed. Ripped the blankets from me and then threw them back in disgust. He had seen a man die, had nearly been burned alive, and I did not think he would ever be the same again. He had talked about the law, about how Cooper should have been tried and hanged, fairly, legally. I wondered if he still felt the same. I certainly did not. These people had killed. They had ruined the lives of untold numbers of women. They had stripped my friends of the comfort they built from the ruins of a ten-year-old tragedy. They deserved to burn, and if the law wouldn't see to that...

I wanted to decide that I would see to it, instead, but it was impossible to know for sure if I could before the actual moment arrived.

Sherlock buried his face in his down pillow with a muffled snarl.

I inched toward him and touched his shoulder, and when he did not jerk away from me, I gripped his hand and lay with my back pressed against his, as I had when we shared a nursery not so long ago. I measured my breaths and counted, in, out, in, out, until his fell into time with mine.

When next I was aware of anything, it was late afternoon. Sherlock had rolled out of the bed and was belting on a dressing gown that fitted him like a tent. He paused and glanced up, then seized a nearly-identical garment from the trunk at the foot of the bed and tossed it at me. Well, that made two. How many of those could Mycroft possibly own?

'Do you think the Greys are up?' I asked.

He straightened and sniffed. 'I smell... breakfast.'

Both of us glanced toward the window, where a sliver of sunset peeped through the crack between the curtains.

He shrugged. 'If they're not, it seems he expects them to be, soon.'

'Or he felt like having breakfast at suppertime.'

'Also a distinct possibility.' He smirked.

It felt good to share a joke. He would forgive me in his own time, I was sure, but he would forgive me.

I belted on my own dressing gown and stuffed my feet into thick stockings to ward off the faint chill seeping up through the deep woollen carpets. The clothes I had worn on arrival had vanished, possibly to be cleaned of their smoke-stench, but more probably to be destroyed. That was one more difficulty to consider, but later, when my stomach was not protesting quite so loudly.

We descended to the breakfast room, which was empty, then migrated to the dining room, where there were eggs, sausages, toast, and coffee on the sideboard. A heap of empty plates at the end of the table indicated that Mycroft had partaken already. The man himself hovered by the wall farthest from the door, fussing over something he had pinned directly to the scarlet wallpaper. His bulk concealed most of the object, but I caught sight of the broad edge of a very large sheet of paper.

I heaped eggs onto a plate and smeared jam onto a piece of toast and settled in to eat while we waited. If the object was relevant, it wouldn't be long before he explained it with appropriate detail. Then again, it might also pertain to his work, and so shouldn't be allowed to postpone breakfast.

The eggs on my plate vanished in moments. I got myself more and ate them more slowly, then downed a couple of cups of coffee to get my brain in order.

The Greys appeared halfway through my second cup, raising the confirmed total number of dressing gowns in my brother's house to four. I shot him a curious glance. A general misanthrope and hermit-in-training, he couldn't possibly have *company* often enough and in sufficient numbers to warrant keeping bedroom clothing handy. Perhaps he simply liked them. One for each day of the week, or something like that. Stranger foibles lurked in the depths of our family than a fondness for brocade.

Theodora seated herself across from me, and Edwin sat opposite Sherlock. Both of them looked as though they had barely slept. They sagged, grey around the edges, with purple smudges beneath their eyes. The hands holding their utensils were limp, grips weak.

'Are you...'

She looked up at me bleakly, and I swallowed the rest of my question with a mouthful of coffee. She was not all right. Neither of them were.

A stack of papers struck the top of the table with a bang, making all of us jump. Mycroft loomed by the wall, having moved away from the object he had been studying. It was an ordinance map of London, not just of the City, but of all the Boroughs, spangled with the shining heads of brass and nickel tacks. I rose up a little in my seat and craned my neck to get a better look at the stack of papers. They bore an official heading, which I could not make out from where I sat, and were covered in small, neat handwriting.

'I have obtained copies of the police reports regarding the events of ten years ago,' he announced.

I very much doubted that those were copies.

'As well as records of other disappearances which were not regarded as connected at the time, but which I suspect were, in truth.'

His suspicions were usually as good as fact.

'Where the exact location of the disappearance was not known, I have approximated, based on what the police were able to learn of the victims' habits, regularly-travelled paths, and so forth.'

He waved a thick hand at the map behind him.

'Those of ten years ago are represented by the brass tacks. Do you see?'

'They're in clusters,' I said.

'Concentrated around the rookeries,' Sherlock added. 'We already knew that. They focussed on the poor, first, and began to attract attention when they tried to expand their reach. This isn't news.'

Mycroft ignored the criticism.

'There is a pattern,' he said. 'In location, yes, but also in time.' He pointed to a single pin in the centre of a single cluster. 'This, as far as I can tell, was the first, or at least the first reported.' He pointed to another pin. 'The second.' His finger moved slowly around the map. 'The third. The fourth. The fifth. The sixth.'

Once or twice, a pin was right beside the one that had come before it, but as I watched his hand move, I saw the pattern he had seen. He was moving outward from a central point that had been invisible among the scattered clusters. As the numbers grew, clusters formed in a widening circle, scattering and tapering away as they moved further from the City.

'What's in the centre?' I asked.

His finger moved to the riverside, in an empty space between clusters. 'The warehouse.'

'Because they secured their facilities first, and used that as a base, starting close to home, and expanding as the operation was able to expand.'

He nodded.

'And the silver pins?'

'The current case. As I expected, a similar pattern emerged.'

Theodora stirred. 'You've found their base?'

Mycroft nodded, but then his massive brows drew together. He flapped a hand at the map. 'I've found a middle point of a similar pattern. As to the usefulness of that...'

## GRAHAM

'Where?'

His finger thumped into the middle of Westminster. 'I have accounted for flows of traffic, the ease with which a cart could pass, to account for some unusual features of the pattern. St James's, I believe.'

Everyone at the table exchanged a startled glance. The gentlemen's clubs and foreign cafés, rows of glittering white townhouses and sprawling mansions seemed a dangerous place in which to root an empire of vice. The Haymarket had its ancient reputation, of course. And if the operation had been very lucrative, a criminal might choose to reside in such an area. But to work from such a place! The movement in and out...

No, they used the cart, and the cart had been covered. A woman bound and gagged in the back would never be noticed. Like any other delivery, the cart would go to the back, invisible from the street, and the human cargo could be unloaded in safety.

I closed my eyes and pictured it. A warehouse was a large, open space inside. Such a space would echo, if a woman chose to scream, and some would scream, no matter how they were threatened into silence. Most abutted a street, perhaps with a strip of pavement between. Workers walked past. There was always a chance that one would wander inside, looking for employment. A warehouse, in retrospect, was a dangerous choice. A house, a nice one, might be separated from the street by a wall with a fence and even a small expanse of lawn. The inside would be divided by walls, papered and carpeted, which would deaden noise. And no one simply walks up to the house of a stranger. If one had the money, a house was more secure.

'Why are there clusters, though?' I asked, opening my eyes. 'They're not all concentrated in the rookeries. What are the other ones?'

'The Hellhounds,' Sherlock replied before Mycroft had even had a chance to open his mouth. 'And others like them. The gangs who have been recruited to do the collecting each have their own territories, I believe.' He stood and stalked up to the map, eyes narrowed, then pointed at one of the clusters in silver, very near to our parents' London house. 'Here they are. They've hunted in their own domain.'

I followed the path of the street I had taken on the night of the storm to where I believed the Wrong Boys' domain must be, adjacent to the Hellhounds. There was no cluster, there.

'It's still a large area to search,' Edwin interjected. His voice was tired and gravelly. 'And I am afraid the police will be reluctant. They do not like to disturb the affluent any more than necessary.'

'We have the Wrong Boys, though,' I said. 'They've seen the cart. One of them, I mean. They must use more than one. They couldn't loiter near the residences, but they could in the busier areas. Wait to see something and follow it.'

He frowned and rubbed at his bad eye. 'I don't like the idea of sending children. Or even adolescents,' he added with a glance toward me and Sherlock, as though either of us could feel slighted, at the moment.

'Adolescents who can go anywhere unseen,' I reminded him.

Mycroft harrumphed. 'Precisely. Unless you think these villains could fail to recognise a policeman, even in plain clothes.'

He made his point. Edwin subsided, though he still frowned.

A coffee cup clinked against a saucer. Wings flapped against the darkening window.

At that time of year, the darkness came early, and it was not all that late.

'There's still time to find the Wrong Boys today,' I said. Or at least Peach, though I could hardly tell him what we had discovered. But I believed that Magpie must have heard of the fire, by now, and would be waiting where he knew we could find him. 'They could be in St James's in the morning.'

'Failing that,' Theodora added drily, 'we now have a map of all the places one is most likely to be kidnapped. In case we must, as you suggested, engineer one.'

# TWO

THEODORA and Edwin accompanied me, though I knew they were more interested in viewing the remains of their home than anything else. They could be forgiven their priorities; some things will always be distractions, like a shattered home, or a body at a wake.

I assured them I would be fine on my own, and they were inclined to agree. The arsonists either thought we had been killed in the blaze or knew we had escaped and gone elsewhere. The carcass of the house would no longer be watched. Peach concerned me—Peach always concerned me—but I expected Magpie or one of the other boys to be there, and if for some reason I felt too unsafe, I could always refuse to go inside.

I went with them as far as the shell of their house. The stink was overpowering. I had always liked the smell of wood smoke, but wood and polish, cloth and paint, dye and hot metal created a repellent miasma. The air above and around the blackened remains was still thick and grey, and the coals still put off so much heat that the constable, who had remained hovering dutifully nearby, was red in the face beneath his cloak and muffler and hat.

Edwin sighed hollowly, but his hand found Theodora's and

squeezed. 'Father will help,' I heard him whisper. 'And there was the insurance, don't forget.'

'I don't want his help,' she hissed in reply, and I resolved to avoid the topic of Edwin's father.

I arranged to meet them back at Mycroft's within a couple of hours, having obtained from him enough money for cabs to spare my ankle.

The ride to the intersection I recalled being closest to Peach's practice was short, much shorter than the walk had been, and I paid the driver to wait. If Magpie was not there, I did not intend to wait for him in Peach's company. If he was there, I preferred to return with him to my brother's home rather than discuss our business in front of someone I was certain was involved in it.

I slipped into the maze of passages where the cab could not go. Instantly, the darkness closed around me, and I had to stop to give my eyes time to adjust. A lantern would have been useful, but the evening had turned overcast, and a certain amount of light reflected downward from the low clouds, making manoeuvring difficult but possible.

Mycroft had procured a complete suit of my own clothing, somehow, which I knew he could not have done with Father's knowledge. It hung very loose on my altered frame, and I had become unaccustomed to the swish of skirts. The sound seemed very loud in the darkness. I'd have preferred to remain a boy until the ordeal was over, of course, but it was what was available, and I could not go looking for Wrong Boys naked. When there was a spare moment, I would ask Sherlock for the use of another of his suits.

And for the first time in what seemed ages, I had boots that fit my feet, laced tightly to support my ankle. Despite the sound of my skirts, I moved more quietly in shoes that fit.

I was quiet enough to hear the footsteps behind me.

That should not have worried me, in itself. There were homes in these back ways. People lived there. It still was not late, and a few places of business were still accepting custom. But these footsteps kept pace with mine, neither falling behind nor hurrying past. With effort, I kept myself from turning round.

I turned a corner, and they followed. I turned again, and they followed. I turned a third time, and the peeling blue door appeared in front of me. Rather than knock, I twisted frantically at the knob, found the door unlocked, and ducked inside. A simple, rusty bolt presented itself at eye level, and I shoved it into the doorframe. But nobody rattled the knob. I could no longer hear the footsteps. Perhaps they had gone past.

A throat cleared itself behind me.

'You look out of breath,' said the unpleasant, sibilant voice.

I turned and found Peach standing there with his arms crossed, watching me impassively. He was right. I was gasping, more from nerves than from exertion. My lungs burned from the cold outside.

'I thought I was being followed.'

'A false alarm, then? Ah, well. I won't ask you to come in, since you already have, but perhaps you would like a cup of tea.'

It wasn't really a question, and I was not sure how to answer.

He extended one of his pincer-like hands toward where I remembered the parlour to be.

'I need Magpie. Is he here?'

He did not lower his hand, and raised an eyebrow in addition. 'No. He had heard about the fire, but could find no one to tell him whether you had burned alive, so he waited here today and will return tomorrow.'

Guilt stabbed through my gut, and I found myself biting my lip, not a gesture I could recall ever having used before.

Tomorrow. I had not planned on remaining with Peach for even a second longer than was absolutely necessary, but I also could not convince myself that there was not a man waiting just outside the door for me to emerge. I leaned heavily on my stick.

If someone had been following me, how long were they likely to wait? I had said I would return to Mycroft's house within two hours. I did not, they would come looking for me. Sherlock had been to Peach's place before, and his excellent memory would lead him back accurately. It might take them half an hour to arrive, so I might have to wait two and a half hours if they took me at my word and departed exactly at the two-hour mark.

In the meantime, Peach had offered me tea. What did he intend to put in it? Did he know that someone was outside? Might he be in league with them? He could not possibly have known that I meant to come looking for Magpie now, indeed could not have known that I would come at all, since he seemed to have only just discovered that any of us survived. So he could not have planned to box me in like this. Was it simple opportunity?

Or was I out of my mind, and there was no one outside at all?

As if in answer, there was a terrific crash, and the door shuddered on its hinges.

'Peach!' a voice roared through the wood. 'Know yer in there, Stephen Peach! Saw the bitch go in there, too!'

Both of us froze. His eyes slid past me and fixed on the door. He licked his discoloured lips.

Another tremendous blow rattled the door, and he suddenly seized my arm with strength I had not expected and dragged me through the parlour, all its lamps extinguished, and to the room that served as his surgery. With a single, practiced motion, he shoved the examination table out of the way and drove his heel into the end of one of the floorboards, causing it to flip up and reveal a handle. He wrenched open a small trapdoor, opening up a space barely the size of a travel trunk, neatly lined with bottles, paper-wrapped parcels, and small boxes. Into the space I tumbled, his hand on my back crushing me against its floor. The trapdoor came down, and I heard the table dragged back into place.

I knew the smells. I was among his medical supplies, hidden to prevent theft. It was terrifyingly close, and my knees digging into my chest made breathing difficult, but applying a tiny bit of upward pressure convinced me that the door could be opened from the inside. I could tolerate the confinement, knowing that I was not trapped.

I heard the door shatter. Heavy footfalls. The voice called again for Peach, and I heard him answer from very nearby.

'Mr Fields, have you been brawling, again? Come through, and I'll have a look. And you've lost an eye? Very unf-...'

He was interrupted by a meaty thud and the sound of something sharp-edged hitting the floor, close enough that I could hear the breath whoosh from his lungs. Dust pattered down onto the back of my neck.

'I 'ear you been awful friendly wi' a particular bunch o' guttersnipes. I 'ear also they been askin' questions to which my employer don' want the answers generally known, see?'

Shoeleather scraped against the floor. 'I treat all manner of people, Mr Fields. I do become fond of some of them. However...'

Another thud cut him off. He choked.

'However, their business is not mine. If you want to know what they know, I'm afraid I am not in a position to help you. I can treat you, though. To judge by the smell of you, *something* is infected...'

'Also 'eard you been askin' questions of yer own.'

'Some of my usual patients have not been to see me, of late. I may have expressed concern...'

'Awful curious concern, Peach.'

'I've a right to care for my patients. Anyway, whatever I may have asked, there were no answers to be had. I can prove nothing. And how would I go to the police, Fields? Tell them *exactly* how I know those women?'

There was a pause, a moment of almost total silence, during which I had no idea what nonverbal communication might be taking place.

'Where's the girl?'

My breathing hitched, and it was all I could do not to choke on my own saliva.

'The one with the stick. She owes me an eye. I want 'er, and yer word you'll ask nothing more, an' that'll end it.'

'A girl came to me some time ago with a bad sprain, possibly a minor fracture. I gave her a stick, and she left with the Wrong Boys. I have not seen her since. I believe she became separated from them, at some point...'

The floorboards creaked as Fields shifted his weight. 'I watched 'er walk this way. Saw 'er stick.'

'Possibly, but she did not come inside. If they brought her here, she may live in the area.'

'All right. Fine.'

There was a terrible noise I could not begin to describe, one I did not know a human body could make, and I understood that Peach was no longer able to reply. I squeezed my eyes shut and counted my breaths as the table above me was overturned with a crash. Glass shattered. Doors slammed open and shut again.

Methodically, Fields worked his way through each of the rooms, the sound of his footsteps approaching and receding, the sounds of his anger growing more and more violent until suddenly they stopped, and there was silence.

Still, I did not move until something wet began to seep through the wool at my back. I pushed through the trapdoor, lightheaded with the sudden rush of air into my lungs, scattering dust and fragments of the bottles I had crushed beneath me.

The wet stuff was, as I had already known, the pool of blood spreading away from Doctor Stephen Peach.

But somehow, he was not yet dead. He sat propped against the wall, his spidery fingers wrapped tightly around his spindly throat, awash in crimson. Red froth oozed over his palm, and with his next breath, a bubble forced its way between his fingers and popped.

'If I could get you to the cab,' I began, the automatic words slicing their way through my shock.

He could not shake his head, but I saw the negative in his eyes.

'Then, is there anything I...'

His lips twitched, but only foam emerged.

'I misjudged you,' I said, needing him to know. 'I'm sorry. I'm so sorry. Thank you.'

But I could not tell whether he understood. In another breath, his twitching eyes went still and his hand fell away, and with a clear view of his carotid arteries, I saw the last beat of his heart.

# THREE

I STAYED AS STILL as the corpse until the sound of footsteps in the other room jarred me into action. I blinked and found myself somehow on my feet, braced against the overturned table, my stick in my hand and raised to strike.

The footsteps were heavy, but also tentative. They did not crash like Fields's had. They staggered. I knew who it was even before I heard the voice.

'Stephen?'

I relaxed, and then tensed again. It would be bad when she came into the surgery. It would be very bad.

'Boys?'

I couldn't let her see him like this. I dropped my stick to my side and hobbled out to meet her, my other arm extended in a gesture of peace.

Sylvia had returned to the front hall, her circular face white as a moon, her huge hands grasping at her skirts and shaking hard. She whirled to meet me with an expression of hope that died as soon as recognition dawned.

'Come sit,' I told her, as gently as I was able. Then I realised there

## GRAHAM

was blood on the hand I held out to her.

She stared hard into my eyes, then back behind me, the way I had come, and shouldered me out of the way. I stumbled against the wall, and by the time I righted myself, it was too late to stop her. A ghastly, forlorn wail rose in the surgery, wordless, empty. I still did not know what they had been to one another. It did not matter.

I followed her. She sat on the floor, near the body, but not daring to touch. The blood had gone sticky, and I could hear it pulling at her knees. Her breathing sounded painful. I touched her shoulder, and she shoved me away, sending me reeling back through the open door. She was incredibly strong. I could not pull her away, and I was not sure I should try. Perhaps that would be crueller than leaving her alone.

'I'm going to find police,' I told her, in case she was listening or cared. 'I'll be back.'

She did not respond. Her large body rocked back and forth, one hand extended, approaching and retreating but never quite touching his cheek.

Her cries carried strongly, even outside. Even if Fields had lingered, he would be gone, now, fled before the noise attracted too much attention. I was not molested as I made my way back to the street and was suddenly reminded of the cab.

The driver looked at me in irritation and then in shock as he took in the state of me.

'Find a policeman and bring him back here, please. The first one you see. There has been a murder.' I shoved a handful of coins in his direction. 'That should be enough for your trouble. If it is not, you may leave your address, and I will forward the balance.'

He stared at me as though I was speaking Latin.

'Please,' I said again, and he rolled away.

There. That saved me some time. I did not know Sylvia at all and could not begin to guess whether she might do something foolish, so the less time she had to be alone, the better. And, I remembered, someone was sure to come looking for me soon. I was not sure how much time had passed, but my original estimate had been two and a half hours, and a large chunk of that must have been eaten up, already.

As I turned to hobble back the way I had come, something caught my eye. A cart. *The* cart. A lamp illuminated the side of the driver's face, and I thought I saw the black circle of an eyepatch. I ducked back behind the corner and pressed myself into the bricks.

There had been another figure beside him, much smaller, in a hood rather than a hat.

It would be a stretch to assume that a smaller person was a woman or a child. But I knew already that Fields was carrying a knife, one that had killed Peach, and he might well have it to that person's ribs.

I winced. There was nothing I could do about it but tell a policeman which way I had seen the cart go. I could not catch up with it, and it would be foolish to try. If the second person had been an accomplice, I would not be able to identify them. If a victim, there was nothing I could do to rescue her. Not yet.

When I got back, Sylvia had cleaned the body. There was no point in fussing at her; I did not think the great gouts of blood could provide any particular information to the police, and anyway, I could identify the culprit by sight.

She had also made tea. She poured a cup for each of us, though hers was mostly gin, and I sat beside her in the darkened parlour and listened to the slow shifting of overturned furniture.

'He had been asking after the missing girls.'

'Aye.' Her voice grated.

'I didn't know that.'

'Din' aks, did ye?'

## GRAHAM

'No. I didn't.'

Muted hostility radiated from her. She was tolerating my presence, but she did not like me. She must have known what I thought of her Stephen. Both of them did. I had hardly been discreet about my suspicions.

Suspicions levelled against the man who died rather than give me up.

I drank her tea and did not try to speak again, not wishing to try her charity too far.

My brothers, the Greys, and the police arrived all at once and poured inside. Sherlock followed the trail of wreckage back to the cooling corpse, and there was nothing I could do to stop him. He stared fixedly, his eyes wide and pupils small, and I could not tell what was going on behind them.

All I could do was relate to the two constables what had happened, desperately wishing for a change of clothes. The blood soaking my back had gone gummy, at first, but it was drying, now, and began to itch terribly.

One of the constables left to fetch more help, and the other dismissed us all to go home.

'Live 'ere,' Sylvia growled. 'Not leavin'.'

The man looked her over, decided she could probably snap him like a twig, and said no more about it.

'I'd like to stay, as well,' I told him, the comment halfway directed toward my brothers. 'Doctor Peach said that Magpie would return in the morning, and I'd like to be here when he gets here.'

He blinked at me. Every time I had spoken to him, he had shown signs of distraction, glancing back and forth between my plain grey dress and my shorn hair. He had not said anything, but having seen my own reflection, I knew I looked very much like a boy in a dress, and he was probably trying to decide whether I needed to be arrested. The other constable had taken me in stride without a twitch, and I wished that he had been the one to stay, instead.

'I'd like to stay, as well,' I repeated. 'Just until morning. There's someone I need to see, and he'll be coming here.'

Mycroft cleared his throat. 'I am sure the officer would be happy to send Master Magpie along to my address, when he appears. I will leave sufficient for cab fare.'

I could tell by looking that *happy* was not the appropriate word, but the young man had been unable to stand up to Sylvia, and Mycroft's presence was no less commanding.

'I can do that,' the constable conceded. 'Sir.'

That would have to be good enough. The way Mycroft had spoken gave me the impression that he preferred I did not stay, and Mycroft usually got his way. And of course, for a second night, I wanted nothing quite so badly as to be clean. The smoke had seared my throat and eyes and left me stinking. I had thought that a terrible way to end a day, but that was before I knew what it was like to have a dead man's blood on me.

'That will work,' I agreed.

In the cab, Sherlock's hand found mine and squeezed, but the light of a streetlamp flickering over his face showed me that he was very far away. His eyes were hooded, half-closed as though he was falling asleep, but his arched nostrils flared with each of his short, quick breaths. He was so far away, I feared he would never make it back.

—

I rose before six, but Sherlock had beaten me and was already downstairs. Taking advantage of his absence from the room, I donned a suit of his clothes without asking. Dressing as myself yesterday had felt strange, strange and dangerous. I had always intended Morgan Grey to

**225**

be a temporary mask, and I held to that intention, but I was not ready to cast him off just yet.

But of course, I reflected, creeping down the stairs in trousers and waistcoat, I would have to be sure not to come to the door when the constable arrived. Perhaps someone had relieved him by then, but I did not want to take the chance of being seen in both skirts and trousers by the same person. After everything else, being arrested for degeneracy did not appeal.

Our elder brother, I often suspected, did not sleep at all. He purchased excellent coffee and consumed it in enormous quantities, but he never betrayed any sign that it truly energised him. Instead, he seemed to store up that energy for gradual release, like a clock that, once wound, ticks away at its measured pace all day without speeding up or slowing down. Sherlock had been up before me, but I knew very well that Mycroft had been awake and working already when he came down.

There was no breakfast yet, but there was, in fact, coffee. It had been there for some time. I poured myself a tepid cup and tossed it back without milk or sugar. It was so bitter I had to swallow a reflexive gag. Mycroft must have made it, himself. I wondered how his household staff tolerated his eccentricities.

Mycroft did not look up from the papers he had scattered all over the breakfast table. There would not actually be a place for eating breakfast, once it appeared. So I let him alone.

Sherlock was in the study-cum-library. He had built himself a small fire, but it had not yet gotten going, and the room was miserably cold. Still, he stood by the window, as far from the fireplace as one could get, peering through a small gap between the curtains.

'Is there a plan for today?' he asked. 'We should, at some point, inform the police of what Mycroft has discovered.'

I nodded. 'And of the murder. I can describe the man who did it, and Robbins will need to know that.'

I crossed the frigid room to stand beside him, wondering what he was looking at.

'Magpie should be arriving, at some point. Though it does occur to me that, not being on friendly terms with the police, he might flee when he sees one waiting for him. I think he was very fond of Peach, though, so he'll be all the more motivated, now. I want to spend the day in St. James's. The Wrong Boys, having numbers, will be able to keep an eye on a large portion of it. You and I and the Greys can walk along where they would stand out too much.'

'I like that idea better than you trying to get yourself kidnapped.' There was a bite to his words that rivalled the bite in the air.

'I don't think I'm quite what they're looking for, actually,' I said as lightly as I could manage. 'I put on a dress, yesterday, and still looked like a boy. And besides, Fields at least is more interested in putting out my eye and probably killing me. I wouldn't be very useful, at that point.'

He snorted, looking at me out of the corner of his eye. His thin lips twisted into a smirk. '*I* think you're pretty, dear sister.'

I flicked his ear, making him flinch away.

'What were you looking at?'

He shrugged. 'These people have found you thrice, though last night was probably coincidence. They're obviously very sneaky. I was making sure they hadn't found you again.'

I shivered. 'I think if they had, they'd have made themselves known at once.'

'Or they're aware that they're attracting too much attention and are waiting for a chance to engineer an accident.'

Nobody would believe in an accident, not at this point. But the person behind all this had revealed his character by killing Jones the editor, by seeking to frighten the Greys before trying to burn them alive, and by sending a man to kill Peach. There was a vindictive streak in the villain, one at times stronger than reason. If he had not sent the albatross head, the Greys would not have connected the new bout of disappearances to the events of ten years ago. Edwin and Jones had not been in close contact in a decade, and the police may never have connected the murder with the arson. People disappeared from London's streets every day. They may never have seen a pattern at all.

He wanted the Greys to be afraid before he killed them, and that desire was what would ruin him. There was something poetic in it.

And I had placed myself into the middle of all of it, just as Edwin had the last time. The figure in the shadows would want revenge on me. But first, he would want me to be afraid. Whatever was in store, it would not be disguised as an accident.

# FOUR

WITHIN a few hours, I found myself in St James's, as planned. The district traditionally bounded by the Mall, Piccadilly, Haymarket, and Green Park was immaculate and exclusive, an expanse of fine businesses, fine dining, fine homes, fine entertainment, and great houses, some of which carried ancient names I knew. It was the domain of the elites, far beyond Mycroft's impressive influence, though he did grumble over breakfast, in a somewhat sinister tone, that it would not be long. Nobody quite wanted to ask what he meant by that.

If St James's was beyond Mycroft's influence, it was doubly beyond my comfort, and trebly beyond Magpie's. He had arrived in a constable's tow, his eyes red and a bruise purpling on his cheek, face set with cold fury. He had tried to run, the constable explained. Mycroft's eyes darted to the number at the man's collar and he smiled broadly, amiably advising that he tender his resignation while he still could.

It took moments to explain to Magpie what we had learned and what he could do to help, ten minutes for him to stuff himself and his pockets with much of the contents of the breakfast table—Mycroft offered a basket, but was refused, with the explanation that a ragged boy with a basket would be quickly arrested for theft—and about an hour for him to go and assemble the rest of his little clan.

Robbins appeared during that hour, trailing along behind a much smaller man with a pointed goatee who obviously outranked him. Cameron. We could all of us tell at a glance, by the expression on Robbins's face, that Detective Inspector Cameron meant to wrap up this matter with his own two hands and not a shred of input from anyone else. We explained what Mycroft had found. I told him about the man who had killed Doctor Peach and described his face as well as I could, crossing my fingers that no one had told him it had been a girl there, last night. It seemed that no one had.

And Inspector Cameron told us all kindly and with much condescension that it would all be all right.

Robbins was allowed to say nothing.

'He's not going to St James's,' Mycroft rumbled when they had left. 'Or if he does, he'll knock politely on each door and ask if anyone has seen a man matching Fields's description, then apologise for wasting their valuable time.'

'He may,' Theodora replied dubiously. 'But he earned his rank somehow. Perhaps he's better at investigating than at conversing.'

'He's on the take,' Mycroft replied.

We all looked at him, and he looked back with incredulity. 'I know how much a Detective Inspector earns, and I know what his suit cost. Either he is earning his money dishonestly, or he is taking it without earning it at all. We cannot rely on Inspector Cameron in this. He likes money too much to interrogate it with any objectivity.'

He may have inherited, I thought, but Mycroft would have thought of that, too, and must have dismissed it. I wondered what it was he had seen, but there was not time to let small matters perplex me.

We could not rely on Inspector Cameron.

And so I strolled slowly along with Sherlock and Theodora,

scanning the houses in their miniature estates from the street and trying to appear as though we were chatting about inconsequential things. Edwin, with his bad eye, had not thought he would be of much help.

We three did not look like we belonged in that place, but that was all right. It was not unheard-of for lesser mortals to visit, to admire, to bask, and then to go home. There were few others like us—it was not easy to pass through St James's on the way elsewhere—but still, we were not alone.

An endless stream of doubts trickled through my head, and I forced myself to pick apart and answer each of them.

What if they only drove the cart at night? I had only seen it after dark, myself.

No, that wasn't likely. It would be less likely to be seen at night, but anyone who did see it at night would be more likely to think it suspicious. And anyway, there was nothing strange about making deliveries during the day. Even if they did, the worst case was that we would have to return and continue to watch at night. In a well-lighted area, that would be easy, even if the season made it unpleasant.

The cart couldn't be going back and forth daily, could it? That would mean they were taking someone every day. That would have been noticed.

No, considering London's population and the operation's choice of victim, it was not at all implausible that several dozens had gone missing without raising any alarms. The cart might very well be in constant use. And if it was not, we would watch until it did appear.

But surely someone would notice the same cart coming and going every day. I could think of no answer to that.

And we had to be wasting our time looking at the houses themselves. Neighbourhoods such as this one did not go unscrutinised. Any hint of something amiss would be seen and documented and appear in the papers. Any curiosity among the elites, any whiff of mystery, might portend a scandal, and so it would appear in print. Nothing could possibly be allowed to appear wrong from the outside.

No, not wrong. But possibly different. Curtains drawn at strange times, perhaps? Would they dare put bars on the windows? I had seen beautifully worked wrought-iron bars on windows before, but on one of these gleaming houses, it would be tasteless. It would draw attention.

We had left the Wrong Boys loitering in front of the shops and watching the streets beyond the residential part of the district, and I wished I could share my thoughts with Magpie. I had thought that the comparative isolation of the houses would provide greater safety, but it was also true that shops had storerooms, basements. I did not know whether they or we were more likely to find success.

The day dragged.

At noon, we tracked down the Wrong Boys to compare notes, and Magpie and I walked together out of the area to find a pie stall and buy lunch for everyone, unwilling to send anyone alone.

People looked strangely at us, but he wore his cap low and his muffler high, and they did not stare quite as long as they would have if his features had been visible. I wondered if he hid himself like that intentionally, or if he was merely trying to stay as warm as possible. What did he do during the summer months?

'I'm sorry about Peach,' I said at length.

He glanced at me out of the corner of an eye. 'You were there.'

'Yes. I was looking for you. A man came looking for him, and for me, having seen me coming. Fields, the one whose eye I put out the night Snail was taken. Doctor Peach had been trying to find her, too.'

'Course 'e was.' There was anger in the words, and a challenge.

'There's a space under the floor where he kept his medical supplies. He put me down there, and when he wouldn't tell him where I was, Fields killed him.'

The information did not surprise him, as I had known it wouldn't.

'You got anythin' to say about that?'

'Yes. I was extremely wrong.'

'That's damn right, you were.'

My lip had cracked in the cold, and I chewed at the edges of the tiny wound.

'I didn' know 'im five years, like I said,' Magpie blurted out suddenly. 'Knew 'im maybe ten, only I don' like to talk about it. 'Bout 'ow I met 'im.'

'Please don't feel that you need to tell me, if you don't want to.'

He did want to, though, and I felt it was the least I could do to listen.

'I was born in America,' he said, and stopped, seeming for a moment unable to continue. His shoulders rolled uncomfortably, and he made a soft noise with his tongue. 'Look, it's a strange thing to say, an' I don' want no pity over it, you understand?'

After a moment, I understood him. I thought him to be about my age, which meant he had been born in or around '56. I knew little enough about America and its recent history, but everyone knew about their war and its results, and the way things had been before. The probability was very high that a Negro boy born around '56 had been born property, and I could not blame him for his difficulty finding a way to say so aloud.

'Go on,' I said.

'Came 'ere when I was a baby,' he said, omitting what I thought must have been a terrible and terribly interesting span of time. 'Mum died on the boat over. I don' remember 'er. My aunt Flora brought me up. Did charwork during the day, worked the streets at night.' There was pride in that statement, and gratitude. 'Then she got sick. One of the other ladies told us about Peach, an' I went an' found 'im. 'E came an' sat up with 'er for a solid week. Never saw 'im sleep. 'E left once, came back all beat up, but 'e brought food an' opium for 'er pain. Did what 'e could for me, after.

## GRAHAM

Tried to get me into a charity 'ouse, but they wouldn't 'ave me, on account of livin' with an 'ore is bad for your morals. That, an' I'm unsightly. So 'e looks... 'E looked after me as much as 'e could. An' the others.'

He looked at me steadily, waiting.

'He was part of your family.'

'Yeah. You could say that.'

'I'm sorry.' That didn't seem like enough, not after I had spent so much time being so cruel in my judgements. 'I wish I had actually known him.'

That seemed to be what he had been waiting for. His shoulders relaxed. 'Yeah. I wish you 'ad, too. You'd 'ave got on, I think.'

I did not think we would have gotten on, actually. Peach's acerbic nature and chilly wit had not appealed to me. But I could have respected him.

We found a stand and purchased our pies, departing with all hands and pockets full. A cup of tea would have been appreciated, as well, but tea was not portable.

"E liked you, you know.'

I stopped short and stared at my companion, eyebrows raised.

His eyes crinkled in a broad grin. 'I know 'e 'ad a funny way of showin' it. Never said 'e was *nice* to no one. But you got away an' found a place to stay, roof over your 'ead, plenty to eat, an' you still came back to tell us what 'appened to Snail. Stuck around to get 'er back. Surprised the 'ell out of 'im, that did. Me, too, if I'm honest.'

Something loosened inside of me at the affirmation. After everything that had gone wrong, all the mistakes I had made, all the gnawing doubts inside, I had almost forgotten that I was involved in something that mattered. I was doing something right. Something clicked, a piece settling back into place, and for the first time in ages, I began to suspect that I was still myself.

'We don't have her back yet,' I said, unintentionally gruff. 'Come on.'

Still the day dragged.

We all found a comparatively sunny spot in Green Park where we could steal a few minutes to sit and eat our pies, Theodora animatedly pointing out the place where the Earl of Bath had duelled the Earl of Bristol in 1730. Her story fell flat. There was too much fresh blood for tales of old violence to entertain.

Then it was back to our endless circuits.

And the day dragged.

'We'll have to find a way to make ourselves less conspicuous if we intend to stay through the night,' Theodora said wearily as we reached a corner and turned to begin another round. 'We'll look strange, promenading around at night. And I'll need a cup of coffee. Or five.'

'And tomorrow?' Sherlock asked. 'We may be able to make it through the night, and possibly through the day, but what about tomorrow night? Do you think Magpie and his know anyone who could take over? We'll have to establish shifts in order to keep this up.'

'We will,' I agreed. 'Mycroft might know someone. Though, come to think of it, I don't know that I've ever heard if he has any friends.'

'He doesn't,' Sherlock volunteered. 'I asked, once. He said he's got plans to found a club in which the first rule is that no one may speak to anyone else.'

I glanced at him, and saw my own thoughts reflected in his face, but I voiced them anyway. 'Why bother founding a club? Couldn't he much more easily stay at home by himself and speak to no one all alone?'

Sherlock shrugged. 'It must make sense to him. We both know better than to question Mycroft.'

Theodora shook her head, not looking at either of us. 'It's none of my business, but you have a very strange family.'

It was easy to joke about our strange older brother, but the word *family* brought Mother back to the front of my mind, and I ducked my head so they would not see the tightening of my jaw or the prickle of tears. She was not dead, I reminded myself. She was not well, but she was also not dead, and where there was life, there was hope. I would see her, somehow. Mycroft would be able to find a way to let me see her without exposing me to Father, without forcing me back home.

And the day dragged. Daylight began to fade.

'We can't ask the boys to stay out overnight,' I said. 'Magpie will insist, but the others are younger. We should give them a chance to get some sleep.'

'Your brother will put them up and feed them, I expect.' Theodora stopped abruptly and shut her eyes, tilting her head toward her shoulder until her neck cracked. I winced.

'One of us should go as well,' she continued. 'That'll still leave two, for safety, and the third can return in a few hours to relieve one of the others. We miss things when we're tired.'

Sherlock did not miss things when he was tired, but he had the grace not to point that out.

I volunteered to fetch the Wrong Boys. The streets were not yet so empty that I feared to go off on my own.

And I was not on my own. The Wrong Boys found me before I could find them, first Weasel, then Dart, then Magpie, and finally Billy. I explained the situation.

The three younger boys looked eager, at first, at the prospect of a third meal in a single day, then dubious, then resolute.

'I'm stayin' ere,' Weasel told me in a tone of defiance. 'Stayin' 'ere till Snail's back an' the bastards what took 'er is arrested.'

'It could take days before we see anything of importance,' I explained. 'We all have to maintain our strength, or we may miss the clue when it comes.'

He was not convinced. The jut of his jaw showed it.

'Dart an' Billy,' Magpie ruled. 'You'll go an' rest now, an' Weasel an' me in the morning. Won't do anybody any good if we're fallin' asleep on our feet.'

He did not mention hunger. That was probably a given, for them.

Dart and Billy pattered off reluctantly into the gathering gloom.

I looked at Magpie, but he was staring over my shoulder, his brilliant eyes wide and icy with purpose. He grabbed my arm and pulled me close, not daring to point. His sibilant whisper raised the hairs on the back of my neck.

'There it is.'

# FIVE

MAGPIE was faster than me. He looked between me and Billy, then tapped Billy's shoulder and pointed away into the evening. 'Get 'em back, get the lady, and tell 'er to get the police.'

Billy gave an answer in French which I could not understand and lumbered away down the street, surprisingly quickly for someone of his size. Like a bear.

The single remaining Wrong Boy motioned me toward the nearest doorway. 'You stay 'ere,' he said.

That wasn't going to work, not at all. If he was caught, no one would know where the cart had gone. Two of us together would have a better fighting chance, and a better chance that one or the other would get away if fighting went bad.

'Rubbish,' I replied, shaking his hand off my arm. 'Come on, or we'll lose them.'

He rolled his eyes — *rolled his eyes!* — but capitulated.

We did not have to run after the cart. It moved at a sedate pace, making its way between the remaining evening pedestrians, and there were enough people still in the street that we could move freely without seeming to follow. After a day of walking, I was glad that I would not have to test my ankle at a run. Not yet, at least.

It wended its way down Piccadilly to St James's Street, turned, passed before the palace, and slowly returned us to the residential part of the district. The great, white houses glowed in the fading light, windows spilling golden beams onto manicured lawn.

Somehow, I had expected that the house where it stopped would be dark, but there were no dark houses. It rolled through a gate, up a drive, and around the back of one of the houses without a name I knew. There were holes dug all over the lawn, and beside them, stacks of huge, flat paving stones, and young trees with their roots wrapped in sacking.

I poked Magpie in the ribs. 'That's how they come and go as they please,' I hissed. 'The cart is full of materials for the work on the garden. Plus some extra cargo.'

He nodded, his entire body tense with fury beside me, then plucked at my sleeve. 'Come on. We 'ave to tell the others where they ended up.'

I turned to follow him.

And my brain rebelled.

What if that cart was full of paving stones and nothing else? I had seen the back of it, but I did not think either Magpie or myself had had a chance to see the driver's face. Had it been Fields? If it had, I'd be sure, but there were other men involved. Theodora's father had been involved. If the driver had not been Fields, that was not necessarily a sign that we had the wrong cart, but it was a nondescript vehicle, exactly like hundreds or even thousands of others in London. There was no writing on it, no paint, no distinctive stains or tears in its canvas. Had Magpie and I thought we recognised it only because we were expecting to see it?

That would be the end of us, and of Snail. I remembered what

Mycroft had said about that Inspector Cameron, and while I did not know how he had been so sure, I had also never known Mycroft to be wrong in his deductions. If we brought Cameron here, and we were wrong, he would never return his investigation to St James's. Even a perfectly straight copper would be embarrassed, possibly professionally censured, for disturbing the kinds of people who lived here.

I pulled up short, and Magpie's hand slid off my arm.

'I want to make sure,' I said quietly.

He looked at me curiously. 'You're *not* sure? I am.'

I chewed hard at my cracked lips and shook my head. 'Did you see the driver? Did he have an eyepatch?'

'No, but that's the cart.'

'What if they knew it was seen and have sold it to someone else? I don't want to go charging in and take them on, just see if I can see Fields. Or see if they take someone out of the back. That'll be enough.'

I had misjudged so much, recently. To fail at this crucial point would be unbearable.

He met my gaze unblinking, the little muscles around his eyes tight. But I thought he saw my point. Quite aside from being an embarrassment, making a scene at the wrong house might very well alert the real villains nearby to our closeness, giving them a chance to flee and correct all the little mistakes that had led us to them. We might not find them again.

He nodded. 'I'll go. Got a lot more practice sneakin' than you 'ave.'

I was sure he did. I agreed.

He shrugged off his tattered coat and handed it to me, then his jacket. In his shirtsleeves, he was as thin as I. His breath blew out beneath his muffler in white clouds as he slipped his scrawny body between the bars of the gate and crept across the lawn. His footsteps in the grass made no sound, and in the deepening darkness, his dull, grimy clothes rendered him all but invisible as he avoided the light from the windows.

In moments, he had vanished.

I strained my ears listening, but there was nothing to hear. That should have been a relief, but the longer the silence went on, the tighter grew the knot in my stomach. It was fine, I told myself. Yes, I worried about nearly everything, but a line had to be drawn between worrying and paranoia. Magpie was, as he had claimed, much sneakier than I was. He'd had a lifetime of practice. The simple fact that he had survived to be my age told of masterful sneakiness. Worry didn't help him, and it didn't help me, and it didn't help Snail.

Breathe, girl.

I tried to breathe. The icy air stabbed my throat, and I had to muffle a cough in my scarf. Terror clutched at me, but I barely heard the sound, so no one else could have, either.

What if someone had come up behind him? Struck him from the back? There might not have been any scuffle, nothing to alert me.

How long had it been, anyway? I should have begun to count the moment he vanished from sight. I couldn't rely on my ability to measure seconds in that state, but at least I would have had some idea, a starting point. How far was it from the gate to the house, and how far to the back? How long would be an acceptable waiting period?

The darkness had become complete. The light from the house's windows cast patches on the lawn that only deepened the blackness of everything around them. I could see the bars of the gate directly in front of my face, but I wondered if that was only because I knew they were there.

It was past time, surely. He ought to have come back.

I wriggled between the bars and heard a button pop off some part of me and skitter away across the pavement. Sherlock would be cross. Sherlock would have been of tremendous use, actually. His ability to see in the dark was as uncanny as the rest of his senses. But Sherlock was not there.

I stepped slowly, crunching as little as possible, until my feet found the grass, and I was able to move more quickly. Even though my ankle throbbed, I held my stick ready as a bludgeon. A few steps in, I remembered the holes, the pavers, and the trees, and I had to slow my pace again. I pushed one foot out, made sure there was nothing to fall into or over, then the other. I did not trust myself to make it directly across the lawn, so I made for the house, instead. If I avoided the patches of light, I could crouch beneath the windows and travel beside the wall.

Suddenly, there was a shout. Only one, a hoarse, bass voice that silenced itself quickly. Of course, they could not risk an uproar, not in that neighbourhood.

But was it Fields? Or was it some poor gardener who had nothing to do with anything?

I quickened my pace, pressing myself against the wall of the house, and made it to the corner where I could see what was happening. Light from what I thought were the kitchen windows spilled onto the scene.

It was not Fields, but I was not fooled for a minute into thinking it was an innocent gardener. Fields's compatriot struggling to restrain Magpie and having a bad time of it. The two grappled, but Magpie twisted like an eel in his grip, his long limbs thrashing. Still, the man was easily twice Magpie's mass. If they could not break apart soon, there was only one possible outcome.

That one shout had not brought anyone else outside, yet. Perhaps it had not been heard.

With that in mind, I sprang forward with my stick held high and brought it down on the man's head with all my strength. I was not strong, not after my illness, but the stick was heavy, and the crack it made was satisfying. He collapsed, just as the door behind the cart crashed open.

## GRAHAM

Magpie and I exchanged a look and understood one another. He could run, and I could not. I nodded, and he vanished into the darkness.

# SIX

There were ten women crammed into the pantry. Granted, it was a large pantry, but eleven bodies and five flat, rancid cots made for a tight fit, all the same. An oil lamp belched smoke on one of the empty shelves. I was relieved to see that none of them were younger than me. Then I was horrified. Snail was not there.

They regarded me with a mixture of curiosity and hollow-eyed despair, some obviously wondering what I was doing there. I wondered the same thing. Fields had not been among those who seized me, and I did not know whether they recognised me as the girl who had put out his eye, or even whether they had recognised me as a girl at all. I knew that they would not kill me immediately. They had to find out how much I knew about them, and who else knew it, who else was coming. But perhaps they did not mean to kill me at all. Perhaps there was a market for boys, too.

'Have any of you seen a younger redheaded girl?' I asked. 'About so tall, very thin. She calls herself Snail.'

One face hardened with the decision not to trust me, but the rest shook their heads.

# GRAHAM

Of course they hadn't. The pantry could hardly be intended for the long term. They were probably moved out within days, either to a brothel or a buyer. It would have been weeks since Snail was last in that place. That meant I would have to find their records. They would be encoded, somehow, but Mycroft would be able to solve that problem.

I felt at the large split the men had left in my eyebrow. It had hurt when I got it, and it would again soon, but it was almost numb, for the moment.

The ten faces watched me. I leaned away from the door and whispered to them. 'My friend escaped. He'll be coming with the police soon.'

Ten mouths opened and then shut again. We all had to hold on only until Magpie returned, hopefully with an army. How long? He would have to reach Theodora first, and she would have better luck talking to the police than he would. She would have to find a constable who could take her to Robbins, who was a better bet than Cameron. But it was late. Robbins would have to be roused, and he would likely have to inform Cameron before he could take action. They would have to assemble a force to storm the house. Cameron would balk at the idea of creating a disturbance in such a place. He couldn't refuse, as I was certain Magpie would have the sense to lie about the fact that I was seized while trespassing. But he would know there was no room for error, and so he would construct the raid carefully. It might not actually happen until tomorrow, or even tomorrow night.

How many of these women would be moved along by then?

And would I still be alive?

Well, I would just have to make myself interesting enough to keep around. Escape was unlikely enough that I did not consider it. There were a lot more of them than there were of me, and they were a lot bigger, and obviously, they had taken my stick.

I could tell that none of them were quite sure whether to believe me.

They were all too wary of disappointment.

I understood, and did not attempt to talk to them anymore. I sat against the wall, instead, and tried to think, but thought was impossible, and sleep was impossible, and without a window, I had no way to know how much time had passed.

Half an hour or an hour or five hours later, they came back for me. At the first rasp of the key in the lock, my fellow prisoners shrank back as far as they could, their bodies pressed together into a quivering wad of grey wool.

It was Fields, this time. I stood to meet him, satisfied that my exhaustion made it impossible for me to show fear. He bent to stare into my face, his single eye squinting hard, searching for familiarity. I reflected with a little cold smugness that he could not possibly have *seen* much of my face the night Snail was taken, and I did not think he had seen much of me yesterday night, either.

I watched him back, aware of a twitch in my lip and an uncomfortable tightness in my throat, praying that neither were visible.

'Yeah,' he said at length, and he struck me hard across the face, sending me reeling backward into the crowd of women behind me.

By the time I could see again, he had both of his massive hands wrapped vice-like around my left upper arm, and another man had me by my right. Together, they dragged me from the pantry, and I heard a third man turn the key behind us. I shook my head to clear it. There was no telling what might be important, and I needed to be aware of everything.

It was not as a house like that should have been. That was immediately evident.

The kitchen was cold, only a few dishes sitting out. It was late, but there ought to have been a scullery maid somewhere. The hidden corridors where servants could pass unseen were dark and empty. Was the entire house unstaffed? Probably so. There had to be deeply untrustworthy servants out there somewhere, but my general impression of the serving class was of starkly moral people. A starkly moral servant would not stand for what was going on in that house. But an untrustworthy one... well, could not be trusted. So the house must have been populated by only those directly involved in the operation. That was a good thing. It meant there were no innocents to become embroiled in the coming conflict. The women were all locked up and conveniently out of the way.

We emerged into a lit hallway, where ghostly shapes loomed, covered in white dust sheets. The light from the windows was a deceit. There was no one in those lower rooms. Possibly the furniture there was covered, as well, but the level of the windows made it impossible to see that from outside. Were these people even supposed to be here? What kind of money was there in this kind of business? Did they own the house, but just kept it inoperative to avoid the need for servants? Or had they broken in and occupied it illegally? God, I could not imagine being the rightful owner of the place, coming back after a long absence to find out what had been done there.

We stopped near the middle of the corridor, in front of an open door, and the other man rapped his knuckles against the frame. So the person inside was important. Possibly the one in charge.

'Come,' came the reply.

I was carried from the door to the centre of the room and thrown face-first onto a deep, plush carpet. As I got my arms underneath myself, one of them, probably Fields, delivered a crushing kick to my bad ankle. I went down again and remained there, listening to their retreating footsteps. The door closed.

'You put out my man's eye,' said a voice from directly above me. It was deep, but not masculine.

I struggled to rise, and got as far as my knees before freezing at the revelation of a pistol pointed at my face. The person behind it was a woman, shorter than I, with grey in her dark hair and the marks of hardship on her face. She wore a plain green gown of an excellent cut, but a closer look showed me that the voluminous skirts were in fact divided, an expensive and fashionable pair of trousers. Her eyes were curiously flat, emotionless, and the longer I held her gaze, the more I wondered whether she ever blinked at all.

'I suspect you set the police on me, as well,' she continued. 'And set a gang of children to search for me. Killed one of my less vital agents. I do wonder how you ultimately found me, though.'

'Mathematics,' I replied.

She waited for an explanation. I had no desire to provide her with one, but she still had a gun pointed at me, and I very dearly wanted to remain alive until help could arrive. 'You probably were very careful to make sure that your activity was scattered randomly through the city, rather than concentrated in any particular area. And taken in sum, that was true. But when the disappearances were taken by date and viewed as they occurred over time, a pattern began to spread from a central point. From here.'

Mycroft had also mentioned using flows of traffic and other such factors in his calculations. I did not want to mention Mycroft, and I did not want to generate any questions I could not answer, so I shut my mouth.

She considered. 'Unfortunate,' she said at last. 'And who else knows we're here? My men said there was another who got away, a shabby little thing with a deformity. You do understand that he can say whatever he likes to the police. They'll never come here looking for trouble.'

'Yes. I do understand that.' That was why he would go to Theodora, first, and let her proceed from there.

Her marble eyes narrowed. 'I asked who else.'

'We two were alone. And as you say, I have nothing to hope from him.'

Word games were unwise, I discovered. She saw through my prevarication and the hand holding the pistol tightened. I tightened, too.

'Then who knew where *you* were?'

Truth, or lies? Definitely lies. If she knew I was waiting for the police, she and her men could simply flee.

'No one.'

I could see her disbelief and hurried to spill out more words.

'No one knew we were here. I had spoken to the police, yes. Quite a lot. But they wouldn't take me seriously. They said I was making up stories, looking for attention. And even when they did notice that women were disappearing, they said those women were the sort that often disappear entirely on their own. They wouldn't take me seriously, so my friend and I decided that if we could prove it...'

More an overextension of the truth than an actual lie, but she did seem to believe that. At least, she nodded. Then she spoke.

'Peter Storm does not know? I believe he escaped the conflagration. Him and his whore wife.'

My back stiffened in indignation, and she laughed.

'I've been watching them for some time. I'm sure they must have told you how they ruined me. You did not escape my notice, either.' Some trace of emotion flickered in her eyes, but it was dull and lifeless. 'Though I did not connect the girl with the stick and the boy with the stick until last night. That was a lapse. I have, myself, taken advantage of male dress on occasion.' The flicker of emotion became a spark. Contempt. 'Though I have to say, you're *much* better at it than I am.'

I blinked. 'Did you have me brought up here so you could call me ugly?'

The contempt became fury. 'No. I mean to shoot you. I know

nothing of you, but I know a lot of Peter Storm, Mr Edwin Grey, and the chit he married. You have not convinced me they are not coming. This will be the third time I have lost everything, you know. I haven't the energy to rebuild again. So when you are dead, just in case you are lying, I will sit by that window and watch for the police, and if I see them coming, I will set the house on fire. There's not much I can do about the men. They will run and probably be caught. The women below are locked in and will burn with me. Of course, I shall shoot myself before the flames reach me.

'Well?'

My brain felt numb. What could I say to that? I had been determined to keep her talking so she would not have time to run, but she had never meant to. That vindictive streak was stronger than I had imagined, and far less reasonable. I blinked slowly, unable to respond. She wanted a response.

The scene played out in my head. It was a large house, and fires spread upward much faster than they spread downward. I was not overly concerned for the women. If this person waited until she saw the police before setting the blaze, there would be more than enough time to free the prisoners before the flames reached them. Of course, I would still be dead, at that point, and the records of sold girls would be destroyed. Snail would not be recovered.

But maybe I could keep her away from the window.

'The third time?' I asked. My voice croaked.

She cocked an eyebrow.

'You said it was the third time you'd lost everything. What happened?'

She smiled grimly. 'You're trying to keep yourself alive. I understand that. I'd prefer to stay alive, myself. But we don't always get what we want.'

# GRAHAM

'Of course I am,' I shot back. 'Why kill me at all? I'm here, I'm in your power. You could as easily make money off me. I've already told you no one is coming for me. I ran away from home and told no one where I was going. I'd rather go back downstairs and share the fate of those women.'

'Your ability to say that demonstrates your ignorance.'

She stepped back, and I flinched, thinking she intended to fire, but she dropped into the chair behind her and balanced the pistol on her knee, still trained firmly on my face. 'You think what waits for them is better than death? You know nothing about it.'

'You know about it, though.'

Still, she would not be drawn out. 'Of course I do. I have engineered it.'

And still, she had not shot me. Why? There had to be something she wanted, either something she wanted me to say or something she wanted to say to me. She did not want to talk about her past, about the things she had lost or about her curious knowledge of prostitution and slavery. What, then?

'You've deliberately engineered what you consider a fate worse than death for these women. Why? You're a woman, yourself.'

There. That was it. Life flared in her eyes, and a mad, burning pride. 'As are you.' Her gaze raked my body like a physical force, making me wince. 'And yet, you've eschewed femininity, very deliberately, I think. You and I may have been born among them, but we are not like other women, are we?'

Good Lord, where was she going with this?

'I put on trousers thinking it might keep me from getting caught and sent back to my parents. I kept them on because *you* were making it dangerous to be a woman.'

'I? It's always been dangerous to be a woman, and yet they, ever weak, have done nothing about that. I only took advantage of the

252

immutable nature of things.'

I tried to stand, but my ankle had finally given up entirely, and I could not. Through gritted teeth I spat back, 'You've hardly done anything about it, either.'

'I've used the way things are to make myself a tidy bundle. Not as cleverly as I thought, it seems, but I am still proud to have accomplished so much. We are not like other women. Look at you. You're a broken, ugly thing, but clever and determined. Compare yourself to those below, huddling terrified in their own excrement. Whatever you say, you've separated yourself from them by transforming yourself into a boy, *because you know what they are.*'

My fingers twitched. If I'd had my stick, I know I'd have shattered her skull with it, whether she shot me in the process or not. 'And what are you, then?'

'An opportunist. Women are weak and docile, and the poor ones most of all. They will all wallow in one form or another of servitude and drudgery all their lives. That also is worse than death, if you were wondering. If by moving them from one misery to a different one I may elevate myself above them, why should I not?'

She said that as though it made perfect sense to her. But she also said it with great ease, as though she had rehearsed it any number of times, an excuse concocted after the fact to give purpose to senseless selfishness. Not like other women, indeed. Certainly not. She was barely even human. I wished I could crush her, but I had to keep her talking if I wanted to live. When she had nothing left to say, I would die. But did she want me to rage and rail at her? Or was I supposed to slowly come to agree with her.

I was saved the horror of having to feign interest by a sound in the hallway. For a moment, I hoped she might turn to look, even though my ankle would not let me lunge to overpower her. But only her head moved, while her gaze stayed fixed on me.

## GRAHAM

'What is it?' she asked, unconcerned.

I wondered whether any of the men were aware of her plans to burn everything to the ground, and what they would say about it if they knew.

The door swung open.

'*You!*' said a voice I had come to know well.

The woman's attention jerked toward the figure in the doorway, and I saw surprise in her face, then venom. As if time had slowed, I saw the maw of the pistol begin to pivot away, the arm holding it begin to stiffen and rise, her aim moving from me to the interloper.

Then a shot rang out, and the woman in the green dress died.

# SEVEN

I SWALLOWED hard and let myself sit, careful not to sit on my ankle. Theodora came to me briefly, then at a noise from without flew back to the door, slammed it shut, and twisted the key with a fierce yank. It was a good door, as high quality as everything else in the house, made of dense, dark oak. It would hold, at least for a short while.

I looked up at her, and she looked down at me, and then she took me in her arms and held me tightly. I became aware of tears on my cheeks, and more in my hair, which I assumed were hers. An object clattered to the floor at my side, a second pistol. Hers had been confiscated by the police, but I remembered that Edwin had owned one, too. He must have been carrying it when their house burned.

'Good girl,' she whispered into my shoulder. 'Good girl, well done. It's all right now.'

I allowed myself to be held for a moment, then there was a dull, reverberating thud against the door, and another. It shuddered on its heavy hinges, but held, the thick wood muffling the angry words being uttered outside.

I pulled away and struggled to rise. With her help, it was possible for me to balance shakily on my good leg. She handed me a heavy fireplace poker that was almost long enough to serve in place of my stick. I looked at the door, wiping the tears from my face and begging my heart to slow. Then I looked at the corpse in the chair. Behind it, there was a desk, and open on the desk was a ledger. She had not had time to burn the records, this time.

'You knew her,' I said as I hobbled toward the book. I made a stop at the corpse and prised her gun from her limp hand. It was no good to her, dead, thank God, but it might be of use to me if and when the door gave out. I did not know how far away the police might be.

Theodora shook her head. 'Last time, all the women rescued were taken together and questioned after the raid. She was among us. We talked for hours while we waited for our turn. I had no idea...'

'Of course you didn't. Do you know anything about her?'

She came to join me as I paged through the ledger, scanning its cryptic notations. The amounts were plain, but nothing else was. I would need Mycroft for this, and so the book must be protected at all costs until I could get it to him.

'It was ten years ago,' she reminded me. 'And I did not see her again after that. She said her name was... Annette, I believe. If I learned her surname, I don't remember. She said she was very wealthy, once, but she married unwisely, and when she divorced, the man took everything from her. She ended up on the streets, and saved and stole until she could rent a place for herself and some other girls to work from, so they would not be at the mercy of men... I really thought that sounded very noble. I can't imagine how she got from there to here, if any of it were true.'

Three losses. A divorce and a plunge to the streets had been the first. Then each of these subsequent failures. She had called herself an opportunist. There must have been a point, sometime during all of this, when she had looked at the poor women around her and realised she could restore what she had lost by standing on their backs.

Theodora's finger came to rest on a line of the ledger, then slid to a single, coded cell.

Rh8y.

'Redhead, eight years?' she asked.

I closed my eyes and prayed that she was right.

—

She was. The police arrived moments after the assault began in earnest on the door, and by nightfall, four men were in prison, and three had escaped, but would not get far.

Recovery began. The ledger's records were necessarily brief and opaque, and when they were deciphered, it was discovered that a good number of women had disappeared onto ships and out to sea, but well over half, more than twenty, were found and freed, and more arrests were made. I did not look forward to the trial.

The difficulties continued. My heart sang when I heard, two days later, that Snail had been found as well, but the authorities would not release a child back onto the streets, and for a tense few hours, it looked as though she would be placed in the workhouse. Mrs Dunn and Dick came to the rescue. They would take her.

I had the immense honour of bringing Magpie and the other boys back to Mycroft's house to meet her.

They piled out of a growler and stormed the foyer with no sense of decorum, whooping as they mobbed the little form standing between the Dunns. When the whoops turned to tears, the adults in the entryway withdrew respectfully, and I began to follow them, but was stopped by a hand on my arm.

A vice-like embrace closed around me, brief as a heartbeat, and then Magpie drew away. 'Give the same to your brothers from me, yeah? An' them Greys.'

'I will,' I said. I wouldn't. There was not much hugging in the Holmes family. But I would pass on the sentiment.

'Magpie?'

He paused.

'We will be seeing a lot of one another, I hope.'

'Yeah, I think. You're a good 'un, Crow.'

'Edwin worked for a newspaper once, you know. He's thinking of starting his own, and he said he could use your help. All of you. For pay, of course.'

He tilted his head with a slow smile. 'Can't read.'

'You could learn to, though. I could help teach you.'

He laughed. 'Bet you're a rubbish teacher. But I'd give it a try.'

He turned to go back to the tight knot of the others, still wound around Snail as though afraid she would disappear again. Then he looked at me once more. 'My name's Benjamin,' he said.

'Morrigan,' I replied, though he must have heard someone else call me, by then.

He nodded and left me to creep back out of the entry and straight into Sherlock. I slipped around him and began to climb the stairs to his room, the room we had been sharing.

'What about you?' he asked.

I shrugged. 'I don't mean to go home. Whatever Mycroft is doing to prevent that, I don't think it can be done forever. The Greys have said I can stay with them as long as I like, and that's what I mean to do. I just have to figure out how.'

'I've already expressed my feelings on the subject.'

'Yes. I know. Don't worry, we'll see one another. We'll both work to make sure of that.'

'We can't be sure. There are too many uncertain variables.'

I laughed. 'Well, if you're going to be like that, we can never be sure of anything, ever. It's *probable*, how's that? Now leave me alone. I'm going to change.'

He nodded, and then a broad grin split his face. 'Fine then, sister. I'll work on installing you with your precious Greys. But you'll work on a system to get me out of school whenever I please.'

I rolled my eyes. 'I think you could probably manage that fine on your own. But it's a deal.'

He rocketed down the stairs and away, and I slipped into our room.

I kicked off shoes and peeled off socks. Laid the jacket on the bed. Waistcoat. Tie. Shirtwaist. I slid out of the trousers and set them aside. Donned chemise, petticoats, skirt.

It was not over, but that, I realised, was not a bad thing. Together, we had fixed something, taken a broken part of the world and made it better, and the power of that realisation flowed through me. I had done something good, and I could do it again.

The Greys would have to rebuild their life, and I would be there to help.

The Wrong Boys were reunited, but they should also be warm and fed and clothed, and I could work to do something about that.

Somewhere, Mother was slowly healing, and she would need support that I could not trust Father to give.

I laid the skin of Morgan Grey in my trunk and told him goodbye. Not a farewell, only an "until later". Then I turned to the mirror to finish buttoning my bodice up to my throat. Just behind my ears, my hair barely touched the high collar. The long hands I saw were white and bony, but strong. The eyes were sharp and alert.

And the face reflected was mine.

GRAHAM

*fin*

# Watch for

# The Death of a Swan

# Coming Soon

Subscribe to the periodic newsletter of M.R. Graham for treats, freebies, and timely notification of the next volume of the Adventures of Morrigan Holmes.

# ABOUT THE AUTHORS

M.R. Graham is a native Texan who traces strong cultural roots back to Scotland, Poland, England, and Germany. A mild-mannered academic during the day, Graham transforms at night into a raging Holmesian loremaster and rabid novelist.

Though passionate about all scholarship and academia, Graham's training and true love lies with anthropology, particularly the archaeological branch.

**Visit M.R. Graham at quiestinliteris.com or connect at facebook.com/authormrgraham.**

Special thanks to my dear patrons,

and to Catherine and Maddie.

You can support the continuing publication of the series and receive early access and special extras by contributing on Patreon at patreon.com/mrgraham.

**Morrigan Holmes chooses, for the moment, to remain an enigma.**